SCONES
and
SCOUNDRELS

Also available from Pegasus Crime:

Plaid and Plagiarism
BOOK ONE OF THE HIGHLAND BOOKSHOP MYSTERY SERIES

MOLLY MACRAE

SCONES
and
SCOUNDRELS

THE HIGHLAND BOOKSHOP
MYSTERY SERIES

BOOK 2

PEGASUS CRIME
NEW YORK LONDON

SCONES AND SCOUNDRELS

Pegasus Crime is an imprint of
Pegasus Books Ltd
148 West 37th Street, 13th Fl.
New York, NY 10018

First Pegasus Books paperback edition April 2019
First Pegasus Books hardcover edition January 2018

Interior design by Sabrina Plomitallo-González, Pegasus Books

ISBN: 978-1-64313-027-9

10 9 8 7 6 5 4 3 2 1

Printed in the United States of America
Distributed by W. W. Norton & Company, Inc.
www.pegasusbooks.com

For readers who know that a book is an open door,
and who gladly step through.

SCONES
and
SCOUNDRELS

1

"Janet, I dare you to read this and tell me you aren't ready to commit bloody murder."

Janet took a step back as Sharon blazed toward her, shaking her fist and the letter gripped in it. Even with the barrier of the sales counter between them, Janet took another step back when Sharon slapped the paper on the countertop in front of her.

Janet Marsh had smiled when the bell over the door of Yon Bonnie Books jingled and Sharon Davis entered the shop, though the smile was against her better judgment. In the few months she'd known her, she'd learned that Sharon had a way of presenting "opportunities" that turned into more than Janet had bargained for. Still, asking Janet if she might be ready to commit "bloody murder" was kicking it up a notch.

"Go on," Sharon said. "Open it. Read it."

Janet couldn't. Sharon's fist held it to the counter.

"I've no doubt," Sharon said, "that Gillian will stop by and give you a copy of your own. But you can thank me for letting you see these ridiculous demands two weeks ahead of your event and not a mere three days prior to." She punctuated each word of the unacceptable time frame with a pound of her fist on the paper.

Janet guessed she could move fast enough to snatch the paper between pounds. Sharon might be ten years younger, but Janet trusted her own reflexes. Even so, she opted for waiting at a safe distance.

With Sharon's last bang, her fist stayed in the center of the paper, pinning it to the counter like a squashed bug. From the way her breath came in ragged puffs, Janet wouldn't have been surprised to see steam jetting from her ears. When Sharon's breathing calmed, Janet stepped forward to give the paper a gentle tug.

"Oh. Sorry." Sharon took her fist away. She shook the hand out then patted it over her short hair. "I'm surprised it isn't standing on end like hackles. Sorry about barging in like a mad dog." She banged the counter one more time. "But Gillian Bennett has a lot to answer for."

Janet had thought the same of Sharon when they first met, but she tried not to hold it against her. Sharon, as director of the Inversgail Library and Archives, was often in a position of having to raise funds or recruit volunteers. Janet knew about the wiles needed by public servants to meet the needs of their institutions. Before following her retirement dream and moving from the prairies of central Illinois to Inversgail on the west coast of Scotland, Janet had been a librarian, too.

Even knowing Sharon's temperament, Janet was a bit surprised she was so on edge. Gillian Bennett was the principal teacher in the English department at the Inversgail High School, and it was thanks to her foresight and organizational skills that a renowned writer was coming to spend the next three months as an author-in-residence.

Janet unfolded the paper, but before she could read it, Sharon snatched it back.

"It's a list of the most preposterous demands from a visiting author I have ever seen," Sharon said. "Listen to this."

Janet sat down on the high stool behind the counter and waited while Sharon fumbled a pair of reading glasses. Sharon seemed not to have noticed that Janet hadn't, so far, said a word. Another indication, Janet thought, that Sharon was unusually rattled. True, Daphne Wood was not a typical visiting author. She was an award-winning environmental writer, known internationally as the icon of ecology, who led the life of a modern day Thoreau. She lived in a log cabin she'd built herself in the wilds of Canada, and she was being brought to Inversgail as an author-in-residence for three months of the autumn school term. But more than that, she was being brought home. She'd lived in Inversgail during part of her childhood and her arrival was keenly anticipated, from what Janet could tell. The library was hosting the inaugural author event Friday evening, but there was no reason for that to be as catastrophically rattling as Sharon was making it out to be.

Glasses found at last, and settled on Sharon's nose, Janet assumed she was about to hear a reason. Possibly several.

Sharon snapped the paper to attention and read. "Requirements for library and bookstore appearances: laptop with Microsoft Office and Photoshop software; access to a color printer with scanning, fax, and copier capabilities; photo paper for printer—glossy—two reams; ice cold Pepsi Free—one six-pack; hot tea—any variety, but *no* Earl Grey; Jaffa Cakes; McVities Chocolate Digestives—*dark* chocolate, *not* milk; quiet room away from the public with smoking permissible—if such is not available, though it is preferable, then a porch or similar fresh air structure, well sheltered from weather, is acceptable; tissues; three Pilot G-2 0.5 pens—black; one Pilot G-2 0.7 pen—blue; assistant with Post-its ready and responsible for ascertaining proper spelling of names and inscriptions, opening books to title page for signing, keeping order among patrons waiting in line, popping Pepsi Free tops, pouring tea."

Sharon snapped the paper again and slammed it on the counter. "And at the end of that lengthy and ludicrous list, she asked for a ceramic bowl with fresh water to which I say *havers*."

"A bowl? And she specified ceramic? That's a new one." The fist came down again and Janet hastily added, "It does sound like nonsense. Havers, absolutely."

"I'm glad you agree. So, are you going to kill her or will I have to do it for both of us?"

Janet's eyebrows had drawn steadily closer together as Sharon read. At the repeated question of killing, Janet's eyebrows shot upward. "Surely—"

"It's a joke?" Sharon said. "I thought so, too. I even laughed when Gillian gave it to me. Gillian didn't."

"But surely Gillian isn't responsible for that list," Janet said. "It came from Daphne Wood, didn't it? Gillian must be as blindsided by it as you are. As you and I *both* are," she added for placatory good measure. "And your event is Friday, isn't it? That gives you five days."

"Only if you count today and the day of."

Which, Janet thought, any reasonable person would. "The list is probably negotiable, though, don't you think? And your event is the dedication and *ceilidh* dance to welcome Daphne and recognize Gillian's father for his work in Glen Sgail. It's more of a party and she won't be signing books. It sounds to me like this covers the requirements for the whole three months of the author-in-residence visit and not something you—we—need to worry about." Janet waited until she saw a grudging nod from Sharon. "I'm sure Gillian's only the messenger. And you know what they say about shooting the messenger."

Sharon's nod became a glower. "Clichés exist for a reason."

"In that case," Janet said, "let's indulge in a few more and look on the bright side. I'll talk to Gillian and see what we can work out. You and I won't let that list put a damper on our day or the excitement of Daphne's visit. How does that sound?" To her own ears, it sounded twee, but a guttural noise rose from Sharon's throat, and Janet chose to interpret it as agreement.

She came out from behind the counter and walked with Sharon to the door. She meant just to open and hold the door for Sharon, but then decided to step outside with her. "*Isn't* it a beautiful day? Better than any cliché we can dream up. Cloudless sky, waves gently lapping, Rab and Ranger ignoring the tourists but looking picturesque on the harbor wall."

"Don't let the sun fool you." Sharon clamped her lips on that statement, but too late to keep another guttural from escaping. With a parting sniff, she left.

"She's right, you ken." An elderly woman with a shopping bag had stopped beside Janet. "Do you see yon cat with Rab MacGregor and his wee dog?"

"Yes."

"Cats are aye right. It's washing its ears. Rain's on the way."

If that were true, Janet thought as she watched the woman continue up the High Street, then the cats of Inversgail, Scotland, must have the cleanest ears in creation. She tipped her head to look as high into the clear blue as she could before going back into the bookshop.

Her daughter came out of the storeroom as Janet disappeared down the aisle where they shelved language books.

"Did I hear the sounds of an irate librarian a little bit ago?" Tallie called after her.

"And you didn't come to rescue me?"

"You were using your calm mom voice, so I knew you had it under control."

"I think I reassured her," Janet said. "Somewhat. She had new details for the Daphne Wood program at the library and our book signing, and they put her in a stew. But you know Sharon." She ran a finger along a shelf until she found the book she wanted, then took it back to the sales counter.

"I don't know Sharon much beyond saying hello or wondering what new stew she's in." Tallie looked at the cloth she'd brought from the storeroom, wiped her hands on it, and then stuck it in a back pocket. "You can't say you really know her either, can you?"

"But she came to me in an agitated state and I consider that the sign of a friend in need," Janet said as she leafed through the book. "Even if I couldn't do much to help in the moment. Ah." She looked up. "Listen to how many words we have for describing rain now that we're here. Black weet, blatter, blaw bye, and dreep. Dribble, drouk, onding, and peuch. Plype, saft, scudder, and smirr. There's more, too, and I've heard some of them, but not all. I'm going to start keeping track. A life list, the way birders do."

"Put them to music and I'll do a jig at Nev's tonight." Tallie looked from the sunny view out the window to her mother. "Is Sharon worried about the weather for Friday night? We've only been in dribbly Scotland a few months and yet we've taken to the scuddering dreeps and blaw byes like ducks to drouks. If *we* can plan around a plype, what's her problem?"

"You have a good head for vocabulary, dear. But her problem isn't the weather. It's a sudden attack of persnickety specifics." Janet didn't mention Sharon's talk of bloody murder, not wanting to give her daughter, the former lawyer, a cause for alarm. "'The Persnickety Specifics'—that's what we can call ourselves when I sing and you do your jig at Nev's. We'll be a hit."

"Nice. I'll go on back to the storeroom and limber up while I finish checking in the order."

The bell jingled again and Janet turned to greet the next customer. Tallie took the cloth she'd stuck in her pocket and whirled it around her head with a whoop as she headed for the storeroom.

The morning's business continued in a steady trickle. Something more than a smirr of business, Janet decided, but less than the all-out frenzy of a blatter. Customers came and went, some passing first through Cakes and Tales, their adjoining tearoom, and bringing with them the smell of fresh cakes and scones. The occasional clinks and clatters from the tearoom were a muted counterpoint to Emanuel Ax tickling Chopin from a piano on the CD playing over the sound system. All in all, and despite Sharon's worries about the impending author visit, it was the kind of morning that made Janet believe she, Tallie, and their business partners Christine Robertson and Summer Jacobs had been sane and completely right when they'd made the decision that brought them to Inversgail.

Six months earlier, and after more months of researching, planning, and finagling, they'd pooled their resources, leapt after their dream, and bought Yon Bonnie Books and the building it had occupied for the past ninety-nine years. Two months after signing their names to the deed, the four had packed up their Midwestern lives and freighted them across the Atlantic. Janet and Tallie, having spent several decades of summers in Inversgail, were familiar with the town. Summer, a journalist, had studied for a year at Edinburgh University and promised herself she'd return one day for "a total Scottish Immersion Experience." Christine, who'd grown up in Inversgail, was returning home to aging parents after living thirty years with her late husband in the same Illinois prairie town as Janet.

The four women liked the symmetry of being the fourth set of owners since Colonel Stuart Farquhar opened the door of Yon Bonnie Books in 1919. They were already convinced the town would suit them. Inversgail was neither as small as a village, nor as large as a city. It was somewhere in between, and that was just right. They'd studied the shop's financial records and further convinced themselves the business would work as an augmented retirement for the two older women and a revitalizing change of career for the younger two. The scheme they'd dreamed up, which included adding a tearoom next door and a bed and breakfast above, called for as much leaping of faith as it did careful planning. But they'd made the leap, and although there were early-morning hours when Janet imagined their lives as a teetering balance of level heads and a yearning for adventure, she felt they were accomplishing their goal.

∞

Tallie, pushing a cart loaded with new books from the storeroom, stopped by the sales counter. "Why *did* Sharon want to share her agitation with us? Anything we really need to worry about?"

"Us? With all we've accomplished?"

"Because more of Daphne's books came in." Tallied patted the books on one side of the cart. Daphne Wood was the kind of versatile author booksellers dream of, one who could write successfully for adults and children. She could capture the imagination of lay readers and the more seriously science-minded. She'd written three beautifully illustrated picture books and a popular series of novels in narrative poetry for the hard-to-please middle school set. "Lovely things," Tallie said, stroking one of the picture books. "Lots of them, too."

"Are there plenty in the window display?"

"Stacks there, too. It'll be a shame if we have to send most of them back. Not so good for the budget either."

"I'll check with Gillian," Janet said. "There might be a hiccup or two, but nothing we can't handle."

"That's because you're Super Book Woman," Tallie said. "Able to read tall stacks of books in a single evening by the fire, although not quite able to reach the top shelf in our lofty philosophy section."

"That's why stepstools and daughters were invented," Janet said. Neither of the Marsh women were tall, but Janet enjoyed her bragging rights for having produced a daughter who, at five foot four, soared over her by two inches.

"Also why we have Rab," Tallie said. "He's coming in today, isn't he? Shall I leave these for him to shelve?"

Janet went to the window and scanned the harbor wall. Rab MacGregor was no longer in sight. Neither was his Cairn terrier or the cat. Rab was an odd-jobs man whom Janet could believe was anywhere from a weatherworn forty to a fresh-faced sixty. He worked for various people and at various jobs around Inversgail. He also worked for them in the shop and the tearoom, "various" again being a good word to describe his hours and duties, both of which were more or less self-assigned. Rab's services came as a package deal; where he went, so did his dog, Ranger. Ranger was as capable of self-direction as Rab, although Ranger's intentions could never be described as "various." When Rab was on the premises, Ranger invariably directed himself to one of the comfy chairs near the fireplace. He was mindful of the chairs, though, and waited patiently beside "his" for Rab to cover it with a Glasgow Rangers tea towel.

Rab had a reputation for lacking get-up-and-go. Christine accepted his reputation at face value. "He drifts to a different drummer, rather than marches," she'd said when he first came to work for them. "But despite his *easy-oasy* ways, he does a fine job when he actually shows up. He'll do."

Janet had a different theory. She'd known Rab during the years her family spent summers in Inversgail. She'd watched him do carpentry repairs, delicate pruning, the mucky and back-breaking work of digging up a water line, and more recently an almost eerie session of reading tea leaves. She believed he'd planted his reputation, that he cultivated, tended, and guarded it, and that behind it there were intricate workings, puzzles, and endeavors they only saw when he let them.

"Rab might be in today," Janet said in answer to Tallie's question. "Or maybe tomorrow. He said it depends on a deadline and whether he beats it or meets it." She heard a snort that sounded like either disbelief or derision. Not from Tallie, though—Summer had arrived from the tearoom with a plate of pastries.

"A deadline?" Summer asked. "Rab really said that?"

"Something like it, anyway."

Janet smiled and took the plate from Summer. She admired Summer's drive to make their business succeed, and the added energy she'd been putting into writing a weekly advice column for the *Inversgail Guardian*. But this attitude toward their lower-octane handyman had crept in recently, and Janet wanted to find out what was behind it. Not on the shop floor, though.

"Time to stop and smell the scones?" she asked instead.

"Smell, taste, and then tell me what you think of them," Summer said. "A new recipe. But tell me later. I have to get back."

"What are you calling them?" Janet asked, passing the plate and a napkin to Tallie.

"If you can't tell what they are, I'll need to tweak the recipe," Summer called over her shoulder. She waved without looking back again, and returned to the clinks and clatters of the tearoom.

"Does she sound stressed?" Janet asked Tallie.

"She sounds like Summer."

Janet took a bite of her scone and considered that. "But you don't think that lately she seems a bit more so?"

"A bit more Summer than Summer? What does that even mean?"

"Maybe she should slow down, look around? I'm not sure."

"Mom, I run three miles every morning to stay in shape, but for as long as I've known Summer, she's burned off the equivalent number of calories just planning what she's going to wear any given day. She's in her element and she's focused. She's fine."

"I'm sure you're right, sweetie. I'll forget all about it and focus on these scones." Janet took another bite. "They're orange, no question. A hint of almond? And something else, but I'm not sure what. What do you think?"

"That you aren't really sure I'm right about Summer. You only call me sweetie when you're distracted."

"What an interesting tic. How long have you been taking advantage of it? But you know, *dear*, you can't always *be* right. That's my job. I'm the smother."

Tallie laughed, as Janet knew she would. "Never in your life have you smothered," Tallie said. "You are the very model of unsmothering motherhood. But going all Mother Hen is another story. You do know that Summer won't appreciate you clucking over her, don't you?" She wrapped her scone in the napkin and put it on the bottom shelf of the book cart, then looked at her mother over the rims of her glasses.

"And she won't appreciate you ignoring that scone," Janet said.

"Saving, not ignoring. It's Monday. I want to get these books put away before the Highland Holidays coach pulls in after lunch."

"Good thinking. Do you want help?"

"Nah. I'll shelve the books. You shelve your worries."

Janet mimed putting a book on a shelf. "There you go. Under *U* for Unfounded."

"And if you ever write your memoirs, I'll shelve them under *N* for Nuts I've Known and Loved."

Janet blew Tallie a kiss and watched her disappear with the cart of books down the aisle between some of the tallest and most eclectic of their mismatched bookcases. She finished her scone, thinking of it as fortification for the onslaught of day trippers the Monday tour bus out of Fort William usually brought. The identity of the spice that complimented the orange so well in the scone eluded her. But that was what labels in the bakery case were for.

She wiped her fingers on her napkin and congratulated herself. She still had a mother's touch. And a mother's ability to reassure her child, no matter how old, how accomplished, or how astute that child might be. What Tallie hadn't heard about bloody murder wouldn't hurt her.

O n the other hand," Janet said to Christine during a lull half an hour later, "it won't hurt for me to run over to the school and talk to Gillian myself."

They stood in the door between the bookshop and the tearoom, Christine not quite towering over Janet. An acquaintance had once called Christine "willowy" and Janet "pillowy." Christine had shot back that they preferred "acutely angular" and "amply cute."

"Take a couple of our new scones with you," Christine said. "If Gillian is dealing with Sharon-the-librarian on a murderous rampage, on top of wrangling a fussy author-not-yet-in-residence, she'll need something to bolster her spirits."

"Good thought."

"If not something for a last meal."

"Tcha."

Janet and Christine had met in an elementary school in Champaign, Illinois. Christine, the transplanted Scot, had been a school social worker. Janet, the public librarian and daughter of a pig farmer, had been her son's show-and-tell demonstration that day. She'd woken ears in every classroom the length and breadth of the school with a reenactment of her state fair blue ribbon champion pig call. Christine claimed it was friendship at first *soooooo-ey*.

"And imagine what else Gillian might be dealing with," Christine said. "What if the list you saw is the least of her worries? What if that's only the preposterous tip of an absurd iceberg of even more ridiculous authorial demands?"

"I'm sure it's not," Janet said. "You're usually more matter-of-fact than this, Christine. What's gotten into you? The committee's been working out the details for this program for months."

"No doubt," Christine said. "For a year, more than likely."

"And with the amount of money that must be involved to bring Daphne Wood here for most of a school term, somewhere along the way they would have asked her for references."

"Must have done," Christine said. "References, background checks, and whatnot galore. That's the way things are done these days, isn't it? And a good thing, too. Especially where children are concerned. Wait here a moment. Incoming." She went to greet two couples who'd come into the tearoom through its front door.

One of the women took a moment to look around before sitting with the others at the table in the tearoom's front window. Janet followed her glance as she took in the brightly painted walls. The woman lifted her nose and sniffed, turned to look out at the harbor, and then sank into the chair Christine held for her. The look of approval on her face was exactly what Janet had hoped to see.

The couples laughed at something Christine said when she left them. She stopped at two other tables on her way back to Janet, leaning in at one to better hear an elderly woman. The woman patted Christine's arm and Christine put her own hand over the gnarled fingers.

"An old friend of Mum's," Christine said when she returned. "She prefers our tearoom to the scandalous T-shirt shop we replaced. Why are you still standing here? We have businesses to run."

"You asked me to wait. You were backpedaling on your worries over further ridiculous authorial demands."

"So I was. Well, no need to worry." Christine flapped the worry away with her hand. "I've been practicing that empathy meditation you turned me on to. Putting myself into some other poor sod's shoes. I tell you, it's really been helping me deal with Mum, the poor old dear. You see? I just called her 'poor *old* dear,' showing that I empathize with her for being as old as the fairies—and away with them, as often as not."

"I'm not sure you've understood the underlying philosophy, Christine."

"Does that matter? I feel calmer and more in tune. And there, did you hear that? I'm reverting nicely to my native accent. Dear old Mum will still say I'm hopelessly Americanized but I can still say *tune* as God intended." She'd pronounced it closer to *chune* than *tune*.

"And by 'God,' you mean Robert Burns."

"Of course. And what you just now called my worries over further ridiculous authorial demands was merely a meditational glitch. My empathy took a wrong turn and put me in Sharon's head. Now, there's a woman who might need help." Christine tapped a forefinger to her temple.

"That wouldn't surprise me," Janet said. "And I hope this whole thing doesn't get off to a bad start. I know you can't judge authors by their books any more than you can books by their covers, but I think I'm going to like Daphne Wood."

"Anyone who's spent her adult life living in the woods like Goldilocks with a bunch of bears has my admiration," Christine said. "I like Gillian, too, so remember to take the scones when you go see her. Anyone who spends her days cooped up with teenagers and their hormones, trying to drum English literature into their heads, also has my admiration and, moreover, deserves an award."

∽

Janet called the Inversgail High School, hoping to catch Gillian on her lunch hour. She didn't, and instead left a message on her voice mail.

"It's Janet Marsh, Gillian, wondering if you can give me a few minutes after school. It's just some last-minute questions about the signing, and I'll be over that way, anyway, so I'll stop by. If that won't be convenient, give me a call." Janet flicked her phone off. When she looked up, Tallie had slipped in behind the sales counter.

"You'll be over by the school?" Tallie asked, giving her mother another look over the rims of her glasses before pushing them up her nose.

"I will be once I walk over there. But I didn't want to worry her and make it sound dire by telling her I'm making a special trip. I'm sure she has enough on her plate. Besides," Janet avoided Tallie's eye and patted her hips, "it's about time I got more exercise, don't you think? Because sampling Summer's scones day in and day out isn't doing me any favors. You don't mind, do you?"

"What questions do we have about the signing?" Tallie asked. "Anything to do with the irate librarian this morning?"

"Things I could easily ask her over the phone. But it shouldn't take more than half an hour there and back."

"Except Gillian's a chatter," Tallie said.

"I'll tell her I have to get back. Keep her on task. Besides, doesn't it look like a lovely day for a walk?"

"Better take your umbrella."

"Good idea."

∽

Janet took her walk during what they'd been calling the nappish part of the afternoon. It came after most of the deluge of tourist buses had departed Inversgail and before the after-work dribble of customers arrived in the shop. It was generally a safe time for one of them to get out to the shops—to "do their messages," as Christine and Scots the country over called shopping.

And there, Janet thought as she passed the chemist. *That's something interesting about Summer. She still says drugstore, not chemist. She still does her shopping, not her messages, and she brings in the mail, never the post.*

The more Janet thought about it, the more she realized she was right. Not that she or Tallie were trying to pass themselves off as natives. Far from it. But Janet did try hard not to be so American that she turned heads. Was she—and Tallie, too—having an easier time making the language segue because they'd spent so many summers in Inversgail? Or was Summer making a conscious effort to avoid adopting local vocabulary? Was this an interesting tic of Summer's? Janet didn't know. If it was, she wondered what it meant.

Or maybe I don't want to know what it means, she thought. *Not if it means Summer's having trouble adjusting to the move. Or if it means she doesn't want to adjust because she wants to go home.*

Janet stopped and faced the harbor. She filled her lungs, enjoying the scents of seaweed, salt, and fish. Slowly, she let the breath out and then filled her lungs again. They weren't in Illinois anymore, and that suited her more than she'd imagined it would. But they were all also working harder than any of them had probably imagined. It was late August and the days would grow colder, shorter, and darker. She could understand regrets and second thoughts.

Another deep breath, in and out.

A breeze lifted the hair from her forehead. That breeze had skipped across the waves from the sheltering Western Isles. It kited an empty crisps bag into the street before whispering between the shops and over the houses and up into the hills and beyond.

Janet filled her lungs deeply one more time. As she released the breath, she pictured her worries catching the tail of the breeze and following it over the hills and far away. It was a fine hope, but about as practical as shelving the worries under *U* for Unfounded back at the shop. She didn't mind laughing at impracticalities, though, or herself, and continued up the High Street with a chuckle and a shake of her head.

"Up the High Street" was, in this case, literal. The main street of shops skirted the harbor and then took a puffing climb up the headland that marked the northern edge of town. A thin strip of white sand beach lay below the headland. Both the Inversgail Library and Archives and the Inversgail High School sat atop it, one behind the other.

Janet pushed herself to climb the hill at an aerobic clip rather than her usual stroll. When she reached the library, she stopped to admire the view of the Western Isles. It was a crisp, clear day, and she knew the view would take her breath, if only she hadn't already lost it in the climb. Giving her prairie-bred legs and lungs another few minutes to recover, she debated which further stamina-improving route she should follow to the school. She had two options: the first leg of a new footpath starting in a garden outside the library and running past the school before it trekked into Glen Sgail, or the more prosaic and straightforward pavement. She checked the time; the pavement won.

The library and high school buildings, not quite five years old, were built on land left to the town by the same Stuart Farquhar who'd established the bookshop. Farquhar's family house—he'd called it his Victorian pile—had crowned the headland until it burned a few years after his death. Only his garden remained.

Inversgailians were proud of their modern school and library, with their state-of-the-art connectedness to the whole wide world. The local council felt shrewd for having slipped under a wire of opportunity to secure government funding for the buildings. That wire had since been pulled tight, cutting off monies for other towns that hadn't been as nimble.

Janet liked the looks of the new school. Its design gave a nod to traditional highland architecture, with gable ends and clean white walls, but on a much larger scale than a croft house. And the school gained a sense of vigor and light from a dozen or more tall windows looking toward the library, the harbor, and the sea. *A much more inviting place to learn than schools that look like industrial office blocks,* Janet thought.

A couple of girls on their way out held the door for her, and she entered an airy lobby hung with artwork. A sign told her it was a show of student and faculty work inspired by the writings of Daphne Wood, the soon-to-be author-in-residence. Janet was impressed by the talent, and immediately pictured student and faculty art hanging in the bookshop or the tearoom. She made a quick note in her phone to bring the idea up with her partners and then followed an arrow to the administrative office.

Several students were there ahead of her, waiting for the attention of a woman behind a barricade-like desk. Janet joined the short queue, only to be waved forward out of turn. With apologies, she moved ahead of the students.

"Janet Marsh for Gillian Bennett," she told the woman. "She's expecting me."

The woman made eye contact long enough to say, "Staffroom, no doubt. I'll ring. Step aside." She gave equally efficient answers to the students while she waited, with the phone to her ear, for someone in the staffroom to answer. No one did, and she turned her attention back to Janet. "Classroom, then. Sign the clipboard, please. Do you know the way?"

Janet added her name to the list of school visitors, then followed the woman's directions to Gillian's classroom, which she gave with the crisp hand signals of a traffic warden—*left out of the office, straight away down the corridor, left again at the first opportunity, door on the right halfway along, number thirty-three.*

Janet enjoyed repeating the room number softly to herself, with its full complement of rolled *R*s, until she remembered the less delightful rolled *R* of that morning. *Murder.* And not just murder, but *bloody murder.* Should she warn Gillian of that plot, she wondered? Let her know that Sharon had asked if she'd like a chance at killing Gillian? No, probably not. Janet did know Gillian, but not well enough to gauge how seriously she'd take such a statement. Because, although of course Sharon's question about committing bloody murder had certainly *not* been serious, Sharon *had* been seriously angry. Likely not angry enough to *kill*, though, so why look for trouble?

Janet turned left where she was meant to turn left. Looking down the corridor, she saw a woman about Tallie's age standing outside an open classroom door, halfway along on the right. Gillian's room, presumably. The woman laughed at something going on in the room and then, with a hand on her hip and an exaggerated flounce, launched into an animated response or remark of her own. Janet slowed her steps, then she stopped, not wanting to interrupt or intrude.

"A prima donna if ever there was one," the woman said, doing a sloppy pirouette. "Right down to her—" On her second revolution she saw Janet and lurched sideways. She steadied herself with one hand on the doorframe, and with the other she smoothed her skirt.

"Are you all right?" Janet asked.

"Looked a bit of a fool, didn't I?" the woman said. "Sorry, can I help?"

"I'm here to see Gillian Bennett. Is she—" Janet tipped her head toward the door the woman was now blocking.

"Bad luck. I think you've missed her." The woman turned and called to whoever was in the room, "She's missed Gillian, hasn't she?"

"Who has?" a male voice answered. A man came to the door, tall with a broad forehead and close-cut dark hair. The woman moved aside and he pulled the door shut behind him. "From the bookshop, aren't you?" he said with a nod to Janet. "Jenny? Janie? Janet." He crossed his arms over his chest, looking satisfied with the last answer, but rumpling his tie.

"Janet, yes. Janet Marsh. You have a good memory." Janet had seen this man before but his memory had the advantage over hers. She was one of a mere four new owners of the bookshop, while he was one of at least several hundred Scotsmen she'd seen in Yon Bonnie Books over the past four months. He'd been in the shop with Gillian, though. He taught math, or was it science? *Tom.*

"And you're Tom," she said, happy to have sifted half his name from her head. "But I've forgotten your last name."

"No worries. It won't be the last name I'm called."

"Gomeril," the woman said to him. To Janet, she said, "He's Tom Laing, but he's short on manners." She held her hand out. "Hello, I'm Hope Urquhart. I work with Gillian in the English department. I knew I'd seen you somewhere. I'm afraid I don't get into the bookshop as often as I'd like. I'll be there for the signing a week Sunday, though. Or will we see you at the ceilidh Friday night? First look at the visiting author, and honoring Gillian's dad and all? Should be a grand time."

"Plenty of drink," Tom said. "Surprising how that helps on these occasions."

"Hush, you," said Hope. "Great food and music. And dancing. I'm far less clumsy when it comes to Dashing White Sergeants."

"I wouldn't miss it," Janet said.

"See you there, then. And you, Tom, behave yourself."

Tom's answer to that was a half-smile. Without knowing him better, Janet hesitated to think of it as a smirk. She watched his face as he watched Hope walk away, though, and the possible smirk turned briefly into what might be a leer. When Hope disappeared around the corner, Tom flicked a glance at Janet and she felt as though she'd been caught spying. She covered her embarrassment by holding up the bag with the scones.

"Do you know if Gillian's just away from her room," she asked, "or is she gone for the day? I hope I haven't wasted a trip. I thought I was meeting her here this afternoon, and I brought some of our new scones from the tearoom as a treat." *And I'm smiling like a loon and talking too much and now he's staring at me.* She lowered the bag and the wattage of her smile.

"A treat, you say." Tom Laing took the bag from her hand. "Or could it be a bribe of some sort?"

"Sorry, a what?"

"You have bribes in America, aye? I reckon they're something like baseball; a national sport."

Likes to hear himself talk, Janet thought. *And bait his audience. But not on my time.* From years of practicing on problematic library patrons, her face settled into lines of polite disinterest. "Nice to meet you again, Tom," she said, reaching for the scone bag.

He moved the bag to his far hand and held it so that she would have to reach around him to get it. "Gillian's gone for the day."

"Ah."

"But I'll see she gets these."

"Thank you."

He nodded down the hall toward the entry. "As I'm heading toward the door myself, shall I walk you out?"

"I'm sure I can find the door, but thank you."

"Aye, well, as I said, I'm going that way." Tom Laing started down the hall. Annoyed, Janet followed. Tom slowed so that he walked beside her, annoying her further, and then he took a scone from the bag and bit into it. "Not bad," he said around the mouthful.

Every muscle of Janet's professional courtesy strained to keep her from swatting the scone from his hand and grabbing the bag. Kicking his shin crossed her mind, too.

When they reached the lobby, he made a sweeping gesture with what was left of the scone. "What do you think of it?" he asked, then popped the last bite in his mouth.

"Think of what? The artwork? The lobby? The school?"

He swallowed and brushed the back of his hand across his mouth. "The lobby?" he echoed, mimicking her pronunciation. "Why would I ask what you think of the lobby?" He gestured again, this time the fingers of his empty hand splayed. "The paintings and drawings. The photographs."

Janet saw no reason to let her annoyance with this man upstage the artwork. "There's a lot of talent here," she said. "It's a lovely show. I don't see how Daphne Wood can be anything but extremely impressed."

Tom went to stand in front of three photographs and seemed to be studying them intently.

"The photographs are particularly nice," Janet said.

"Some of my best."

"They're yours?" She knew she sounded incredulous, but he didn't seem to notice. And just because she thought his photographs were stunning didn't mean her opinion of him needed an upgrade. On the other hand, there was no need to be purposely rude. "They're beautiful. Where is that?"

"Sgail Gorge," he said. "Or as we're calling it again, Glen Sgail, and it's about bloody time. One of the most beautiful places on earth. We owe a debt that can't be repaid to Gillian's father for all he's done."

"The presentation to Alistair and the ceilidh will be nice, though," Janet said. "And isn't the whole Daphne Wood author-in-residence thing a tribute to the work he's done?"

"The ceilidh will be a load of bollocks with all the tradition stripped out of it. The author-in-residence 'thing,' as you call it, is another story. Anyone who doesn't make the most of this opportunity has bollocks for brains. Your shop won't be doing too badly selling her books, I reckon."

"Speaking of books," Janet said, proud of herself for not speaking her mind, "I'd better get back to them. Your pictures are wonderful, Tom. All the artwork is. The light and the white walls in this lobby"—she gave the word the full Midwestern treatment—"set everything off beautifully. The whole school is lovely."

"Smoke and mirrors, that's all it is," Tom said. "Just the planners wanting to give the impression the building belongs here. It doesn't. Like so many new *things* in Inversgail, it's nothing but a transplant. See ya."

Not if I see you first and find a place to hide, Janet thought. Tom Laing certainly saw nothing wrong with being purposely rude.

On Monday evenings, the four women met at Nev's, a pub that
wasn't on the High Street, and didn't look like much on the
outside. Tucked between Smith Funerals and the *Inversgail
Guardian*, Nev's didn't advertise itself to tourists, but welcomed anyone
who discovered it, along with their dogs. At some point in the past, the
sign with the pub's original name—Chamberlain's Arms—had disappeared. *Came down in a storm*, some said. *Stolen by outlanders*, said others.
Taken down for repainting, still others said. Locals didn't need the sign,
though, and Danny, the publican of most recent record, saw no reason
to bring it out of the cellar where it gathered dust in a dark corner.

Janet called their Monday nights at Nev's their quality of life check.
Christine called them their weekly wind-down with occasional whisky.

"It's an honest place," Christine had said when she proposed the
meetings. "We can be honest at Nev's and admit that not every moment
of our new lives is Scotties, scones, and purple heather."

"Meetings at Nev's will provide the antidote to the *dreich* that's bound
to creep up on us from time to time," Tallie had said, using her favorite
weather word from her childhood summers.

Janet and Summer had easily agreed. Nev's gave them greetings from
locals and occasional smiles, a chance to unwind or unburden, a game of
darts if anyone liked, and neutral ground. Nev's provided ale and whisky,
too, and comforting pub food to go with them. Rab MacGregor, true to

his nature of being variously here or there, joined them sometimes, but not always. They'd been coming into Nev's on Mondays long enough to have a "usual" table near the door to the darts room. Summer occasionally joined the players, and Tallie usually went along, to cheer her on.

"You're feeling guilty about something," Christine said that evening.

"Am I?" Janet asked. "I wonder why?"

"You might be trying to hide something." Christine studied Janet more closely. "Aye, that's probably it. It's what usually makes you look guilty."

"People read me like a book these days. I'm not sure I like it."

"But it's appropriate," Christine said. "So let's not get sidetracked by that complaint. Unburden on us. That's what these evenings are for."

"It isn't much, really," Janet said. "Just that feeling—"

Christine stood up. "Sorry, Janet. Dad's having a time getting Mum's coat off over there. I'll be right back."

Meeting at Nev's also gave Christine a chance to get her parents out of the house and down to their old local for a bit of company. Her mum didn't always remember that Christine wasn't just home on a short visit from America, but she knew Nev's and recognized a half pint when she saw it.

The music on the sound system switched from plaintive vocals, in what Janet assumed was Gaelic, to an even more plaintive fiddle piece. She sat back, half listening to Tallie and Summer laughing over solutions to hypothetical burning issues, and half listening to the music. A fairly dreich piece, she thought, and perfectly lovely. Nev's didn't go in for real musicians. The times they'd tried live music, tourists had flocked in. There would be live music at the library Friday night, though, and Janet was looking forward to that.

She wondered about Christine's question. *Am I feeling guilty? No, not really. Or only partly.* What she felt, she decided, was the odd mixture of guilt and annoyance that comes when a message one leaves isn't clear or goes astray. So she'd missed Gillian that afternoon. Then she'd gotten back to the bookshop and found Tallie being rushed off her feet by a surprising flurry of customers. Those missteps were compounded by her dislike for Tom Laing. The walk to and from the school had been otherwise refreshing, but considering the outcome, she felt she'd made a bad decision in going. She disliked making bad decisions more than she disliked Tom Laing. But she also disliked ruining a pleasant evening at Nev's with negative thoughts, so she closed her eyes and attempted to push them away using what she'd gleaned from her book about empathy meditation.

The next thing she knew, someone was touching her shoulder, and she heard Tallie stifle a giggle and say, "She's snoring." Janet opened her eyes. Christine and Danny the publican were nose to nose with her.

"Are you all right, then, Janet?" Danny asked. When she nodded, he and Christine stood up. "Good, because Christine reminded me, none too subtly, I might add, that tonight marks four months you lot have managed to stay in business, much to my considerable surprise." He smiled at Christine and received a good-natured snarl in return. "No, really, much to my considerable pleasure, and so I'd like to stand you a round of drinks in congratulations."

Danny Macquarrie was yet another reason Christine enjoyed their Monday evenings at Nev's. Tall and broad, he had served with distinction in the Royal Navy and then come home to Inversgail. Even after a brilliant naval career, Christine claimed he had occasional fits of inadequacy, stemming from the time she'd pushed him off the harbor wall when they were small and she'd had to jump in to rescue him.

She'd also confided in Janet that they were both independent enough, stubborn enough, and set enough in their ways that the casual and quiet relationship they'd settled into, since she'd returned, suited them. She and Danny had what she called an uncluttered relationship. "We've known each other since we were *weans*," she said. "We're happy with the amount of time we spend together, and equally happy keeping our friendship free of strings and the snarled mess strings so often make."

Danny's relationship with Nev's appeared to be just as casual, and he kept its true nature quiet, too, so that many of his patrons had no idea he owned the place and wasn't just one of the barmen.

Christine helped Danny bring pints of the local ale, Selkie's Tears, to the table. Five, because Rab and Ranger materialized, as if out of nowhere, in time to join them in a toast to their business. The toast earned a round of applause from other patrons. Another fiddle piece merged into a lively accordion tune and they drank their celebratory pints, the picture of relaxed contentment. Right then, Summer looked content, too, Janet thought. Then Janet caught Tallie watching her watch Summer and she knew what her daughter was thinking—*I told you so.*

James Haviland, editor of the *Inversgail Guardian*, stopped by their table with Martin Gunn, one of his reporters, in tow. James was an unassuming sort of renaissance man about Inversgail. He wrangled the paper, played fiddle in a ceilidh band, threw darts not quite like a champion, and when he sat and knit his fingers over his stomach, he looked like a favorite uncle about to tell a story. Janet knew the younger man, Martin Gunn, by sight and his apparent devotion to Nev's and darts, but nothing beyond that.

"Are you playing at the library Friday, James?" Christine asked.

"Fair warning," James said, "I am. Fancy a game, Summer?"

Summer shrugged, but got up and took her pint with her.

Nev's was filling up. Christine went to check on her parents. Rab and Ranger had dematerialized. Janet looked around for them and saw Gillian and Tom walk in, Tom's hand at the small of Gillian's back.

Tallie saw them, too. "Good," she said. "Here's your chance to catch her."

Gillian and Tom stopped at the bar, and while Gillian gave their order and paid for their drinks, Tom looked toward the darts room. He might have seen them at their table near the door, but Janet detected no flicker of recognition. When he had his drink in hand, he said something to Gillian, patted her backside, and took himself off to the darts, leaving her standing at the bar.

"She looks a little bummed," Tallie said, after Tom passed them.

"He's a big bum," said Janet. "Hop up and invite her over here."

"Hopping."

Gillian was one of the bookshop's best customers. Janet and Tallie knew that, because she'd told them so when she first introduced herself. She was one of half a dozen or so self-proclaimed best customers, and Janet had decided early on that it didn't matter whether those customers spent their entire paychecks in the shop or only came in once a month to browse; anyone who believed that firmly in their love for Yon Bonnie Books was indeed a best customer.

"It was from you!" Gillian said when she came back to the table with Tallie. "Tallie told me the scone that saved my life this afternoon was from you, Janet. Bless you. Tom let me think he had it left over from his elevenses, the great numpty." She sat between them and took a long swallow from her pint of something darker than the Selkie's Tears.

"I'm glad you got it and liked it," Janet said. "Did you get the message I left, too?"

"With Tom?"

"On your phone."

Gillian brought her phone out and shook her head with each flick of her finger as she scrolled. She was a few years older than Tallie, with an attractive touch of gray starting to frost her temples. The movement of her eyebrows, as she continued flicking through her phone, gave the impression she was getting more and more lost in her trail of messages. When Christine rejoined them, she put the phone away.

"How are you, Gillian?" Christine asked, "You're looking a little haunted around the eyes. Has this whole visiting author song and dance got your knickers in a twist?"

Gillian's smile looked haunted, too. She took another swallow of her drink and then answered with a game lift of her chin. "After more than a year of planning, and months of preparation and keeping a vigilant eye out for pitfalls to pave over, I can truthfully say that I am ready for the term to finally be over."

Christine stared at her. "Term one only started last week, didn't it?"

Gillian nodded. "Small problem, eh? Well." She nodded, again, and took another swallow. "A few more hurdles to get over and then every-thing will be fine. I'm sure it will be. And here's what I keep telling myself: It's as well to remember that Daphne has been living alone in that cabin of hers for a long time."

"Decades," Janet said.

"Can you imagine?" Gillian asked. "I'm a bit of a nature girl, myself. In fact, Dad and I often took her rambling with us. But the way she lives now is light-years beyond a weekend hill walk."

"She isn't entirely off the grid, though," Tallie said. "She writes, she gets published. She does interviews. She's acclaimed by reviewers. Readers love her. She might live like a recluse, but she hasn't cut herself off."

"Even so," Gillian said.

"Even so, what?" Tallie asked. "Is there something you're trying to tell us? Or trying to not tell us?"

"Only that we shouldn't be surprised if she's—" Gillian measured an inch with her thumb and index finger then squinted at them and brought them together so they almost touched. "I reckon she might have become a wee bit eccentric over the years. She and I were inseparable, did you know that? I spent a lot of time in her house and she spent even more in mine. Dad called us the two musketeers."

"Wonderful," Janet said. "How eccentric is a wee bit?"

"Not much." Gillian rummaged in her bag and came out with several sheets of folded paper. "But she has a few—" Gillian waved the papers as though diminishing or dispersing whatever it was that Daphne had a few of, then handed them to Janet.

Janet unfolded the papers and saw the list Sharon had stormed into the shop with that morning. She handed them to Tallie.

"You aren't going to read them?" Gillian asked.

"Sharon stopped by first thing today and let me read hers," Janet said. "But thank you, it's good to have a copy of our own."

"Ah." Gillian traced the grain of the table's wood with a finger and didn't say any more.

"I'm not really worried by some of what's on the list," Janet said. "For big signings, having a person on hand to open the books to the title page and someone to get the right spelling for names is fairly standard procedure. And a lot of authors are particular about the pens they use for signing. Although, if they're *so* particular, then it makes sense for them to supply their own. But the rest—"

At that point, Tallie, who'd been reading the list, whistled and passed it to Christine.

"The others didn't see Sharon's copy," Janet said, hoping that explained Tallie's whistle and Christine's dropping jaw. "Does Daphne really expect to have everything else on the list at the signing? What's she going to use all that for? Unless she's planning to do a program of some sort, but this would be the first we've heard about that. Maybe none of her requests are as totally outrageous as Sharon seems to think they are—"

"Oh, I think they might be," Tallie said.

"Anyway," Janet said, "it leaves us wondering where all this is supposed to come from. Your grant? Because we can't supply it."

"A ceramic bowl with fresh water?" Christine read aloud. "What's that for? This isn't eccentric, Gillian, it's barking mad."

Gillian looked at the three of them and put a hand to her mouth. The hand wasn't enough to stop a squeak that turned into a laugh. For a brief moment, Janet thought they'd been let in on a joke, although not a particularly good one. When Gillian's laugh threatened to become hysterical, she knew better.

"Gillian," Janet said, then more sharply, *"Gillian."*

Gillian pointed at Christine. "She said 'barking mad.'" She started to laugh again, but Christine employed the best quelling look in her Elizabeth II repertoire. It was enough to make Gillian draw in a breath and straighten her shoulders. "Barking mad," she said, looking at Christine, then Janet, and then Tallie.

"We understand your words," Tallie said. "But what do they mean?"

"She's bringing a dog," Gillian said. "It goes everywhere she does."

"A service dog?" Janet asked.

"I don't think so. But it goes to book signings and only drinks out of ceramic bowls. No empty margarine tubs to be substituted. Or aluminium mixing bowls." Gillian was beginning to look and sound unhealthy. She tried smiling, which didn't improve anything. "Can you believe it? Not once in all our correspondence, in all the negotiating over her accommodations for the three months she's going to be here, did she mention a dog."

"Can she bring a dog here from Canada?" Tallie asked. "Won't it have to be quarantined?"

"Yes, she can bring it. No, there's no quarantine. Yes, it's arriving with her. No, the flat we found for her does not allow pets. On top of that, Daphne emailed yesterday to say she's arriving two days early. At first I thought that was a good omen. Then she told me about the dog." Gillian started to sway, her brow pale and sweaty. Tallie moved her glass a safe distance away.

"Will the agency bend the rules just this once, I asked, oh pretty please?" Gillian said in a singsong. "Will they let a well-loved, well-cared-for, literary dog stay for a mere three months? No, they won't. Not even for our illustrious visiting migraine will they bend their sacred rules. And how much time have I got to sort this out before she arrives?"

"Not long," Janet said.

"Not long," Gillian echoed. "Two days. And this on top of final arrangements for Friday night. Oh, my God."

"What are you going to do?" Tallie asked.

Gillian swayed toward Tallie and grabbed her arm as though it might save her from drowning. "Is there room at your B&B?"

"Oh, Gillian, I'm so sorry," Tallie said. "We're fully booked at least this week and next."

"Then the only thing I can do is hope for a great big bolt of lightning and a tremendous crash of thunder, followed by a miracle."

"A thunderplump," Janet said.

"I don't even need a blattering downpour," Gillian said. "Just something huge and divine and directed at Daphne. What do you think my chances are?"

"That doesn't sound like the competent, organized, rational woman we've come to know and admire," Janet said.

"But wouldn't it be nice? The two musketeers. We went to different universities, went different ways. Maybe it seems odd we didn't keep in touch, but not really. She had a difficult patch in our last year, and I see it happen all the time with the kids I teach. Daphne was a lot of fun back then. Until she wasn't. But I've been hoping we could have that back."

Tallie slapped her hands on the table. The slap fell short of sounding like thunder, but Gillian jumped. "I think I have your miracle, Gillian," she said, "and her name is Maida Fairlie."

Maida Fairlie was a small Scottish woman weighed down by the rectitude of dour ancestors. She was also the mother-in-law of Janet's son. Tallie told Gillian about the house Maida had been trying, unsuccessfully, to sell.

"It belonged to her parents," Tallie said. "It's empty. Maybe she'll consider a short term lease."

"It's the house right behind ours," Janet said. "Call her, Tallie."

"Call her," Gillian said, "and hope for a Maida miracle."

When Tallie got through to Maida, and told her the situation, and heard her wavering one way and then the other, she handed the phone to Gillian.

"Gillian's the one working the miracle," Christine said as they watched her end of the conversation. "Look. She's got Maida to say yes. You can tell because, just like that, the cares of the world lifted and she looks ten years younger. I must say, I've never lost ten years talking to Maida."

"Just as well," Danny said, overhearing Christine when he came to clear away empty glasses. "You only need to lose two or three years."

"That was inspired problem solving," Janet said to Tallie. She tapped the list of requirements. "Now tell me where I'll find these G-force fighter pilot or whatever they are pens Daphne Wood is so keen on."

"I'll ask Basant," Tallie said. "If he doesn't have them, maybe he can get them."

"Order them online," Danny said. "Be here faster than you can blink Selkie's Tears from your eyes."

Tallie thumped her empty glass on the table. "Shop locally."

"Mind the glassware, lass." Danny rescued the glass from Tallie. "But she's right, Janet, and I shouldn't need reminding. Locals need to stick together. Another round, anyone? No? You know where to find me if you change your minds."

Gillian finished her conversation with Maida Fairlie. She handed the phone back to Tallie, and waved at someone behind Janet. "Tom," she called and then shook her head. "*Och* well. Darts. But, Tallie—" She sat back with a sigh and a smile for all of them at the table. "My load is lightened by the miracle you've wrought. You and Maida. I'm to go for a walk-through tomorrow, but the house sounds perfect. I cannot tell you what a relief it is to have that off my mind. Thank you. And now I can let Daphne know and relieve her mind, too." She stopped for a moment and made a face. "I reckon I might have left her with the impression I was angry with her."

"Imagine that," Janet said. "So then, not to shovel anything back onto your load, but what should we do about Daphne's list of requirements? How seriously should we take it?"

"Ah, but here comes Tom. Good." Gillian waved him over and he came to stand behind her chair. She turned to look up at him as he started to knead her shoulders. "The latest and largest Daphne problem is solved, Tom, thanks to the bonnie bookshop clan."

"Moral support on my part, only," Christine said.

"And where would we be without morals?" Tom asked.

"But back to the list," Gillian said. "Janet, if you can provide the more mundane requests, I'll tackle the rest."

"You'll *speck-tackle* the rest," Tom said. "Because our whole Daphne term will be spectacular. She'll be great. She's brilliant, our Daphne is."

"And he's blootered," Christine said to Janet, but not quietly enough.

Tom pulled the chair out next to Gillian, dropped into it, and laid a heavy arm across her shoulders. "I'm blootered, but brilliant, as well, and proud of my wee girlie here, for her beautiful brilliance, too."

Gillian leaned her cheek against his arm and then slid from under it, taking his hand and getting to her feet. "It's away home for you, Tom. Give me your keys and I'll get you there so you can sleep it off and be brilliant at school tomorrow."

"You get some sleep, too, Gillian," Tallie said. "Tom's right. Everything's going to be brilliant."

~

Rab MacGregor reappeared at their table shortly after Gillian left with Tom. He needed their help, he said. He'd had an urgent call from Maida Fairlie.

4

Sea mist from the harbor met them as they left Nev's. The mist didn't so much creep in on cat's feet as twine around their ankles and brush past them. It followed Christine as she helped her parents into their ancient Vauxhall. She told Janet she would settle her mum and dad at home and then join the others in their late evening rescue of Maida. The mist swallowed Ranger the terrier up whole as he trotted ahead of Rab, but it couldn't quite catch hold of Rab, who said he'd see the others soon. Summer gave her regrets, shrugging into the mist as though it were a blanket. She had to be in bed early, to get up and bake for the tearoom and feed the guests staying in the bed and breakfast. Janet and Tallie watched her go and then kicked home through the mist to change into clothes more suitable for the work ahead.

"How many words do we have now for mist or fog?" Janet asked as they walked up Fingal Street toward their granite cottage on Argyll Terrace.

"Murk's one of my favorites," Tallie said. "But we own a bookshop, so we can look it up. Don't you love saying that? *We own a bookshop*."

Janet linked her arm with Tallie's. "This particular mist has more personality than some. A more interesting personality, anyway. It isn't like a wall of fog."

"A wall of fog is dense and thuggish. It only wants to blot things out."

"That's exactly how it is," Janet said. "But look how this stuff gathers and pools and seems to be following us. It's curious, wonders what we're up to."

"We're shifting furniture," Tallie said to the mist, "to save Maida's bacon."

∾

Maida, in her excitement at being asked to let her house for more money than she would have dreamed (or dared to suggest), had neglected to give Gillian a piece of information. That wasn't to say that the missing information would have immediately turned Gillian against renting the house, but it had created a situation of near panic for Maida. Or as near to panic as Maida Fairlie ever came. The once comfortable, though rather plain, semidetached house stood completely empty, and after months of no interest from prospective buyers, Maida had stopped dropping by to air it out or sweep.

When Maida had phoned Rab for help, she hadn't told him the full extent of her emergency, either, so that what he passed along to Janet and the others was further watered down. When Janet and Tallie arrived in jeans and old shirts, ready to "shift a wee bit of furniture," Maida was unlocking the front door.

She looked past them to the pavement and the street. "No one else with you?"

Janet turned to look at the street with her. "I thought Christine and Rab might be here by now, but they'll be along soon. We came through the back garden."

Maida looked at their shoes. "Mind and wipe your feet, then." She opened the door and went in ahead of them, turning on lights.

"Wipe them on what?" Tallie asked.

"Oh, aye," Maida said. "I'll add a doormat to my list of things to bring along."

"How long has it been empty?" Janet asked, trying to gauge the cobwebs, dust, and dead bluebottles.

"A wee bit of sweeping and dusting will set it right," Maida said. "The broom and dust mop are in the cupboard, there. I'll go watch for Rab."

Janet and Tallie looked at each other, and Janet was about to mutter something when Maida came back. "Thank you for coming round," she said, the full weight of her dour ancestors imprinted on each word.

"Well," Janet said when Maida had gone again, "bare floors are easier to clean."

Tallie went to the cupboard. "Choose your weapon, Merry Sunshine."

∞

Two of Maida's teenaged nephews arrived with Rab and the first load of furnishings in a small utility van. Christine rolled to a stop in her parents' car behind the van.

"Ranger not supervising tonight?" Christine asked Rab, as he watched the nephews maneuver a bedframe from the back of the van.

"He's minding the van."

They each took two straight-back chairs from the van and followed the nephews through the front gate and up the short path. Maida could be heard following the nephews with cautions to mind the woodwork, corners, floors, and walls. Bedframe safely landed, Maida sent the nephews and Rab out for the rest of the bed, then she greeted Christine with the same dour thank you she'd doled out to the others.

"This is very good of you, too, Maida, and on such short notice," Christine said.

"I've always said I'm well-blessed." Maida picked a cobweb from her sleeve. "The house has what you might call a few—" She hesitated before elaborating on what the house had a few of. "I dinnae like to call them problems, per se. Eccentricities, perhaps."

That word again, Janet thought.

"So, what's my tenant to be like, do you know?"

"We don't know much beyond her professional reputation," Janet said, feeling Tallie's and Christine's eyes on her. "She's a wonderful writer."

"Prolific," Christine said, "and wide-ranging."

"She has something for every reader," Tallie added.

"And a dog," Maida said.

"Will that be a problem?" Janet asked.

"I have nothing against dogs, so long as they don't yap or bite," Maida said. "Or drool, or jump up, or lick. Or shed."

"What about housetrained? You'd like that, wouldn't you?" Christine asked.

"What's the best way we can help you tonight, Maida?" Janet asked, after giving Christine a discreet poke in the ribs.

They moved aside as the nephews carried in a narrow end table on top of which they'd balanced a dish pan containing several pots and pans and a drainer stacked with dishes. Janet saw Maida bow her head and close her eyes. When the load came to rest with only a thump and no additional sounds of crashing or breaking, Maida's eyes popped open and then fixed on the trail of mud from one of the nephews.

"I have two thoughts at this point," Maida said. "First, I could use help organizing at the other end so that Rab and the lads know what to take and what not. Second, we'll have to clean the floors again when we're finished."

"How will we know where you want things put on this end?" Christine asked.

"I reckon it'll be obvious. If not," Maida said with one of her rare smiles, "use your imagination."

Tallie volunteered to go with Maida and the two drove off into the mist. Janet and Christine split up to clean kitchen and bath and start putting things away. Rab and the nephews brought in the last of the load from the van and went to pick up another. By the time the van had made half a dozen trips, stopping once to get more boxes from the bookshop, they'd brought a second bed, a dining table, a kitchen table, two more straight-back chairs, an overstuffed armchair, a toaster, an electric kettle, a teapot, flatware, a short sofa, a wardrobe, two bookcases, blankets, linens, and pillows. Janet wondered if Maida had anything left in her own house.

Maida and Tallie brought the last load, including teabags and milk, and two of Maida's prayer plants, African violets for the kitchen window, and a purple passion plant.

"To make it more homelike," Maida said.

"As opposed to the derelict pensioner's flat it must have appeared when you got here," Christine whispered to Janet, after Maida went into the kitchen and wondered aloud about bringing over cookbooks. "It's no wonder it hasn't sold. And Maida in the cleaning business. Tcha."

"She might be like one of those barbers who stays so busy, because he's the best, but then he never has time to get his own hair trimmed," Janet said.

"You're a kind soul, Janet."

"Thank you."

"If somewhat delusional."

"Shall we give the floors a quick clean tonight and call it good enough?" Tallie asked.

"Surely tomorrow's good enough for that and setting right anything we've put wrong," Christine said. "We're all exhausted and most of us have work or school tomorrow."

"I'll stay," Rab said. "Finish it tonight."

"I can get the worst of this out the front door right now," one of the nephews said. He opened the front door and swept a few straggles of leaf and mud out. Then, not bothering to shut the door, which they'd been leaving open as they worked, anyway, he faced his brother and proved his strength by hefting the broom as though it were a set of barbells.

As the others discussed or avoided further cleaning, Janet went to close the door. It was then that she saw another vehicle appear out of the mist and roll to a stop in front of the house—a Land Rover of some sort, she thought. The driver got out, came around to the passenger door, opened it, and her traveling companion hopped out, too.

"I can't ask any of you to stay longer," Maida said above the others. "Mind, if you do, the windows need going over, too. *The broom is not a caber!*"

Janet watched as the travelers looked up and down the street, sniffed the air, and appeared to study Maida's house.

"Not that cleaning the floors will make any difference," Christine was saying, unaware of the travelers now coming through the front gate and up the short path to the door. "Not after the wretched dog tracks its muddy paws all over. What time are Daftie Daphne and the wretch due to arrive tomorrow? Do we know?"

Janet stepped out onto the stoop and held out her hand to the woman whose face she could now see clearly. "Hi, you must be Daphne Wood. I'm Janet Marsh. We're very happy to have you here."

"Yip," said the dog.

The woman looked at Janet's hand and stuck her own in her jeans pockets. Janet pulled her hand back. She turned to let the others know the author had arrived, and saw there was no need. They stood like an uncertain chorus behind her. Christine met her glance with one raised eyebrow.

"I haven't introduced myself," the woman said. "How do you know that I am this Daphne Wood?"

It was a fair enough question. Before anyone else answered, one of Maida's nephews jumped in.

"She looks like the picture on the back of her books," he said. "We have them at school, and she had her hair wrapped round her head just like that. She can't be anyone else, can she? But what kind of dog is that?"

Neither Daphne Wood nor the dog answered.

"Pekingese," Rab said.

At that, Daphne Wood nodded.

"Looks like a wee lion," the nephew said. "Did *you* cut its hair like that?"

"Pekes are lovely dogs," Maida said. She gave the dog a dubious look as she pushed past Janet. "Hello, Ms. Wood. I'm Maida Fairlie. It's my house you'll be staying in."

Daphne said nothing.

Maida renewed her efforts. "Welcome back to Inversgail. Welcome home—and to your home away from home. It seems like there should be an official welcoming committee, but I suppose we'll have to do. You're a wee bit early, aren't you? Only you've caught us putting the finishing touches on the place. Rab, boys, why don't you help Ms. Wood in with her luggage? I hope you had a good trip, Ms. Wood? Did you fly into Prestwick? That's a long way to drive on such a night. How long did it take? No trouble finding us, I hope?"

Daphne Wood let Maida's words wash her in through the front door, the dog following at her heels. She still hadn't said anything beyond questioning Janet's knowledge of her identity.

"Tallie, will you show Ms. Wood the bedrooms and bath?" Maida said. "And while Ms. Wood freshens up, Janet, why don't we find the kettle and make tea? Then we can just run the dust mop round and make sure things are nice and tidy. All right? We'll have tea shortly."

"Janet," Maida said when they were in the kitchen, "that's a peculiar person out there. Are you sure it's Daphne Wood? Maybe we should ask for identification."

"I think peculiarity *is* her identification," Janet said. "But, yes, I'm sure that's Daphne. She does look just like the picture on her books. Besides, she has a maple leaf shoulder patch on her jacket."

"I didn't notice," Maida said.

"You were probably looking at the dog," said Christine. "You were probably wondering what a back-to-nature, living-in-the-wilds woman who wears buffalo plaid is doing with a Pekingese."

"The dog looks as though it should appear at that poncy show in Birmingham," Maida said, as she looked for the teabags. "Crufts, isn't that what the show's called? What do you think the dog is called?"

"Rachel Carson," a voice said behind them.

Janet, Maida, and Christine flinched and turned to find Daphne Wood standing in the door. Rachel Carson stood beside her. Maida smiled and held up the box of tea she'd finally found. Janet flinched again. No one had warned Maida about Earl Grey.

Daphne held her phone up. "Low bat. I need to make a call."

Her shortage of verbiage proved contagious. "Use mine," Janet said. She pulled her phone from a pocket and handed it Daphne.

Daphne consulted a number written on the palm of her hand and keyed it in. While she waited for an answer, she and Rachel Carson stared at the wall. Janet realized that *she*, Maida, and Christine were staring at Daphne and Rachel Carson. She pulled Maida and Christine out of the room, but no farther than just around the corner.

"Peculiar with a capital P," Maida whispered.

"Shh." Janet put a finger to her lips. "I want to hear what she says."

Maida gave Janet a scandalized look.

"Janet's right, Maida," Christine whispered. "This is a peculiar person come to stay in your house. Hearing what she has to say might give you peace of mind."

Daphne had called Gillian and made no effort to keep her end of the conversation private. They might have stood in the back garden and heard her, Janet thought.

"Someone has risen to his or her level of incompetence," she enunciated into the phone. "No, I do not know to whom I am referring. What I do know is that the house is not ready. You said it would be. . . . I am barely more than twelve hours ahead of my revised estimated time of arrival. Within the great scheme of things, I hardly call that a day early. There are people here who insist on yammering at me and giving me Earl Grey tea. I thought I made it clear. I loathe Earl Grey tea. . . . I see. . . . I don't know their names, no. . . . That's entirely up to you. Good night."

Daphne stopped talking and they heard footsteps and the *clickety-clickety-click* of tiny dog toenails crossing the linoleum. Janet, uneasy now at their eavesdropping, looked at the others. Christine, head cocked for more sounds from the kitchen, wasn't bothered in the least. Tallie had apparently joined Rab and the lads outside—a smart move, Janet thought. Maida had her phone out and appeared to be turning it off, possibly to avoid calls from Gillian. Also a smart move, if somewhat cowardly.

They heard the refrigerator open. It stayed open longer than seemed necessary, considering all it contained was a pint of milk. The refrigerator door closed. More *clickety-clicks* followed, and then Daphne and Rachel Carson were standing in the kitchen doorway again. She held Janet's phone out. Janet waited to see if Daphne would come hand it to her. She didn't.

"Gillian says hello," Daphne said.

"Oh? That's kind of her." Janet took her phone and smiled. Her smile wasn't properly returned, either.

"Now I am tired and want to go to bed," Daphne said. "It was a pleasure meeting all of you. Perhaps I'll see you again someday. I will unpack myself in the morning. Please take everyone with you when you go. Good night."

∽

"Maida didn't leave the loathed Earl Grey back there, did she?" Tallie asked.

"No, she took it with her," Janet said.

"A missed opportunity," said Christine. "If she'd followed her own advice about using some imagination in where to put things, then she might have shoved it—"

"Thank you, Christine," Janet said on top of her.

After being dismissed by Daphne, they'd gathered their things quickly, and left even faster. Maida, who had always reminded Janet of a mouse, reinforced the image by scurrying off with her nephews. Before Rab drove away in the van, Janet saw Ranger staring out the passenger window at Maida's house. He hadn't barked when Rachel Carson arrived on the scene, but it was difficult to tell what he thought of the situation. Janet and Tallie rode with Christine back around to their house and asked her in for a nightcap.

"As long as it's a proper nightcap," Christine said, "and doesn't involve the loathed Earl Grey."

Janet's house, up the hill and a century older than the one they'd just abandoned to the unusual visiting author, was a traditional detached stone cottage, with four rooms down and two up. Janet had worried, on making the move to Inversgail, that bitterness toward her ex-husband would color her feelings toward the house. They'd spent happy summers there with the children, and planned for longer stays in retirement. It would have been such a shame if she'd only wanted to stare coldly at the house and wish it grief, and then a pox and a painful death. The granite cottage proved sturdier than her resentment for her husband, though, and Janet had caught herself patting one of its blocks as she went in the door, as though patting a dear old shoulder to lean on. She patted one now, damp with the mist, and the three went through to the snug family room—the lounge, as Christine called it—where Tallie got out the sherry.

"I've never heard Maida talk so much as she did when that woman arrived," Christine said. "No doubt she'll have to sleep in to get over it."

"Daphne might improve with a good night's sleep, too," Janet said.

"Speaking of delusional," Christine said, looking at her sherry against the light and then fixing her eye on Janet, "do you think Gillian should have asked for a certificate of mental health before engaging Daphne?"

"I want to know how she knew to go to Maida's," Tallie said. "No one knew that until this evening."

"Gillian was going to text her," Janet said. "She would've given Daphne the address when she did."

"And Daphne didn't bother to mention she was already in the country, on the ground, and arriving any second." Christine sipped her sherry, marveled, and then pronounced, "Daphne is definitely a daftie."

"She was probably exhausted after the trip," Janet said, "and driving in the fog on top of it."

"Exhausted or not, the woman could have shown some common courtesy."

"You're right," Janet agreed. "But let's see how she is in a day or two. It can't have helped that she heard you call her Daftie Daphne."

"Don't go blaming any of this on me," Christine said. "She's spent too much time alone in the woods, pure and simple."

"She couldn't have expected to get in the house tonight," Tallie said. "She didn't have a key."

"She was doing a drive-by," Christine said. "Casing the joint. I propose a toast to poor Gillian. She's going to have her hands full."

"Should we call Gillian?" Tallie asked. "What time is it?"

"Going on midnight," said Janet. "Good Lord. Much too late. We'll all turn into mist or murk if we're up much longer."

Christine's phone trilled.

"Danny's brain must be murk to call so late," Christine said. "If you don't mind, I'll just take it over here." She wiggled her eyebrows at the Marsh women and took her phone to the window that looked out on the back garden.

"Mom?" Tallie got up and nodded toward the kitchen. "We have no reason at all to overhear this phone call."

"But I think we do." Janet rose and started toward her old friend.

Christine had turned from the window, her face slack with shock. "It's no bother," she said into the phone. "You're no bother, Danny. I'll call round tomorrow." She shut the phone off. "A man's been killed. At Nev's. At Danny's."

5

In Danny's hurried call to Christine, he'd only been able to give enough detail to chill the three women and add further dismay to the evening. Christine wouldn't sit down again after she disconnected. Though she couldn't stop rubbing her arms, she didn't want the sweater Tallie offered, or something warm in place of the sherry.

Danny had found a man curled on the pavement behind Nev's when he took the rubbish out at closing. The blood had convinced him the man hadn't merely chosen a poor place to sleep it off.

"But could he have fallen and hit his head?" Janet asked.

"Something told Danny no, I think."

There'd been no reason to call an ambulance. He'd called Norman Hobbs, the local police constable, but someone else answered.

"Did you know Norman's away?" Christine asked.

They didn't, and they mulled that over as they finished their sherry.

"We'll hear more in the morning," Tallie said. "Let's hope it isn't as bad as we think."

Christine put on her coat without saying anything else. Janet gave her a hug at the door, then went back to the lounge, turned off the lights, and stood by the window. Before going up to bed, Tallie asked her mother if she was all right. Janet said she was. She listened to familiar, soft creaks as Tallie climbed the stairs, then turned back to the window.

Curtis, her ex-husband, had often teased that she wasn't any good at reading weather signs. *Curtis, you might be right*, she thought as she stared through the window, trying to see through the mist, down through the back garden to Maida's house with its strange occupants. *I might not be good at reading weather signs, but I'm brilliant at feeling them.* She shivered and followed Tallie up to bed.

∾

Morning came sooner than Janet would have liked, but on pulling back the curtains, she saw that it was bright and clear. *And bright and clear is more than that unfortunate man behind Nev's will ever care about again*, she thought. Her initial good spirits properly put in their place, she let the smell of fresh coffee take her by the nose and down to the kitchen. Tallie always started a pot before going out for her morning run. As intrigued as Janet was by the possibilities of empathy meditation, she fully believed in the reality of coffee.

She poured a cup and as she and took the first sip, her phone rang. She thought it might be Christine, but it was Gillian, who didn't sound at her best. Janet guessed she hadn't had a decent night's sleep, either.

"I spoke with Daphne this morning," Gillian said, with little preamble. "She said you were there when she arrived last night. Now she isn't answering her phone. Neither is Maida Fairlie. What exactly is going on?"

Janet decided the anxiety in Gillian's voice warranted a double-barreled approach; she took another sip of coffee and channeled every ounce of empathy she could dredge up. She gave Gillian an abridged version of the previous evening, leaving the full story for Maida to tell, if she saw fit. "We were tidying," Janet said. "Giving Maida a hand, making sure things were nice for Daphne."

"She said the house wasn't ready."

"Did you know she was arriving last night?" Janet was proud of herself for the mildness of her question and the lack of accusation in her tone.

Then she immediately felt bad for *wanting* to accuse Gillian. "Things might have gotten off on the wrong foot last night, Gillian, but don't worry about it. Daphne surprised us. We surprised her. She'd had a long day and probably wasn't at her best. Flying in, renting the vehicle. Driving here. The fog."

Janet realized she was gesturing with her coffee mug for each added trauma Daphne must have endured. She put it down. "When it comes down to it, Gillian, Rachel Carson appears to be capable of many things and Daphne might think she's capable of *anything*, but she couldn't have shared the driving from Prestwick. That was all on Daphne and it would've exhausted anyone." Janet took another sip of coffee and heard nothing on the other end of the line. "Gillian?"

"Rachel Carson is a dead environmentalist. Were you talking to Daphne like that last night? No wonder she said people were yammering at her."

"Daphne named her Pekingese Rachel Carson."

"Pekingese."

Janet heard an amazing number of subtle undertones in that single word. Doubt was the only one she could identify with confidence, so she tried to reassure Gillian. "Rachel Carson only yapped once. She seems quite well trained."

Gillian disconnected without saying goodbye.

Janet looked online for news of the death at Nev's, but learned only that police had put out an appeal for anyone with information to contact them or Crimestoppers. She hesitated, and then decided not to call Christine. She would see her at the shop or hear from her soon enough. Instead, she skipped her usual breakfast porridge and went to the shop early to ask a favor of Summer. Scones had worked on Gillian the day before. Maybe Summer's scones would have a sweetening effect on Daphne, too. But in Daphne's case, Janet hoped that what her father had liked to say was true—if some is good, more is better.

"Half a dozen? Sure," Summer said.

While Summer put an assortment of scones in a bag, Janet started to tell her about the death at Nev's. Summer cut her off.

"I heard."

"I should have guessed you would."

Summer folded the top of the bag. "My grandma was big on taking food to newcomers in the neighborhood. After a death, too." She handed the bag to Janet. "So this is doubly nice. Are you sure she'll be up?"

"Oops."

"Bring them back, if she's not," Summer said. "I'll never tell."

"Thanks. See you in a bit."

On the short walk to Daphne's, Janet wondered about telling her of last night's death. *But with what aim, and is that being a good neighbor?* She decided not.

A gray cat sat on the harbor wall, washing its ear. It might have been the one sitting with Rab and Ranger the day before; she couldn't tell. Rab and Ranger weren't there or she could have stopped to ask and maybe rub the cat's chin. She passed the chemist, the chiropodist, and the cheese shop—the "chops" as the children had called them—feeling very much a local for hardly giving them a glance. The cheese shop wasn't open, yet, or she couldn't have helped giving it a sniff. She hurried back up Fingal Street, and made the uncustomary turn on Ross, the street below her own. And stopped.

Halfway along the street, standing in the middle of it, was a woman dressed for some form of martial arts, waving what appeared to be a sword.

Janet studied the situation and started forward again. The "sword" was no doubt wooden, as it didn't glint in the sun. And the woman's movements with it were more deliberate than random waving. They looked like a choreographed routine. And, of course, the woman was their peculiar author, Daphne Wood.

"Glorious morning," Daphne called upon seeing Janet. A night's rest had apparently done its best for Daphne. That would be a relief for Gillian.

"Enjoying the fresh air?" Janet asked.

Daphne did several deep lunges, thrusting with the sword each time. "This isn't fresh air." She slashed the sword from right to left and then from left to right. "You haven't breathed fresh air until you've filled your lungs with the crystalline purity that is the atmosphere of the Canadian woods."

That crystalline purity had done more to preserve Daphne's soft burr than the windswept prairies had for Christine's, Janet noted. "You could be right." She held up the bag. "Have you had breakfast? Perhaps you should move out of the street. There's a car coming."

Daphne brought the sword upright and touched it to her nose. Without a look at the approaching car, she strode to her front gate, where Janet saw Rachel Carson waiting. Daphne gave a hand signal to the dog, and then opened the gate, went through, and closed it, leaving Janet on the other side. Janet decided she didn't mind.

"Have you discovered the back garden?" she asked. "You might find your, er, swordplay more enjoyable there."

"Forza," Daphne said.

"Sorry?"

"What I'm doing is Forza, an exercise routine based on samurai sword work. And no, the back garden is out. The trees won't give me enough room to swing properly and I never like to hurt trees."

"I suppose the front garden's too small? I'm just thinking about your workout being interrupted by traffic. And safety."

"I'll tell you something about myself, Janet. You are Janet, aren't you?"

"You have a good memory."

"An excellent memory, which is a feature people notice about me immediately. But I find that people notice very little else about me. In fact, I often feel invisible. Compound that with my theory that most people, these days, are more interested in divining the truth on their screens, and I suspect that no residents on this street even noticed me this morning. Other than the fellow in the car, and he's probably already forgot that he saw me."

Janet was pretty sure Daphne was wrong about at least some of the residents. She'd noticed a curtain twitch in one window and an elderly man had come out of his house and must have swept his stoop to a nub by now. On the other hand, judging by the number of public service announcements Police Scotland broadcast about distracted driving, Daphne might be right about the man in the car. Rather than argue either point, Janet held up the bag.

"I brought fresh scones as a welcome-to-Inversgail present," she said. "We make them—well, I don't make, but a couple of my business partners do. For our tearoom. It's down on the High Street. Cakes and Tales, next door to Yon Bonnie Books, which you might remember from when you lived here." She was yammering as badly as Maida had the night before. She stopped and smiled, then reined that in, too.

Daphne reached over the gate and took the bag. She opened it, sniffed, and appeared to consider what she'd smelled. Then she took out a scone and offered it to Rachel Carson. The dog ignored it. "This doesn't bode well," Daphne said, studying the scone and then sniffing more closely.

Janet jammed her hands into the pockets of her khakis so she wouldn't be tempted to grab the bag back.

Daphne stuck her tongue out and took a quick, delicate lick, not unlike a snake flickering its tongue as it explored. And then she ate the scone in two gulps.

"You'll find napkins in the bag," Janet said.

Daphne waved the suggestion away and licked her fingers. A second scone went down at the more sedate pace of three gulps. "They're quite good, after all," she said, not offering one to Janet.

"After all these years, how does it feel to wake up in Inversgail again?" Janet asked.

"The jury is out, I think. Or, as I like to say, the loon has yet to laugh." Daphne waved a scone as she talked, though not with the same finesse as she'd used the wooden sword. Rachel Carson followed the arc of the scone as it passed back and forth over her nose. When she saw Janet watching her, she turned her head and feigned indifference.

"I don't think I've ever actually heard a loon," Janet said. "Do they live in Scotland?"

"You obviously aren't a birder. As a matter of fact, they're found throughout northern Europe, but in this part of the world, they're called divers. So you *might* hear one laughing in Inversgail, because they are native. Unlike you." Daphne laughed at that, several trills longer than Janet thought necessary. Then she cocked her head and thought for a moment before saying, "I prefer the name loon, but it can be confusing in a town like Inversgail, where there are plenty of the bipedal, mammalian-type loon." She laughed again, then snorted before taking another scone. "There certainly used to be, anyway. More than one town's fair share, and I can't see how that would have changed over the years. Gillian's father is still here, for instance. One might have hoped for improvement, but then one might encounter someone like that woman who owns this house. Jada."

"Maida Fairlie?"

"No, I'm quite certain her name is Jada. It's an unusual name for a woman of her age from this part of the world. I wonder what the story is behind that aberration. And your name is Janet. You see, they both begin with the letter J."

"Well, yes, that's one way to remember them," Janet said, wondering how Maida would like being rechristened.

"The best way, I assure you." Daphne tapped her forehead. "Remember, excellent memory. Now, what do you know about this affair at the library Friday night?"

"It should be a good time. People are looking forward to meeting you and welcoming you back. Welcoming you home."

"But I'm not the only attraction. I'm sharing the stage with Gillian's father. In fact, as the presenter of a plaque of some sort *to* her father, I might be considered ancillary to the whole affair. Invisible."

"I'm pretty sure you're considered the draw and the star, Daphne. Honoring Alistair for his work is the added attraction."

"These other people, though. This group calling itself something unbearably long so they can use the acronym GREAT-SCOT."

"They've worked closely with Alistair. They did a lot of the replanting in the glen."

"All earnest, I'm sure. They'll most likely wear green shirts. I've met the type."

"Anyway," Janet said, "it's a good combination of celebrations. Welcoming home the internationally acclaimed environmentalist while recognizing the work of a local one—it seems like an energy-efficient sort of event. And then there's the music and dancing. It'll be lively, and a lot of fun."

Daphne peered at Janet with the same consideration she'd given the first scone she'd bitten into. "You make a good point. If nothing else, it will use fewer plastic plates and forks."

Time and schedules permitting, the four partners had developed the habit of meeting briefly before opening each morning. They met at the interior door between the bookshop and the tearoom to wish each other a good day and pass along news or information. This mostly consisted of Christine and Summer telling the bookshop two what specials were on in the tearoom and Janet and Tallie telling the tearoom two about sales going on in the bookshop. Occasionally, one or the other of them shared an inspirational quote. More frequently, someone told a joke to start the day with a laugh. This morning, keeping an eye on the clock, Christine said she had more details that Danny had given her over coffee in her parents' kitchen.

"This morning?" Janet asked.

"He was sitting outside in his car when I arrived home last night."

"Do they know a name yet?" Tallie asked.

"Danny says no. The police haven't released that or a cause of death." Christine took a deep breath that turned into a yawn. "Sorry. He said after we left last night—left Nev's—a group on a pub crawl celebrating some lad's twenty-first came in. Danny didn't know any of them. They'd found their way from the pubs on the High Street. He wasn't keen on them being there, but they weren't causing a problem. At first. And then a couple of the lads got loud and started in shoving each other. Danny says he doesn't know what it was about. He sent them on their way. The others left, as well, and he thought they'd cleared off. When he went out the back later, he found that poor lad. He remembers serving him, but he told the police he didn't think he was part of the group."

"And it couldn't have been an accident?" Janet asked.

"There was a brick involved in such a way—" Christine put a hand to her mouth, then took it away. "An accident is unlikely."

"Is Danny all right?" Summer asked.

"He's stunned. It takes a lot to stun that man, but nothing like this has happened at Nev's since he's been there. Well." Christine drew herself up.

Janet saw Elizabeth II flicker into focus for a moment, and then it was familiar Christine standing next to her, tired but solid. Janet gave her a hug like the one she'd sent her home with the night before.

"I'm not the one who needs hugs," Christine said gruffly.

"I know that," Janet said. "And it isn't for you. It's for Danny the next time you see him."

∽

Janet's and Tallie's personalities and talents meshed in their new business. Janet liked to say that, having known her daughter since she'd only been a bit of indigestion and then a kick in the ribs, she'd been fairly certain they *would* get along. They shared most duties and staked out a few they each preferred over others. Tallie, burned out after years of teaching contract law, liked opening boxes of "new" and keeping the computer inventory up to date. She also revived the Saturday morning children's program that the previous owners had offered haphazardly. She never had great numbers of children, but discovered unexpected joy in reading stories and doing crafts. Janet, with her librarian's eye for matching books to patrons, enjoyed ordering stock.

"What are you buying for us today?" Tallie asked.

"Fitness," Janet said vaguely. She'd brought a stack of publisher's catalogs from the office and then ignored them in favor of sitting at the computer for an online search.

"I half-expected to hear that dog yapping all night, but I didn't, or it didn't."

Janet looked up. "I don't think Rachel Carson is much of a talker. Daphne was more talkative this morning, though, and more . . ." She pursed her lips, debating what Daphne was more of, and then went with the catchall. "More interesting. If you change your running route tomorrow, you might see what I mean." She told Tallie about taking the scones to Daphne and described the spectacle of finding her in the middle of Ross Street flourishing her sword. "I would love to see what Norman Hobbs would make of her."

"Forget Constable Hobbs and back up a moment," Tallie said. "After the cold and decidedly odd reception she gave us last night, you took her scones? And you approached her as she stood in the middle of the street waving a sword?"

"A wooden sword. She said it was a samurai sword workout and, frankly, it looked like a lot of fun. I think I could get into something like that."

"But not in the middle of the street."

"No, we have more room in our back garden. She looks very fit, dear."

"Well, that was a nice thing for you to do, Mom. I'm sure it made her feel welcome on her first morning back in Inversgail."

"She probably doesn't get many fresh scones delivered to her doorstep out in her woods."

"I'm surprised she even eats them," Tallie said.

"You'd be surprised how *fast* she eats them."

"But, generally, you think she improved with a good night's sleep?"

"Yes," Janet said after some thought. "She's very sure of herself. I'd say she's mostly sunny, with a smirr of condescension."

The door jingled and a man they hadn't seen for some months stepped in.

"Reddick!" Janet said. "What a delight. Is Quantum with you?" They'd all been quite taken with Reddick's collie when they'd met. Reddick, a slim man with dark hair and dark circles under his eyes, was a member of the Major Investigation Team from the Specialist Crime Division of Police Scotland.

"I don't think he's here for a chat," Tallie said quietly.

6

M rs. Marsh and Ms. Marsh." Reddick nodded at Janet, then Tallie. "It's good to see you both looking so well. Quantum sends his best *woof*."

Janet stood up. That was the difference between Reddick and Norman Hobbs, she thought. Norman was proper and professional, but he would just as likely sit down, cross his legs, share a cuppa with you, and ask for extra biscuits. Norman had used every page of the pink princess notebook given to him for his work by his niece. Reddick had been an occasional customer during his convalescence after a bad fall some months earlier, and Janet liked him. But standing to meet him balanced the formality she sensed between them. And his tired eyes told her more than his pleasant words or the supposed greeting from his collie.

Tallie came to stand beside her mother. "What can we do for you?"

Reddick opened a zippered portfolio and removed three clear plastic bags. He laid them on the counter, one beside the other. The first, which was also the largest, contained a book by Daphne Wood—a copy of *Gathering My Thoughts and Thimbleberries*. The second contained a receipt from Yon Bonnie Books for a copy of *Gathering My Thoughts and Thimbleberries*. The third held one of their bookmarks.

Janet glanced quickly at Tallie—calm, relaxed, but gazing seriously, steadily at Reddick. Waiting. Janet waited, too. Reddick looked around, and appeared to listen.

"No customers," said Tallie. "Tuesday mornings tend to be slow."

"Valuable time for paperwork, then? I'll try not to use it up. I take it you're aware of the death last night at Nev's?" They'd seen Reddick at Nev's occasionally, as well, along with Quantum, whose posture was every bit as professional. "These items were recovered in the course of our inquiry. Actually, with one other item." He took another bag from the portfolio and laid it down beside the others. It held a credit card receipt for one night's lodging at Bedtime Tales.

"Oh my." Janet glanced at the ceiling and then squinted at the receipt.

"Have you identified the victim?" Tallie asked. "Are these his?"

"The name has not yet been released. Ownership hasn't been determined."

The door jingled and a couple of women speaking German came in.

"I'll stay with the customers," Janet said. "See if Summer can get free, Tallie, and the three of you can go upstairs."

Tallie went and Reddick started to gather his plastic bags.

"Before you put them away," Janet said, interrupting him. "What's the date on the book receipt?"

"The same as for the B and B: four days ago. Any chance, at all, that the room—"

"Hasn't been cleaned at least once since?" Janet shook her head. "More like two or three times." Then she thought of another question. "Will Constable Hobbs be helping with your investigation?"

"I'm not authorized to give out that information."

Janet nodded as though that answer was fine and made sense. It was, and it did, but it was also unsatisfying. Reddick went upstairs with Tallie and Summer. Janet chatted with the Germans and rang up two of Daphne's books for one and a book of folktales for the other. When they'd gone, Janet sent a text to Christine in the tearoom, asking her to call when she had a moment. Her phone rang almost immediately.

"That's the difference between Reddick and our Norman," Christine said when Janet told her Reddick's unhelpful answer. "Besides the fact

I used to change Norman's nappies when I babysat for him back in the Mesolithic."

"You aren't that old," Janet said. "You're barely more than Neolithic."

"You're a good friend, Janet. The difference between them is that Reddick is eminently trustworthy, while Norman wouldn't worry at all about telling us who else is working on this or if those items will identify the victim or someone else. Customer, I have to go."

Janet had more customers of her own. She helped one set find guide books for a trip to the Orkneys and Shetlands and sold ten postcards to a pair of sisters up from London. After suggesting the sisters write the cards over tea in Cakes and Tales, she saw Reddick returning with Tallie and Summer. Summer started back toward the tearoom, but at a word from Reddick, came with him and Tallie to join Janet at the sales counter.

"I've one more question for you," Reddick said. "Do you maintain a community directory of any sort? A list of area organizations? Information about clubs, associations, societies, interest groups?"

The three women shook their heads throughout his catalog.

"You've tried online?" Tallie asked.

"With no luck."

"A list like that might be useful," Janet said with a shrug at Tallie and Summer. "If you tell us what kind of group you're looking for, we might be able to come up with something."

Reddick shrugged, too. "It's as much for myself as not. I heard a whisper about a whisky society. Single malts?"

"Ian Atkinson," the three women said in unison.

"Atkinson," Reddick echoed, and Janet wondered that he didn't shudder. While Ian Atkinson hadn't been directly at fault, actions he'd taken had led to Reddick's fall and prolonged convalescence. "He writes those books, those Single Malt Mysteries, doesn't he? Well, it was a longshot, in the first place. Thank you for your time."

"What do you think?" Janet asked after he'd left. "Do we know the victim's name?"

"We can probably guess," Tallie said. "Sam Smith stayed here four days ago. If Summer's description matches Danny's, that would clinch it."

Summer wrapped her arms around herself, drawing her shoulders in. "He'd been hiking. He wanted a comfy bed for a night, and a hot shower."

"Smith. I wonder if that's how he found Nev's?" Janet got a blank look from Summer and raised eyebrows from Tallie. "Smith Funerals is next door. Did he say anything about a family connection to Inversgail, Summer? Or ancestor hunting?"

"No."

"Do you remember anything else about him?"

"Why? What does it matter?"

"It doesn't. Summer, I didn't mean to be—"

"I need to get back." Summer pulled away as Janet reached a hand toward her. Arms still wrapped tight, she went back to the tearoom.

"Now look what I've done," Janet said.

"It's all right," Tallie said. "You haven't done anything."

"Except be insensitive."

"She needs to go bake something. She'll bake through it and she'll feel better. Reddick had a lot of questions. She's just had enough."

∞

Gillian came into Yon Bonnie Books over her lunch hour. She didn't look annoyed, but she *had* disconnected that morning without saying goodbye. Janet held her breath and smiled as she came toward the sales counter.

"How goes it, Gillian?"

"I owe you thanks and apologies. If I'd had any idea how difficult all this—" Gillian's hands and fingers splayed in alarming directions. She looked at them and tucked them in her armpits.

"You've been under a lot of stress," Janet said.

"Thank you. For that and everything. Is Tallie in? I need to thank her again, too, for finding the house."

"Out doing a few messages."

"I'll catch her later, then. You might be happy to hear that I finally reached Daphne. She said you called round. With scones." Gillian looked at her hands, again, took them from her armpits, and rubbed her face. "Have you thought about marketing your scones for their remarkable curative properties?"

"I'll mention it to the others. So you think Daphne will settle in all right? She seemed cheerful this morning."

"I have hope," Gillian said. "I also have an extra half-hour for lunch today, and Tom told me I needed to come see your window display. He said it's Daphne Wood's woods incarnate, and he's right."

Janet laughed. "That's a good title for it." She went over to the window with Gillian. "Tallie had a lot fun of putting it together. You get the same effect whether you're looking at it from outside or in."

Their window displays weren't ordinarily more elaborate than books on easels or in stacks facing the street and more books facing the interior of the shop. But to celebrate their visiting author, Tallie had let her inner crafter loose into the wilds of Canada. With help from Rab and children at her story and craft times, she'd made a miniature forest clearing with Daphne's cabin standing in the middle.

"Rab made the cabin," Janet said. "Out of a box, I think. He used the cover of *The Deciduous Detective* to get it right."

"Did he make the wee beasts, as well?"

"Tallie and some of the kids at her programs. They used polymer clay. They're baked so the kids can take them home later. She let them use whatever colors they liked."

"Hence the green squirrel and multicolored moose," Gillian said. "They're brilliant. The whole window's brilliant."

"The kids are proud of it. They've been bringing their families and friends to see it."

"And to shop?" Gillian asked.

"Shopping is always encouraged."

"And so I should hope. I'm all for anything that keeps my favorite business going strong." Gillian adjusted her glasses and looked more closely at one of the animals in the window. "What's that, then, poking its nose out from behind the stack of books?"

"A wombat," Janet said. "The boy put so much time into getting it exactly right, that Tallie couldn't bear to tell him it's the wrong continent. But, really, how can you go wrong with a wombat?"

Gillian winced.

"What? You think Daphne will mind?"

Gillian lifted one shoulder infinitesimally.

"But if we have a porcupine with purple quills, how can a wombat be so bad? I've read some of Daphne's books; she seems to have at least a bit of a sense of humor."

"You've also met her."

"Point taken. But I hate to take it out of the window. The little guy will be so disappointed."

"Tell you what," Gillian said. "Never mind. Leave it. It isn't worth worrying about."

Janet didn't find the words or Gillian's smile especially convincing. The initial wince struck her as more genuine. "You're sure?"

"Aye, absolutely. Leave the wombat. Now, I'm on my own time. Let's not spend it worrying about wombats, or batty authors, or anything else. I'd like to visit with some of my books, if you don't mind."

Janet went back behind the counter to the hold shelf where they kept books that customers asked them to special order. They'd been surprised and gratified by how many customers did that, what with the ease of online ordering. Gillian had a permanently labeled space on the shelf, where half a dozen titles waited patiently for her budget to catch up with her lust to own.

"Which ones, Gillian?"

"I'm in an all-or-nothing kind of mood."

Janet handed the stack to her. Gillian took them to one of the arm-chairs in front of the fireplace and let herself collapse into it.

Unlike some of their self-proclaimed best customers, Gillian made good on the title. She loved everything about books, but especially owning them. New mass market paperbacks or rare antique volumes—if a book interested her, its pedigree made no difference. She'd been a chain smoker until she'd sat down one day and calculated how much she spent on cig-arettes each year. Then she'd quit, cold turkey, and spent the money she saved on books and the spare time building more bookshelves. It had made her lungs happy, she said, and it made her happy. It made the new owners of Yon Bonnie Books happy, too, although Tallie said it made her feel like an enabler.

Gillian kept herself to a strict book budget so she wouldn't end up starving toward the end of each month. That meant she usually had a small family of books sitting on the shelf for which she only had visiting privileges. Janet and Tallie didn't mind being soft touches, though, and they let Gillian spend as much unsupervised time with her brood as she wanted. They pretended not to notice when they caught her stroking the covers or smelling the ink.

ℒ

Tallie came back from her errands and dropped her shopping bag on the counter in front of Janet. "Success. I got Daphne's pens. I swear, Paudel's is like the bottom of Mary Poppins's carpetbag. If you need it, Basant has it."

"I often think I don't need anything," Janet said, "but he sells me something anyway."

"That's because there's no point in going in if you aren't going to buy something."

"A sentiment I understand and endorse," Janet said quietly, then she nodded toward Gillian still sitting in the chair by the fireplace. Most of her books sat on the arm of the chair, but she cradled a Wodehouse first edition in her arms, her eyes half shut, shoulders relaxed. *The picture of biblio-bliss,* Janet thought.

A few minutes later, Gillian gave herself a shake and yawned. She gathered the rest of her books and took them back, going around behind the counter to personally tuck them onto the hold shelf.

"Feel better?" Tallie asked.

"Mm." Gillian seemed to be struggling to throw off the biblio-haze, her verbal skills not quite functioning.

"Tallie was just telling me that she found the pens Daphne specified for the signing," Janet said, watching to see if Gillian would reach for her wallet and take one or two of her books home. "She *bought* the pens, so that's them taken care of."

"Ah, that's great," Gillian said. "Thanks, Tallie. And thanks for the tip about the house. I owe you one. I owe you more like a dozen. See you Friday, yeah?"

After the door closed behind Gillian, Tallie said, "Subtle, Mom. Real subtle."

"Too much?"

"Nah. She didn't notice. We know she loves books, though, and we know she's good for them."

"I love them too, dear. Those particular books I'd love even more going out the door."

∽

The business day yawned toward an end. While Janet went around the shop straightening shelves, she toyed with idea of leaving Tallie to finish closing so she could go home and have an early glass of wine. *Wine and cheese.* She took a knitting book from the philosophy shelf and returned it to crafts and hobbies. Leaving early would give her a chance to stop at the cheese shop and pick up something sharp and smelly before they closed, too. She could also stop at Paudel's Newsagent, Post Office, and Convenience to see what Basant would sell her that she didn't need. He had a wall of old-fashioned sweetie jars behind his counter and she definitely didn't need anything from them.

The door jingled. Janet heard Tallie start to greet the customer, but the customer's own greeting washed right over Tallie's and drowned her out.

"You must be very happy to see me. People in bookstores usually are."

That voice. It could only be their visiting author. Janet, hidden from the sight of anyone at the sales counter by the row of tall shelves, cravenly stayed where she was.

"What do you know about this murder last night?" Daphne asked.

"As yet, details are sketchy," Tallie said in her best lawyer's voice.

"And I think we need to change that, don't you?"

7

Janet waited in her craven position behind the bookcase, hoping she'd hear the sound of Daphne reversing course and marching back out the door. She didn't hear anything other than the cool jazz bass playing over the sound system. She imagined her sensible, serious daughter and the unpredictable Daphne staring at each other over the counter. She sighed, found her backbone, and went to join them.

"There you are," Daphne said as Janet appeared. She'd turned her back on Tallie, apparently finished with her. She'd exchanged her martial arts outfit for jeans and the buffalo plaid jacket of the night before. Her tone of voice suggested she'd had an appointment with Janet and suspected her of trying to wiggle out of it. That tone added an extra rod of stiffening to Janet's backbone.

"Nice to see you again, Daphne. How's Rachel Carson adjusting to her new surroundings?"

"Jet-lagged."

"I'm sorry to hear that. I'm not sure you met my daughter last night." Janet gestured toward Tallie. Daphne ignored the gesture.

"I was asking your clerk—"

"My daughter."

"Daughter? Where?"

This time Daphne tracked Janet's hand and turned back toward the counter. But she didn't see Tallie, who'd moved faster, mouthed "tearoom" at her mother, and disappeared in that direction.

Like mother, like daughter, Janet thought. *But there is strength behind counters for the craven.* She moved past Daphne to take up her position behind the polished oak set in place ninety-nine years earlier by Colonel Farquhar himself. She felt instantly centered and in control.

"You must have been mistaken," Daphne said. "It's only you and the clerk here, and now she's gone off. So." She leaned an elbow on the counter as though they were good mates sharing a pint. "What do *you* know about this murder last night?"

"Details remain sketchy." Janet remained librarian erect.

"I keep hearing that." Daphne stroked her chin. "And who's in charge? Someone in the local constabulary who has risen to his level of incompetence, no doubt."

"That's unnecessarily harsh," Janet said. *Not to say rude.* She'd heard Daphne use her "level of incompetence" assessment the night before. It didn't sound any better the second time around. "We've found the local police to be responsive and community oriented."

"Have you? And where's your local copper now? He's not in his tidy station."

"Out investigating would be a good guess." Janet didn't like defaulting to sarcasm, but Daphne begged for it. Daphne also didn't react to it. "From what I understand, Daphne, the Specialist Crime Division of Police Scotland handles these cases."

"Solving murders."

"Yes."

"With which you and your business partners have some experience. Ah." Daphne wiggled a finger at Janet. "I've done my homework on Inversgail current events."

The door jingled, bringing in what Janet hoped were the last customers of the day.

"We'll talk again," Daphne said. "I'll just nip next door for more of your delicious scones."

The new customers were delighted by the window display and bought one of Daphne's picture books. Daphne hadn't said a word about the window.

∽

The cheese shop was closed by the time Janet passed it that evening. She didn't stop at Paudel's, either. She would have felt virtuous about bypassing empty calories, but she didn't have the energy. When Tallie had scooted to the tearoom, she'd been able to convince Summer to describe their bed and breakfast customer of four nights earlier. Christine relayed the description to Danny. When they'd locked their shop doors for the night, they knew that Sam Smith, the American who'd wanted a comfy bed and a hot shower, was the victim.

"Were you talking about that when Daphne came in?" Janet had asked.

"No," Christine said. "She breezed in, said nothing, and breezed right on out the front door."

Maida was right, Janet thought. *Peculiar with a capital P.*

Tallie had thought they should all eat at Nev's. Not as curiosity seekers, but as locals supporting locals. Christine said she needed to get home for an evening of supporting her local oldies, and would talk to Danny later. Summer said she would go, which Janet thought was a good sign. She'd let them go without her, though. A quiet evening in sounded good.

When she got home, she kicked off her shoes and puttered in the kitchen, heating a bowl of leftover lentil soup and buttering a piece of toast. She poured the glass of wine she'd wished for earlier, tipped a splash of it into her soup bowl, and balanced everything through to the lounge. Feet up on a hassock. Crossword puzzle and a pencil waiting on the end table. A sip of the wine. A spoonful of soup. A knock on the back door. She would have ignored it, but before she could get up, there was Daphne, hands cupped to either side of her face, staring in the window.

"I'm good at this, aren't I?" Daphne said when Janet opened the door. "You probably didn't notice me following you home."

Janet thought that remark should merit alarm, but was too tired and annoyed to dredge it up. "What can I do for you Daphne?"

"It's what I can do for you. May I come in?"

Against her better judgment, because Daphne sounded like the worst kind of persistent door-to-door salesman, Janet nodded her in, but not to the lounge where her cozy meal sat congealing. She took Daphne to the small dining room. There, for lack of a polished oak sales counter, she could put the dining table between them, settling for Danish modern.

"Your home has more character and charm than mine," Daphne said, "but how lucky for us that we're connected through our back gardens."

"I know I sound unneighborly, Daphne, but I've had a long couple of days."

"Exercise and proper diet will solve your problems with that, but that's not why I'm here. I'm here to offer my expertise."

"In what?"

"I love it," Daphne said. "I see how you do it and why you're successful. You are quintessential."

"No, just tired. What are we talking about?"

"Crime investigation. You and your business partners solved another murder in this town."

They had, but Janet didn't think it was widely known. It hadn't been reported that way in the papers. And, actually, they'd been working alongside Constable Norman Hobbs. Or, if not quite alongside him, then at least tangentially. They'd been well aware of the problems that might cause him with the Specialist Crime Division, so they'd effaced themselves and let Norman take the credit.

"Where did you hear that, Daphne?"

"I won't give away my sources. That proves I'm trustworthy. But I heard that you came down on the villain like the four horsemen of the apocalypse."

"We did not."

"Forgive me. I'm a writer and I was using literary license. The four of you are cozier and more likely resembled Flopsy, Mopsy, Peter, and Cottontail. But you enjoyed yourselves? You enjoyed the danger?"

"I'm not sure I'd go that far."

"But you obviously have a flare for this, and I'm offering my services for the current investigation. Attaching myself to your cadre, as it were."

"There is no cadre."

"You're right. Cadre isn't the best word, but the four of you need an identity. A name."

"We really don't."

"Interesting." Daphne cocked her head. "I'd rather hoped the gung-ho American can-do spirit that brought you to Inversgail would have you jumping at the chance to prove yourselves again."

"Don't you have enough to do preparing for three months of programs and classes?"

"Do you see how well-tuned you are for this? Your lowball questions. The way you hide behind your graying hair and well-upholstered figure. Your lovely outrage. Give me one good reason for your reluctance."

Daphne's accent made *outrage* sound more like *oat rage*, and almost made Janet smile. Instead, with her hand unseen below the table, she took pleasure in counting on her fingers the *excellent* reasons she wouldn't be jumping at a chance to investigate *anything* with Daphne.

"The police are competent. We have a business to run. We know nothing about the victim." This last wasn't quite true, because they now knew he'd been hiking, had taken a break for a comfy bed and a hot shower at Cakes and Tales, and he was an American named Sam Smith. Janet briefly wondered what else Summer remembered about him. If he'd been traveling alone, or if he and the other guests had talked over breakfast. But then she realized she'd trailed off and Daphne was watching her the way a hawk watches a rabbit—if hawks licked their lips.

"The cause of death hasn't been made public, so it might not be a murder investigation," she continued. That was also only partly true, since Danny had been absolutely sure it was murder. Now Janet had four reasons, and four fingers jabbed toward Daphne, and she remembered an old joke about giving someone five good reasons that ended in a fist. "If it is murder," she said, "we have no reason to insert ourselves in an ongoing investigation and possibly trip up the professionals." With that, she curled her fingers into a fist and shook it at Daphne—still below the table.

"There, that last reason must be why you're able to work so well with the professionals. You sound just like them. Well." Daphne stood up. "Take a few days to think over my proposal and get back to me."

Janet had no intention of thinking it over. When she'd closed the door behind Daphne, she reheated her soup and toast. She drank her wine and refilled her glass. She attacked and conquered her crossword puzzle. She was in bed and sound asleep before Tallie crept up the stairs at ten.

And over the next few days, she very carefully *didn't* think about Daphne's proposal. But it would have been next to impossible not to hear what others were saying about their peculiar visiting author.

Danny let Christine know that Daphne and her dog dropped in for a drink at Nev's. She circulated, listened in on conversations, and generally acted nosy. She made people uncomfortable. When she started taking photographs, Danny took her aside and asked her to stop. On a hunch, then, he stepped out the back and found her snapping pictures there, too.

Summer told them she'd heard through the *Inversgail Guardian* grapevine that Daphne had paid a visit there, too. She'd introduced herself to James Haviland, the editor, and offered to write a series of articles about her experience as a visiting author. James had welcomed the idea and set her up to meet with one of his reporters. The visit had ended on a sour note, though.

"She as much as accused James of being in a policeman's pocket," Summer said.

Tallie asked what evidence Daphne had offered. Christine wanted to know whose pocket Daphne had in mind. Summer told them Daphne had been short on specifics.

Sharon from the library stopped by Yon Bonnie Books another morning. The day was bright and she was early. She knocked on the door until Janet unlocked it, and then she spread her worries about arrangements for the Friday night program—and Daphne—from the stoop to the sales counter. Once again, Janet found herself on one side of the counter, listening, while Sharon vented on the other.

"The combination of food, music, dancing, and prima donnas creates a level of stress that might be lethal," she told Janet. "I'm happy to do it, of course. And I've read one or two of her books. But beyond that, I find I'm not terribly interested in Daphne Wood, especially after meeting her. Not that I have anything against the environment or against people working to preserve it. It's just that I prefer my 'greens' in a less natural and aggressive form. Saturday cannot come soon enough."

"Your program is Friday night," Janet said.

"And Saturday it will all be over, and then I'm away on my holiday."

∽

"Daphne's behavior is certainly interesting," Christine said Friday morning, when the four partners met in the communicating door. "Interesting from my social worker's point of view, anyway. Personally, I wouldn't want to spend much time with her. Norman Hobbs would find her behavior interesting, too. Where is he when we need him?"

"Jess might know," Summer said.

"Yes, why haven't we called her?" Christine asked.

Jess Bailie, the estate agent who hadn't been able to sell the house where Daphne was staying, had started seeing Constable Hobbs over the summer. They saw each other so tentatively, though, that Janet thought if either of them blinked, they'd pass each other by.

"Jess might not know," Janet said, "and it would be a shame to give her something to worry about."

"Back to Daphne," said Tallie. "If she thinks she's investigating the murder, someone should tell her to have another think."

Janet found it somewhat irritating that the other three looked at her.

Rab and Ranger came in to work for a few hours that morning. While Ranger chased something fleet in his sleep, Rab rearranged the clay animals in the window display.

"The kids love coming to see where they've moved to," Janet said.

"And wondering where they'll go next," Tallie said. "It makes *me* wonder what we can do for the next window. The 'look, look, look, Mum!' factor of this one is great. The kids love showing off what they've done."

"Makes me wonder about this author," Rab said, "and her prodding and poking."

"Makes you wonder what?" Janet asked.

"Hard to say." Rab puzzled over it, micromanaging the animals' movements. "Look in this window, you see her books. We made sure of that. Look tonight, you'll see her up on stage. Gillian and Sharon made sure there was plenty of notice for that. And then Daphne Wood pokes and pries and prods, and people stop and look."

"Look at what?" Janet asked. "The poking and prying?"

"Could be." Rab scrutinized the wombat then nudged it so it peeked from behind a tree. "No question she's clever, though. Makes me wonder. Is there something she *doesn't* want us to see?"

8

Rab's question got lost in a busy day of bookselling. Janet was glad it did. Any thought of Daphne investigating the murder at Nev's, for whatever reason, reminded her of the proposal she was trying to forget. So far, Daphne hadn't come by for an answer, and Janet was glad of that, too. She hadn't bothered to tell the others about the evening visit, because she was sure Reddick and his team would solve the crime soon, leaving it a moot point. She was also hopeful, though less confident, that something else would happen to capture Daphne's attention and time. With luck, that evening's kickoff celebration at the library would do the capturing, and then Daphne's focus would turn to the reason she'd been brought to Inversgail at such expense.

The double-billing for the evening—world-renowned environmental writer and homegrown environmental activist—was a coup for Gillian and the group known succinctly as GREAT-SCOT. As Daphne had earlier observed, the group's unabbreviated name was laboriously long, but members of the Green Resident Environmental Alliance Trust—Start Conserving Our Tomorrow were happy with their acronym (and some didn't let on that they couldn't remember the full name and wouldn't torture themselves to try). The homegrown activist being celebrated was Alistair Gillespie, Gillian's father.

Alistair, a wiry, compact man in his early seventies, known for his hiking shorts and love for acronyms, was a founding member of

GREAT-SCOT. A former teacher himself, he'd been a tireless promoter of environmental education throughout his life. When Gillian was a schoolgirl, he'd worked on preserving the Farquhar garden, working closely with the Girl Guides and Boy Scouts. For the past two decades, he'd led the effort for the restoration and regeneration of the Sgail Gorge, down through which the River Sgail tumbled before calming itself to splash under the bridge in town and then chuckle into the harbor. After years of replanting, repair, and stewardship, the gorge and woods were recovering. The name was being restored, too, with the wild, deep valley being rechristened Glen Sgail.

Janet drove that evening, taking Tallie and Summer in the Audi she'd bought secondhand in Fort William. Tallie and Summer planned to sit with some of the *Guardian* staff. Janet said she'd keep an eye out for Christine and her parents and give a hand getting them settled with plates from the buffet.

∽

"I thought I might be bowled over by a tad too much tartan. Overcome by a plethora of plaid."

"Oh. Hi, Daphne." Janet didn't jump when Daphne sidled up to her at the library that evening, but her smile didn't commit itself to anything, either.

Despite what Daphne said she'd feared, Janet was happy to see a few kilts mixing with the trousers, jeans, and other skirts in the room. She also saw a smattering of T-shirts with the blue and white flag of Scotland, some with the yellow and red of the Royal Banner of Scotland, and a blossoming number of the green shirts Daphne had predicted members of GREAT-SCOT would be wearing. She'd changed from her usual khakis to black trousers and a loose tunic, knowing they'd be comfortable if she joined the dancing. Daphne, she noticed, still wore her jeans and buffalo plaid jacket, and had a backpack slung over one shoulder. She had a pen and notebook in one hand and the end of a leash in the other. Janet looked down. Rachel Carson, on the other end of the leash, looked up at her and then away. Janet had never seen a dog in the library and wondered if Daphne had asked permission or if she'd used the backpack to smuggle Rachel Carson in. She also wondered how Sharon would feel about a dog attending a program at her library.

The event room at the Inversgail Library and Archives was a simple rectangle. It had been given its utilitarian shape so that it could accommodate the widest variety of programs (*a plethora of programming possibilities*, Janet refrained from saying to Daphne). This evening, the room was arranged for a lively time. Tables with food and drinks stood along one short end and a stage at the other. Smaller tables and chairs ran down both the long sides of the room for anyone stopping to eat or sitting out when the dancing began in the bare middle of the room.

"Are you sitting with Gillian and her father?" Janet asked.

"I'd rather not. His hiking shorts are disquieting and she seems tense. It's upsetting Rachel Carson."

Rachel Carson sat next to Daphne, gazing into the distance. If she hadn't arrived in Inversgail that way, she might have had lessons in being laid-back from Rab's Ranger or Reddick's Quantum. Looking more closely at Daphne, Janet saw she was also gazing into the distance, but she didn't look laid-back. She just seemed to be avoiding eye contact with anyone.

"I'm making a list," Daphne said. "I'd like your help."

That request was an improvement over being asked to kill someone or being asked to track down a killer. Janet relaxed, somewhat. "Here comes Christine. We're going to fix plates for her parents and ourselves. You can join us if you want, and then I'll take a look at your list."

"Why eat now?" Daphne asked. "I thought speeches and presentations were first. The important parts."

"Ah, but food is always important," Christine said as she came to meet them. "Nice to see you, Daphne. Come on; let's dig in. I promised Mum she can eat her pudding first."

Daphne trailed behind them as they filled plates. She'd hadn't greeted Christine and didn't say anything more to Janet, who noticed that she'd reverted to speaking in the clipped, blunt sentences they'd heard the night she arrived. Janet wondered if the crowd was making her claustrophobic.

As part of her grant, Gillian had been able to arrange for the culinary classes at the high school to cater food for the ceilidh dance and the bookshop signing. The students, in white shirts and long white aprons, stood behind their tables, looking like fresh-faced, serious chefs. For the pleasure of their guests, they'd prepared a supper of haggis balls with a whisky and mustard sauce, baked beans, Brussels sprouts, oatcakes, pickle, three types of cheese, and blackberry tart with pouring custard.

Janet and Christine filled four plates between them. Christine also took a bowl with the blackberry tart and custard for her mother's starters. Janet glanced at Daphne. "You're not eating?"

"I ate before I came," Daphne said.

"That was smart. This way you can circulate more easily and meet people. Although, from what I understand, you've already met quite a few people." If Janet thought that was an opening for Daphne to admit to irritating people up and down the High Street, she was disappointed. "Are you sure you don't want something?" she asked. "There's plenty of good food here."

"I avoid potluck," Daphne said.

"It isn't potluck. The high school cooking class catered it."

"Then why did I bring a green salad?"

Janet saw a practically untouched bowl of green salad looking lonely and out of place between a pan of baked beans and the Brussels sprouts. Maida Fairlie, looking dour and somewhat out of place herself, eyed the salad and then took a small portion.

Feeling sorry for the salad and slightly less sorry for Daphne, Janet took a large scoop. She and Christine had their plates, bowl, and utensils under control, but help juggling it all to the table would have been nice. Daphne didn't offer.

"What kind of list are you making?" Janet asked.

"Local interest."

"What do you have on it so far?"

"That's why I need your help."

"I'll be happy to, if I can, but there are many more qualified people than me."

"You're assuming you're my only source."

"Ah. Well, Christine's got our seats staked out over there." Janet nodded toward the table Christine had commandeered by sitting her parents down and spreading their coats on the rest of the chairs. "Do you know Christine's parents? Helen and David McLean—you might have known them when you lived here."

Daphne followed Janet without answering.

"Got your hands full there, Daphne?" Christine asked, nodding at the pen and notebook Daphne set on the table. Christine helped Janet land the plates and utensils she was about to drop. There were two seats left at the table. Daphne sat in the one next to Christine's mother, leaving a chair farthest from the others for Janet.

"Helen and David," Janet said, leaning forward across the table and looking around Daphne at them, "may I introduce our visiting author, Daphne Wood? Daphne, these are Christine's parents, Helen and David McLean. Helen was a district nurse and David was head teacher at the primary school."

"What a beautifully behaved dog," Helen said. "Would it like a haggis ball?"

"We're vegetarians. Excuse me." Daphne turned to Janet and held up her notebook. "It's a list of people of interest."

"I thought you said it was a list of *local* interest."

"It's the same thing."

Janet took a bite of the green salad. She was interested in Daphne's pen, to see if it was one of the vaunted G Force Battalion whatever-they-were that she insisted they supply for signings, but Daphne flapped the notebook to catch her attention—but only so much of her attention. She held the notebook at an angle that made it difficult to see what was written in it. When Janet tried to get a better look, Daphne pulled it back.

Daphne had swiveled in her chair so that her back was to Christine's mother and the rest of the table. Over her shoulder, Janet saw Christine and her parents looking startled and possibly affronted. She also saw Gillian Bennett and Tom Laing. They'd stopped at another table to chat, but it was easy to see from the look Gillian cast in their direction that a chat with Daphne was on her agenda.

As far as Janet could tell, the pages she'd seen of Daphne's notebook were blank. So was Daphne's expression. The green salad, on the other hand, was full of personality, so Janet took another bite. "Does this list have anything to do with the murder?" she asked quietly, after swallowing. "Because—"

"You've reconsidered. I thought you would."

"No, I haven't. It isn't our business."

"The town is implicated. Your local is implicated."

Janet shook her head. "You've misunderstood."

"Your business is implicated."

"What? Where did you hear that?"

Daphne tapped her ear. "Ear to the ground. Two ears or three, four, or five would be better than one."

"What you heard isn't true, and what I meant is that we aren't in the investigation business."

Daphne threw herself back in her chair with a loud exhalation. If she wanted to draw attention to their muted conversation, she succeeded.

"*Who* is that woman?" Christine's mother asked.

"Daphne Wood," Christine's father said loudly into her ear.

"Would what?" Christine's mother asked.

Daphne leaned toward Janet again. "We'll leave that discussion and return to the list. I'm asking you because you run a bookstore. Bookstores are a good source for local information."

"They certainly can be," Janet said. "Libraries, too."

"Librarians lack imagination."

"They do not. You just don't know the right librarians."

Daphne considered that. "There is only the one within a hundred miles of my cabin, so you might be right."

"What would you like to know, Daphne?"

"The names of people I might like to spend time with while I'm in residence."

Janet mulled Daphne's request. She also wondered how much longer it was going to take Gillian and Tom to chat their way over and provide reinforcements, or at least offer some relief from Janet's odd ceilidh companion. They were still a few tables away. Christine and her parents, having been ignored, had turned around and were talking to people Janet didn't know at the next table.

"Are you looking for people to spend an evening with, Daphne? Or someone to grab a meal with, or go to the movies?"

Rachel Carson appeared to consider these options. Daphne waved them away.

"Are you looking for someone to get outdoors with? You could join the Three Sisters Hill Walkers. They hike most weekends. Parts of the West Highland Way, that kind of thing. I'm sure the GREAT-SCOTs would love to have you sit in on their meetings. They bought the beautiful plaque you're giving to Gillian's dad this evening. I understand they're really pleased you're making the presentation."

"I'm aware of their pleasure." Daphne acknowledged their pleasure or her awareness with a brief nod, then closed her eyes and pinched the bridge of her nose.

"Are you all right?" Janet asked.

Rather than answer, Daphne signaled "wait" with a raised palm, let go of her nose, and then wrote furiously in the notebook, scratched out half of what she'd written, and wrote a few words more. When she stopped, she pinched the bridge of her nose again, but this time with her eyes open and looking expectantly at Janet. "Go on."

Janet thought while she finished a haggis ball. "There are a couple of book groups in town and a local theater group."

"You're off track. You're listing groups. And you might find them interesting, but I might not. Interesting isn't exactly right, anyway. I want *useful* people." Her pen came to life in a light but insistent staccato on the notebook that gave Janet the idea she was floundering pretty quickly toward useless herself.

"Useful in what way?" And why were Gillian and Tom still dithering two tables away?

"Useful in the non-irritating way."

Janet hid her own blossoming irritation with another mouthful of green salad and nearly choked. Some of the leaves in the salad felt and tasted like astringent peach fuzz. She bolted another haggis ball to get the feeling off her tongue, shuddered, drank the rest of her lemonade, and almost reached for Daphne's. Daphne waited. Rachel Carson yawned.

"How about a photographer, then?" Janet asked, making an effort to recover some couth.

"Photographers, as a general rule, are splendid," Daphne said with no change of expression.

"Good. Put Gillian's friend Tom on your list." Although she, personally, found him about as irritating as whatever she'd just encountered in the salad.

"Surname?" Daphne asked.

"Laing."

"Now," Daphne said, pen poised for more action, "tell me why he will be useful."

"For whatever reason you thought a photographer would be useful in the first place," Janet said. She felt a light touch on the back of her shoulder and looked up. *Salvation.* Gillian was there, holding Tom's hand.

"How about this?" Gillian said. "Tom teaches science at the high school. He's a walking gazetteer who knows every burn, brae, water-fall, and waterspout you can name along this part of the coast. He's a brilliant photographer who's sold his work to West Highland Calendars. He's contributed photo essays to Historic Environment Scotland and *Scotland Magazine*. And he's usually around when you need him, except when he's occasionally not, as has been the case this week. But here he is now. Daphne Wood, I'd like you to meet Tom Laing. Tom, this is my dear friend, Daphne."

Daphne smiled. She'd started smiling as soon as she saw Tom, and she continued smiling as she watched them bring a couple of empty chairs from another table.

"We've already met," Daphne said after they'd sat. "Tom took me on an extraordinary photo shoot."

"He—"

"Took me on an extraordinary photo shoot."

"How nice," Gillian said.

To Janet's ears, it sounded more like *how ice*. Appropriate, she thought, because Gillian's smile froze for the fraction of a second it took her to look from Tom to Daphne and back again.

"She was asking questions," Tom said, "talking to people who'd been at Nev's that night. One thing led to another. More of a sightseeing trip, really."

"To get my Inversgail legs back under me, so to speak," Daphne said.

"We're going to do a calendar together," Tom said. "That's brilliant, isn't it?"

9

W hat do you think a predatory smile looks like?" Janet asked Christine.

"Like this."

"Whoa. Where did you learn to do a thing like that?"

"Shark Week, a few years back. Tony adored those documentaries," Christine said, referring to her late husband. "Why?"

"The way Daphne smiled at Tom Laing, just now."

Janet had hopped up after Tom announced he and Daphne were working together on a calendar. Gillian's reaction to that news had convinced her it was the perfect time to get more lemonade for everyone, and she'd interrupted Christine's mother in the middle of describing her latest bout of vertigo to ask Christine for help carrying. When they reached the drinks table, Janet filled Christine in on the developing awkwardness. Then, still haunted by the unpleasant salad greens, she downed another whole glass of lemonade while Christine looked back toward Gillian, Tom, and Daphne. Tom and Daphne were talking and laughing. Gillian appeared to be stabbing Janet's blackberry tart.

"Huh," Christine said. "I didn't see Daphne smile, but my professional diagnosis is that she isn't predatory; she's crazy. Or to quote from the official *DSM* translated for Scots, she's a bampot."

"You're a social worker, not a psychologist," Janet said, "but she's definitely an odd duck. The dog, for instance. A husky, in the wilds of northern Canada, that I can understand. But a Pekingese? And she brought it tonight? Has Sharon or anyone from the library noticed?"

"Good points," Christine said. "Did no one check her out beforehand?"

"There probably wasn't a sanity box to check off on the application."

"But surely there was something like an interview."

"You know how much a clever person can hide in an interview."

"Good Lord, yes."

"It'll be a relief when the signing's over," Janet said. "Then I can stop being so unnaturally nice to Daphne. It's too much hard work."

"*You're* a bampot," Christine said. "You'd be nice to Nessie if she paddled in to buy books."

"That's called good customer service and for Nessie, it wouldn't be hard at all. Not compared to Daphne."

"Well, she's not quite normal," Christine said, "but who would be after living alone out in the woods for so long?"

"I wouldn't be normal. I like watching people too much."

"We call that being nosy," Christine said, patting Janet on the back as though she was a good puppy, "and we love you for it. So why aren't you back there sticking your nose in right now?" When Janet didn't say anything, Christine looked at her. "You're staring into your lemonade."

"Trying to see myself," Janet said. "I don't like the image of me sticking my nose in where it doesn't belong."

"No one's at her best reflected in the bottom of a lemonade."

"I don't like the idea that I *stick* my nose in, and I don't like the idea that people might think I do it for fun. Like a hobby. I don't want to stick myself anywhere I don't belong."

Christine took the lemonade glass from Janet, making her look up. "Now then. You are standing *here*. You are not sitting over there. You left the scene of that awkward moment because you felt your nose didn't belong there. As for 'stick,' that was a poor choice of words on my part. I'm sorry."

"It makes me sound like a buttinsky."

"Which you're not. I really am sorry."

"Or worse, a busybody scandalmonger."

"I wonder how many times I should apologize," Christine said, appealing to the acoustic tiles in the ceiling. She looked back at Janet. "Will it do if I choose another word? I'll agree that 'stick' isn't the right one, but there is some truth to the 'nose' part of the equation. You and I both know that we are inquisitive." As Christine spoke, she drew herself up into her Elizabeth II pose. Janet was never quite sure if Christine was aware when she did it. The pose would be perfect with the addition of a hat, if only Christine didn't despise wearing them. "We're also insightful, thoughtful, and helpful, and we have proven that discreet and nonjudgmental nosiness is sometimes necessary."

"From time to time," Janet agreed. "Back to Daphne, though. She heard that our business is implicated in the death at Nev's."

"Did she? And I mean that literally," Christine said. "Because if she did hear that, I'd like to know where. And if she didn't hear it, but she's saying it anyway, I'd like to know why."

"And if it was true, we would probably know. Police crawling all over the place is something we'd notice."

"Eagle-eyed as we are. So," Christine said, "I propose replacing 'stick' with 'nudge.' We *nudge* our noses in where they're needed."

"That does sound better," Janet said. "And knowing us, we'll continue doing it, if we think we can make a difference."

"Whether our noses belong where they're nudged, or not."

∽

Rachel Carson was finishing the salad on Janet's plate, now on the floor, when she and Christine returned to the others. Christine's parents had been joined by their equally elderly neighbor. Daphne was licking the last of Janet's blackberry tart from her fingers.

"We seem to have lost Gillian and Tom." Christine set down the four cups she'd juggled to the table and took two more from Janet's precarious grasp.

"She's gone off to ably organize," Daphne said. "No idea where he went, but that sort always turns up again." She helped herself to a lemonade and then, without thanks, another word, or bothering to pick the plate up off the floor, she and Rachel Carson left the table.

Janet watched them navigate past people toward a less-populated spot in the room. Daphne didn't seem to give any more thought to the people she brushed by than she did the furniture. "Definitely an odd duck," Janet said.

"That's the nature of ducks," Christine's mother said. "I've never quite taken to them, with their wee black pudding eyes. Mind, they're a treat roasted at Christmas."

As Christine's mother and the neighbor started comparing notes on the proper roasting methods for various fowl, Janet caught sight of Sharon near the stage and pointed her out to Christine. "She's looking less frazzled than I expected. Let's go find out how that's possible."

"Dad," Christine said, giving her father a kiss on the head, "don't let these two challenge each other to a roast-off."

⁓

Sharon and a group of GREAT-SCOTs were chatting, her russet cardigan like a dead leaf among their verdant shirts. *Autumn leaf,* Janet corrected herself. *Like an autumn leaf. Nothing dead. No dying.*

"What a wonderful, *lively* turnout," Janet said when Sharon saw and greeted them. "You must be pleased."

"Fair pleased, ready to dance, and looking forward to the whole thing being over in a matter of hours," Sharon said. "We just need to get Daphne to the microphone on time and then away again so James can start the music." Except for a twitch in her eye when she mentioned

Daphne, she appeared to be calm and enjoying herself. "We're moving like clockwork," she said, "ticking down the minutes, and then it will be over with. Done. Finished. Finis. And would you like to know what happens after that? A good night's sleep and then tomorrow, I'm away for my holiday."

"Yes, you told me," Janet said.

"I did? When?"

"When you came in the shop the other morning. Never mind. That's the sure sign your holiday is overdue." Janet patted Sharon's arm, then looked at Christine. "Overdue—a little librarian humor."

"Very good," Christine said. "I'll *borrow* it sometime. So where are you off to on your hols, Sharon? Did you *book* someplace warm and sunny?"

"Isn't that the only way to travel? I'll send you a postcard and make you jealous."

"It's good you had your trip to look forward to," Janet said. "I know all the arrangements and special requests haven't made this easy for you. Keeping your eye on the prize was smart."

"Eh?" Sharon looked confused. "No. It was never the trip that helped me get through all this, but I'll tell you what it was. I made a wonderful discovery."

"Tranquilizers?" Christine asked. "Whisky?"

"Guilt." Sharon cast glances left, right, and behind her before continuing. "Specifically, Gillian's guilt over saddling me with that ridiculous list from Daphne. I sent her a very long, very stern email telling her exactly what I would and would not be responsible for in terms of this occasion." She crossed her arms, the picture of an implacable librarian. Janet thought she ruined that image, though, with another round of uneasy glances. "As a result," Sharon said, "Gillian stepped up, as well she should, and I had very few details to deal with for this evening. The power of guilt is golden. Thank you for the suggestion to go after Gillian, Janet."

"I'm not sure I said anything—"

Sharon swirled around to the table nearest them, picked up a plate and cup, and handed them to Christine. "You don't mind clearing these away for me, do you? The program is about to start and I'm needed."

"I'm sure I didn't say anything *remotely* like 'go after Gillian,'" Janet said.

"It doesn't sound like you," Christine agreed, staring at the plate and cup in her hands.

"But it doesn't matter what I said, because now *I* feel guilty."

"That does sound like you," Christine said. "Sharon's theory of golden guilt is interesting, too. Let's test it, shall we?" She studied Janet in a way that suggested measuring or weighing. "Aye, I see the guilt you're feeling, and between you and me, it doesn't do you any favors. But I reckon you're feeling just guilty enough you won't mind taking care of these." She handed Sharon's plate and cup to Janet. "The program's about to start, and I might not be needed, but I'll go on back to Mum and Dad, anyway."

Janet picked up a few more stray plates and cups on her way to the bin, running into Tallie, who was on the same mission.

"Did you see Reddick come in?" Tallie asked.

"I didn't." Janet scanned the room and spotted the policeman standing at the back of the stage. He and James Haviland seemed to be sharing a joke while James tuned his fiddle. "Is he on the job, do you think, or here for the ceilidh?"

"Hard to tell with him. You know who isn't here, though? Norman."

"Doggone. You're right. It isn't like him to miss music and dancing."

"And food."

Janet looked for Reddick again. Now he and James were sitting at the table with Summer and others from the paper. "I might have to corner Reddick, see if I can get him to cough something up."

"I'd love to watch you sweating it out of him," Tallie said, "but maybe you should wait until you can get him in a dark alley. And promise you'll make sure your phone is charged so you can call me from the pokey."

By then, the GREAT-SCOTs were heading for the stage, so Janet promised to keep her phone charged and she and Tallie went back to their respective tables. Christine and her parents were deep in conversation when Janet arrived. Catching the words *irritable* and *bowel*, she moved on to the next table and sat beside Rab.

"Did you see that Daphne brought her dog?" Janet asked.

Rab nodded.

"Is that allowed, or—"

He shook his head. "If it were, Ranger wouldn't be interested, anyway. He prefers a wooden floor for the dancing."

"Maybe she's taken the dog out. I don't see either of them."

Some of the GREAT-SCOTs on stage scanned the room, too, faces not quite to the point of being worried. Janet didn't see Sharon, but maybe she'd gone to find Daphne. Then Rab pointed and Janet saw Daphne emerge from the short hallway where the toilets were located. From somewhere, probably her backpack, she'd produced and put on a floor-length, moss-green robe. With the backpack slung over one shoulder and Rachel Carson's leash in hand, she headed for the stage. Gillian and her father intercepted her, and Gillian's father took Daphne's arm. She deftly substituted the leash for her arm and shooed Alistair and Rachel Carson ahead of her and Gillian. The four of them made for an interesting procession up the middle of the room, Alistair making small overtures that Rachel Carson ignored.

"Microphone on that podium is a wee bit sensitive," Rab said. "We'll hope the dog doesn't bark directly into it."

"Unless Daphne picks her up, she probably can't," Janet said.

"Pekes are great jumpers."

One of the GREAT-SCOTs, flushed and beaming, moved to the podium in the center of the stage and welcomed the audience.

"The head GREAT-SCOT?" Janet asked.

"Aye. Rhona McNeish. She's a wee bit sensitive, too."

Rhona's brush of red hair stood as erect and looked as excited as she did to be introducing Daphne Wood and Alistair Gillespie. "The mission of GREAT-SCOT," she told the audience, "is to work for conservation and sustainability, but especially for the education of future generations. That is why we are proud to be part of the grant that brought Daphne Wood home to Inversgail." Rhona stopped to beam anew, her GREAT-SCOT shirt looking barely large enough to contain her swelling pride. "Tonight, Daphne will give us a taste of what we can look forward to during her stay, after which she'll present the plaque honoring Alistair for his life's work and his life's love—the restoration of Glen Sgail. And then it's on to the ceilidh. Ladies and gentlemen, please welcome Daphne Wood."

The audience clapped. Daphne made brief eye contact with Rhona, then she and Rachel Carson walked around the podium and stood in front of it. Daphne raised her arms toward the audience, opened them in a wide, sweeping gesture, and stood that way, palms up, staring straight ahead. As far as Janet could tell, Rachel Carson stared at the pattern of the tiles on the floor. Daphne stayed in her pose long enough that people began to look uneasy. Then she raised her arms higher and every eye watched as she brought her palms together and lowered them. She breathed out, smiled, and took her place behind the podium.

"Thank you, Joan McNeish," she said without another glance at Rhona. "Thank you for your kind words. If I'd known you and your eco-contingent were going to wear such a startling shade of green, I would have chosen another color myself. Where is Gillian?"

"Here, Daphne," Gillian said from not many feet away.

"Gillian, my old friend." Daphne sounded delighted to find her, although the delight didn't extend to more than a quick smile. "Thank you for bringing me back to my roots—to the place of my own origin story—Inversgail." She swept her right hand out, which Rhona only narrowly dodged. "And Inversgail, thank you for welcoming a daughter and her dog home again."

She scooped up Rachel Carson and waved one of her paws at the audience. Rachel Carson leaned toward the microphone, looking as though she might have a few words to add. Janet cringed in anticipation of an amplified yip, but the dog only sniffed the equipment and then licked Daphne's chin. The audience loved it, laughing and clapping again.

Daphne put Rachel Carson down, raised her arms, and there was instant hush.

"So kind. Thank you. Now, let me save you time and me untold repetitions by slaking your curiosity with the answer to a question I hear a *great* deal." She turned a brief, bright smile on Rhona. "The question is, why do I live the way I do? Why do I choose to live alone, save for my companion dog, in a simple cabin in the deep woods of Canada? The answer is found in St. Bernard's epistle 106. Also, for those who read carefully, in the front of each of my books.

"St. Bernard says, 'You will find something more in woods than in books. Trees and stones will teach you that which you can never learn from masters.' A wicked quotation to find on the title page of a *book*, but true, and over the next few months, you will find that I am an honest person who believes in living an honest life. Allow me to illustrate."

Though she was right about their green shirts looking bilious behind her mossy robe, Rhona and the GREAT-SCOTS remained a friendly backdrop to Daphne's lengthening remarks. Alistair stood by, too, smiling and waiting, ready to step forward to receive his plaque and deliver his own short speech. Daphne didn't seem ready to give up the microphone, though. Her voice rose and fell in time with dramatic arm gestures that looked almost balletic, or possibly like a form of tai chi. Janet couldn't tell if the arms added anything to Daphne's message or if she was trying to hypnotize the audience. She gave herself a shake to dispel the effect, either way.

Daphne went on and on and on, and now that Janet was paying attention to the words, it didn't sound at all like a speech recognizing someone's contributions or life's work. In fact, it didn't sound like a written or rehearsed speech so much as a stream of consciousness oration, with the stream well on its way to leaping the banks.

"These are frivolous efforts," Daphne was saying. "The spokeswoman for your local club"—she looked at Rhona again—"You call yourselves GREAT-SCOT, the Green Resident Environmental Alliance Trust—Start Conserving Our Tomorrow, is that correct?"

Rhona, her eyes wary, nodded.

Daphne shook her head. "I'm sorry, Joan, but SCOT might as well stand for Stop Cheating Our Tomorrow, because your wee green plans and efforts are already too late. You might as well invite construction and industry."

She turned back to her audience and explained to them how Inversgail, by existing at all, had contaminated and brutalized the landscape and that every one of them was guilty of further degradation. "You own cars. You burn fossil fuel. You walk on pavement. You have indoor plumbing and refrigeration. You're celebrating the construction of a footpath that will allow and encourage more people to intrude on nature, on our paradise. And now, you would hardly know there is a murderer in our paradise. A man, a stranger, has died here, was *killed* here, and when I questioned the response—or the lack of it—I was told by several people, 'We don't know anything about him.' 'We didn't know this person.' 'We have no reason to get involved.' That is a sad commentary on a single life and an even sadder reflection of an attitude toward the poor old world we live in, and this, *this* is why I absent myself from it."

Daphne paused and stared straight ahead again. The entire room might not have been breathing. The only sound Janet heard was a gentle snore from Christine's mother, whose head lay on her husband's shoulder.

"Please believe me," Daphne said, still staring forward, but now with a hand on her heart. "I do not mean to make you uncomfortable or to belittle you or your efforts. But consider this—cleaning up crime is part of cleaning up a community. Murderers are no better for the environment than other toxins.

"And now, before I leave you, I'd like to share two more quotations with you. You might say these are my mantras. One is a quote from the physicist Richard Feynman. It is this: 'The first principle is that you must not fool yourself—and you are the easiest person to fool.' The second quotation is from T. S. Eliot. I've been told it's quite dark. Nonetheless, I find it deeply resonant: 'All our knowledge brings us nearer to our ignorance, All our ignorance brings us nearer to death.' Ladies and gentlemen, thank you for your warm welcome home."

Daphne stepped back from the microphone with the look of someone expecting applause. On either side of her, Rhona, Gillian, and Gillian's father exchanged the looks of people expecting something rather different. Rhona recovered first. She handed Daphne the plaque, somewhat aggressively, Janet thought, then whispered something to her, took her by the arm, and brought her back to the microphone.

"Can you believe I forgot the most important part of the evening?" Daphne bounced the heel of her hand off her forehead. "But first, let me assure you that I'm looking forward to the experience of being back home in Inversgail. Living amongst the weasels and the moose has given me many opportunities for new experiences, and I look forward to sharing them with your children in the schools. You'll find that I'm game for trying almost anything once. Although once is often enough. Roast weasel, for instance. Not something I recommend.

"And now, Alistair, you old sinner, on behalf of all garden gnomes, I present you with this plaque and the honor that goes with it." She looked at the plaque, shrugged, and handed it to him, then turned back to the microphone. "Ladies and gentlemen, enjoy yourselves at the ceilidh and dance like there's no tomorrow, because there just might not be one." Daphne clapped and, because they were polite and possibly couldn't think of anything else to do, the audience joined in.

Rab caught Janet's eye. "Are you going to let her do a talk before the signing in the shop?" he asked.

"Over my dead body."

10

Daphne's unusual presentation didn't put a damper on Alistair's spirits. He recaptured the audience by handing the plaque off to Gillian and then clicking his seventy-something heels twice in the air. He told the audience the recognition and thanks were, by rights, theirs, and then he turned and spoke to Daphne.

"Tha thu gòrach agus mì-thlachdmhor," he said with a slight bow. *"Fàilte gu Inversgail. Coisich gu faiceallach."*

There were a few titters and Janet caught a bemused look or two, but Daphne bowed her thanks to Alistair and air-kissed his cheeks. At that, the audience roared, and then James Haviland and his fellow musicians took over the stage.

"I understood some of that Gaelic," Janet said proudly. "Welcome to Inversgail. That was certainly nice of him after the gloom and doom she poured on the evening."

"Murk and smirk, more like," Christine said, "because she's a bampot. I'm away, Janet. My old dears need their beds."

"See you," Janet said and then turned to Rab. "Did you catch the rest of what Alistair said?"

"Bit long to go into." Rab got up, his feet looking ready to join the first dance. "Will the gist do?"

Janet nodded.

"She's a bampot."

∞

Janet watched the first few dances, her toes tapping. There was no formality to wait on before joining a set, but she hadn't danced a reel or jig
in years. Her plan was to absorb the footwork and lilt by osmosis and so
avoid making a fool of herself when she did join in. She watched Tallie
and Summer march, turn, and polka as directed by the caller in "Gay
Gordons," and then step, slide, turn, and swing in an "Eightsome Reel."
Gillian, Tom, and Alistair were out there, as well as the other teacher
Janet had met when she'd gone to the school. Rab went past in a set with
Rhona. Daphne didn't dance, but Janet saw her and Rachel Carson
mingling. Rachel Carson shook hands and Daphne made small talk, her
earlier odd behavior no longer evident.

When the next dance neared its end, Janet's toes told her to get up and
go for it. She stood and saw Reddick sitting alone. On a whim, she asked
him to join her. He agreed and they lined up opposite each other for "The
Flying Scotsman." Reddick bowed, the dance began, and they received
a thumbs-up from Tallie, who was guzzling a lemonade on the sidelines.

Janet and Reddick circled each other and every so often came together
to slip-step down the middle of the rectangle formed by the other couples
in the set.

"You seem to be moving well," Janet said during their first slip-step.
"Are you fully recovered from your fall?"

Reddick said he was and they separated again.

"An unusual woman, Daphne Wood," Reddick said during their next
slip-step. "What were you discussing so seriously while you ate?"

"Civic organizations," Janet said, but before she could ask him why
he wanted to know, they'd separated again.

"Any progress on Sam Smith's death?" she asked as they made another
trip up the middle.

"That name hasn't been released yet." Reddick's footwork was briefly
confused on that slip-step.

Coming back together, Janet said, "The name was easy enough to guess. We haven't told anyone."

"It will be released soon, but thank you."

"Do you know where Norman Hobbs is?"

"I'm not at liberty to say."

They separated again, and Janet found the pattern of both the dance and Reddick's answers frustrating. He sounded as though he took lessons in reticence and loyalty from a BBC butler. But when they came together for one last slip-step journey up the middle, he surprised her.

"I understand your concern for Hobbs. I assure you, there's nothing wrong and he'll be back soon."

"Thank you for that," Janet said. "Quick question. Is Yon Bonnie Books implicated in Smith's death?"

"If that becomes the case, you will be the first to know."

"The Flying Scotsman" came to an end and Reddick thanked Janet for the dance. She hoped she hadn't put ideas in his head with her last question, but she had the sneaking suspicion he'd been working to keep a straight face. That was fine with her. She joined Tallie and Summer in "Gay Gordons" and saw that Reddick had taken a seat near the stage. She wondered what or who he was watching, because he didn't appear to be watching the dancers. The next time she looked over, he'd gone—from the library, apparently, because she didn't see him again.

⸺ ✍ ⸺

"She didn't eat anything," Gillian said when she and Janet met at the drinks table. "I asked her weeks ago, when the students were setting the menu, if she had a favorite dish she remembered from childhood. Was there anything, I asked, anything she'd particularly like to have here this evening? So we have her to thank for the Brussels sprouts. And then she brought that horrible salad and ate nothing at all."

"Don't let it bother you," Janet said. "It's a wonderful event."

"That's what Dad says. He just laughs and says Daphne's the way she is because the fairies took her when she was a bairn, but when they found out what she was like, they kicked her out again. He's loving this evening, isn't he?"

"Has she always been so—"

"Thoughtful?"

If there'd been a glint of sarcastic pleasure on Gillian's face when she said that, Janet missed it. But she didn't miss the narrowing of Gillian's eyes as she saw Tom swing past with their fellow teacher on his arm.

Toward the end of the evening, Janet spotted Daphne at the buffet. Daphne looked over her shoulder, then took a plastic container from her backpack and scooped it full of haggis balls, adding a dollop of the whisky mustard sauce for good measure. Rachel Carson sat at Daphne's feet, looking left, then right, then left again as though ready to let Daphne know if anyone was on to her. Daphne snapped the lid on the container and stuffed it into her backpack.

A short time later, Gillian, Tom, and Alistair left, taking Daphne and Rachel Carson with them. They all looked happy enough in each other's company. *Maybe they're going for a pint*, Janet thought. If they were, she hoped it was somewhere other than Nev's. Danny was a good publican who knew how to make everyone welcome, but making Daphne welcome might tax even him.

Tallie came over, as Janet watched them go, and handed her a folded note. "Daphne asked me to give this to you."

"Oh dear." The paper appeared to have been torn from Daphne's notebook. Janet unfolded it and read: *I finally have the name for our crime-solving collaboration: S.C.O.N.E.S.—Shadow Constabulary of Nosy Eavesdropping Snoops.*

"Did you read this?" Janet asked her daughter.

"Strangely, even after her warning about ignorance and death, reading that note didn't tempt me," Tallie said. "What is it?"

Janet passed it to her. "She thinks the four of us should be jumping at the chance to help her find that poor soul's killer. Of course, I told her no. And told her no again this evening." She took the note back, crumpled it, and jammed it in her purse.

"Of course, you did."

Janet saw her daughter giving her a thoughtful look. *But not the sort of "thoughtful" Gillian seems to think Daphne is, I hope.*

"Some of us are going for a pint," Tallie said. "Want to come?"

"Who's we?"

"Summer, Martin, James. Maybe Pat the accordion player."

"No thanks, darling. Bed and a book sound good to me."

"Who's under the covers with you tonight?" Tallie asked.

"Jeeves and Bertie."

"Kinky. Don't you three stay up too late."

Janet called her bedtime reading running away from reality. Tallie told her if she ever felt guilty about it, she could call it business prep and feel virtuous. Janet thanked her and said that wouldn't change anything. She'd just feel guilty about enjoying her work so much.

∞

One of James Haviland's fiddle tunes ran through Janet's head as she drove home. It was a mournful piece he'd played after the dancing was over, suitable for the mist that was moving in again. *Suitable for evoking ghosts,* Janet thought, and so she wasn't entirely surprised to see a small, agitated shadow tapping its foot as it waited at her front door.

"Maida?"

Maida, arms wrapped tightly around herself, blocked Janet's way. She wasn't just agitated; she had no sweater or coat and she was shivering.

"What is it?" Janet asked. "Come inside where it's warm." She put a hand out to guide Maida aside so she could put her key in the lock, but Maida flinched, pulling away. Janet got the door unlocked and pushed it open. Another shiver ran like a spasm through Maida. "Come inside right this minute," Janet said, taking Maida firmly by the elbow. "I'll make tea. Unless you'd rather have—"

"Something stronger might be better," Maida said.

Janet hadn't been expecting company and wondered about the state of the kitchen. Maybe it would be best to settle Maida in the living room. *But what does it matter, really? She's family, after a fashion. Odd family, maybe, but not as odd as Daphne.* Janet poured a small whisky for Maida and one for herself. She brought a knitted throw and put it around Maida's shoulders, and then sat down with her.

"Maida, tell me what's happened. Are you hurt?"

"No! No, I'm not." She put a hand to her mouth and took several gulping breaths.

"Where's your car? I didn't see it when I drove up. Where's your coat?"

"My coat's with my purse. I left them both over there and I couldn't make myself go back."

"Where? To the library?"

"Did you eat any of the salad Daphne brought?" Maida stopped, overcome by an emotion that did alarming things to her color and coherency.

Janet reached out and took her shaking hand. "Maida, what is it?"

"That woman. Do you know what she did? Do you know what she is?"

"Christine thinks she's become eccentric from living alone for so many years. Actually, she called her a bampot, and frankly I'm inclined to agree. But, please, don't repeat that, Maida."

"No," Maida said, shaking her head. "You don't understand. Bampot's just the beginning of it and that's too mild. I'd call her a cannibal, but then *I* would sound like a bampot. But she took my houseplants—my African violets, purple passion, and prayer plants— and she chopped them up and disguised them with a bit of spinach and lettuce and served them up as salad at the ceilidh."

Janet's first concern, after calming Maida, was whether Daphne had poisoned anyone, including herself. She shuddered, remembering the last wretched mouthful she'd eaten before setting her plate aside. She didn't *feel* any different, now, several hours later, but how long would poisoning by prayer plant take? Surely Daphne wouldn't have let Rachel Carson finish what was on her plate without knowing her exotic greens were safe.

Janet poured another small whisky for each of them and then opened her laptop. "I'll just check to see if the plants are toxic."

"They're not," Maida said. "I wouldn't keep them if they were. Not with Freddie and Wally." Freddie and Wally were her three- and one-year-old grandsons.

"That's very good and thorough of you, Maida. Still, I'll feel better if I check. I don't mean to doubt you, but in times of crisis, librarians look things up."

Maida sipped and watched as Janet tapped her keyboard, stopped to read, and tapped some more. "She's definitely not right in the head, and no telling what she'll get up to next. She's a danger."

"Ah, I've found what we need," Janet said with a rush of relief.

Maida took a last sip—more of a gulp—and put her glass aside. "It's our duty to stop her. I'm going to call nine-nine-nine."

"But they're not poisonous," Janet said. "You were absolutely right, Maida, so there's no need to call the police. No one actually recommends eating any of the three plants, but they aren't toxic. I know the plants meant a lot to you—"

"They were like my babies."

"I can tell," Janet said. She was beginning to regret refilling Maida's glass.

"I want Norman Hobbs to arrest her for destruction of private property."

"You don't think the plants will grow back?" From Maida's reaction to that question, Janet guessed not. "It isn't exactly an emergency, though, Maida, so nine-nine-nine probably isn't the appropriate number. We could call Gillian."

"I will certainly call Gillian. I will call her and I will call Norman Hobbs. He has a cutting from one of my prayer plants. He'll understand the tragedy and he'll know how to handle this."

Janet suggested a pot of tea and a little more thought before making the call. Maida wouldn't hear of it. Her phone, however, was in her purse, and her purse was with her coat.

"And I left them both behind when I ran out of the house. We'll use yours."

Janet made the call, wondering if Reddick's prediction was accurate. Maybe Norman Hobbs would finally answer his phone.

He didn't. Reddick did.

❧

"What did Ms. Wood say to you about the plants?" Reddick asked after hearing Maida's story. He'd taken the chair nearest to her and spoke calmly and quietly.

"She said they'd be no bother," Maida said with a quaver. "She said it was like living in a garden."

"I think he means what did Daphne say when you went over there this evening?" Janet said. "How did she explain the, um, harvest?"

Maida moaned, looked at the floor, and shook her head.

Reddick turned a stern eye on Janet. She mouthed "sorry" and clamped her lips firmly so he'd know she meant it.

"Ms. Wood didn't say anything?" he asked, turning back to Maida. "Are you sure, Ms. Fairlie? I know this is upsetting, but you needn't be uneasy or afraid. Did she threaten you in any way when you confronted her?"

Janet had liked Reddick each time she met him, even with his BBC butler's rectitude. She liked him now for the gentle kindness he showed Maida. She couldn't help thinking, though, that Norman Hobbs, having known Maida most of his life, would see something Reddick was missing. It was Janet's theory that the ghosts of Maida's Presbyterian ancestors stood shoulder to shoulder with her as she navigated her way through life—a way that Janet estimated at roughly ninety-five percent straight and narrow. Janet had seen the remaining five percent take Maida down interesting byways. And right now, Janet was sure Reddick was wrong. Maida didn't look uneasy or afraid; she looked shifty-eyed and a bit piddled.

Maida glanced up and caught Janet studying her. Judging by the way Maida's cheeks turned a deeper shade of pink, Janet was sure she was right.

"Ms. Fairlie?" Reddick prompted. "Did Ms. Wood say or do anything?"

Maida looked at the floor again and shook her head.

Reddick went to the window.

"We each have a back gate," Janet said.

"Right, and a light's just come on over there. I'll just nip through, then, and have a chat with Ms. Wood. You say you left your coat and purse there, Ms. Fairlie?"

"And her keys," Janet said.

After he stepped out the back door, Janet asked Maida if she'd changed her mind about a cup of tea. Maida answered with a barely audible no. Janet picked up a crossword puzzle and the two sat in silence.

∾

Maida might have dozed off by the time Reddick returned. Janet decided to be charitable and believe that was the reason she seemed to jump when he rapped on the door and stepped in. The extra pink was back in her cheeks, though, and her gaze didn't rise quite so far as to meet Reddick's when he cleared his throat.

"You have Maida's things," Janet said. "Wonderful."

Reddick laid Maida's coat neatly over the back of a chair. He kept hold of her purse. He waited until Maida looked up at him, then he handed it to her. Purse regained, she regained some of her original, bristling anger.

"What did she have to say for herself?" she demanded.

"She said you gave the plants to her." Reddick's tone was even, as though he delivered a traffic report. "She thought they were a house-warming gift and hers to do with as she saw fit."

"What about restitution?"

Reddick's face remained impassive. His tone didn't waver. "Ms. Wood had a guest."

"Tom Laing?" Janet asked. Impassive though Reddick's face might be, a glance from him was enough to clamp her lips again after a quick, "Sorry."

"According to Ms. Wood, a reporter with the *Inversgail Guardian* happened by. Martin Gunn. He waited in another room while we talked. The question of restitution for your loss didn't arise, Ms. Fairlie, but the question of pressing charges did."

Maida gave a yip of pleasure. It was short-lived.

"Ms. Wood said that if you'll forgive her for treating the houseplants like fresh groceries, then she won't pass details of the story along to Martin Gunn and she won't press charges against you for burglary and attempted murder."

11

Reddick had found Maida's coat and purse right where she said she dropped them in Daphne's kitchen. He also found the liquid contents of an unlabeled bottle spilled on the cutting board and across the counter.

"My special plant food," Maida said. "I make it myself with powdered bat guano. I brought it for her. But when I found nothing but the stumps of my beautiful plants in their pots—it was too horrible. I dropped everything and ran, just as I told you."

"Ms. Wood claims you were trying to poison her. That you were going to mix the liquid in her organic muesli but got cold feet."

"I was not! I didn't open the bottle because there were no plants left to feed. What's more, it's quite dear to make and pouring it on muesli would ruin the muesli *and* be a waste of the plant food."

∽

Janet was still in the family room when Tallie got home, feet curled beneath her in her favorite chair and working her crossword. After deciphering the hysteria of Maida's story, the black and white grid was more calming than any amount of empathy meditation she had the patience for, and safer than another whisky.

"What happened to your threesome with Jeeves and Wooster?" Tallie asked.

"Change of plans. What's a four letter word for 'recurring pain'?"

"Ache."

"No, I don't see how that will work. Ah, got it." Janet filled in the letters and put the crossword aside. "It was 'pest,' and that reminds me. Try to avoid the creaky step when you go upstairs. We have a guest." She picked up the two whisky glasses and took them to the kitchen. Tallie followed.

"A real guest, or did you fix drinks for Jeeves and Bertie and then have them both yourself?" Tallie looked at her mother's eyes. "You aren't just still up-awake, you're up-excited, the way you are when something's happened and you're trying to fix it. So what's going on, who's upstairs? And please don't say it's Daphne."

"No, it's Maida and—"

"Maida?"

"Shh. She was still upset and I didn't like the idea of her driving home on a night like this. Although, come to think of it"—she held up one of the glasses—"I gave her more than I'm sure she's used to. She was a wee bit squiffed, so it's just as well she did stay."

"No such thing, Mom. To be squiffed or not to be squiffed, but a wee bit squiffed is out of the question. And now why are you staring out the window and why does it look like you're trying to burn through the mist between here and Daphne's house with laser vision?"

"Because I wish I could find out what she's up to. But if I could see *her*, then she could see *me*." Janet shivered, the way Maida had earlier, and backed away from the kitchen window. "Come back to the living room. We'll close the curtains and I'll tell you what Maida told Reddick."

"Reddick?"

"Shh, yes. But please, squiffed or not, let's not wake Maida. The poor thing needs her sleep and I don't need any more of her hysterics. Reddick, bless his heart, knew exactly how to handle her, and got her calmed down enough to talk. Between hiccups. And it's all because of the salad."

"That's how all the best bedtime stories begin," Tallie said. She drew the curtain for her mother then settled in a chair with the knitted throw Janet had put around Maida earlier.

"I saw Maida looking at the salad on the buffet tonight," Janet said, "and I thought she just didn't like the looks of it. But it turns out she was puzzled by it, because it looked oddly familiar."

Maida had told Janet and Reddick that she finally had a moment of horrible, dawning recognition. She knew where the salad greens had come from and she'd tried to approach Daphne, to confront her. Daphne eluded her, though, so Maida went to find out for herself.

"She said she knew she shouldn't let herself in while Daphne was out," Janet said, "but she couldn't help herself. In case she was wrong about where the greens came from, she stopped at home, first, and picked up a bottle of plant food—a concoction all her own—to leave for Daphne."

"A heart of gold, our Maida has," Tallie said.

"A broken heart of gold. She loved those plants."

"Where does Reddick come into the story?"

"As a stand-in for Norman, whom Maida insisted on calling." Janet told her about Reddick's arrival, his departure for Daphne's, and his return with Maida's belongings and Daphne's accusation.

"Does Maida need a solicitor?" Tallie asked.

"Reddick didn't seem to think so. He thinks it's a game of brinksmanship on Daphne's part. If Maida doesn't say anything more about destruction of property, Daphne won't repeat her ridiculous claim about poison. Reddick didn't come right out and say it, but it's pretty obvious he thinks Daphne's as nutty as we do."

"But he didn't say that?" Tallie asked.

"No."

"Then we don't really know what he thinks."

"No, we don't. We don't know what Daphne's thinking, either, or what she believes happened. But even if Daphne *doesn't* believe Maida was trying to poison her, I'm pretty sure she's capable of making people believe that's exactly what Maida was doing. Martin from the paper, for instance."

"Why Martin?"

"Didn't I tell you that part? He'd come home with Daphne. Hadn't he been with you and Summer?"

"He got a text. Left early."

"I wonder if it was from Daphne," Janet said. "I don't like not knowing what she's thinking or what she's said to Martin about all of this. Or what she's going to say to anyone else. It worries me, and makes me wonder what she's up to."

"We don't know that she's up to anything, but I think maybe you're up way past your bedtime and worrying too much."

"Maybe." Janet let her head nestle against the back of her chair and closed her eyes. "This feels awfully comfortable all of a sudden, so you're probably right. But half of me wants to cancel the signing, send all Daphne's books back to the publisher, and absorb the loss." She opened her eyes again and saw the reaction to that idea on Tallie's face. "Don't worry. The business person in me who likes to pay bills and eat knows we'll have to play nicely with our back garden neighbor and make this work. If I say that firmly enough, I'm pretty sure I'll believe it, too."

"Well, it won't hurt to be careful around Daphne."

"After Reddick left, Maida said she felt like she'd stepped in a patch of nettles and she couldn't stop rubbing her arms. She looked absolutely sick when she heard Martin Gunn was over there. She's worried it'll end up in the paper or as breaking news in one of its tweets—except she called them *twits*."

"Come on." Tallie took Janet's hand and pulled her to her feet. "*The Guardian* has the murder to keep it and its twits occupied. This sounds more like gossip and misunderstanding. You'll see. You'll feel better in the morning. So will Maida."

"Mmm," Janet said. "Or worse."

Tallie jogged in place at the bottom of the stairs as Janet came down
the next morning, then she was out the door for her run. Maida had
already crept out, having stripped the bed and dusted the room before
going. Janet found a note from her on the kitchen counter, thanking her
and also reminding her that she'd promised to talk to Gillian for her.
Janet didn't remember making that promise, but decided it wouldn't
hurt and might help if she, rather than Maida, made the call. She tried
Gillian twice and then left a message. That would give her time to think
through more carefully what to say, anyway.

At their morning meeting in the communicating door, Janet was ready
with words of wisdom for the others: "Buffets and bampots don't mix."

Tallie snorted and went to run a dust mop around the floors while
Janet explained to Christine and Summer.

"Any chance you can talk to Martin?" Janet asked Summer. "Is that
kind of thing done? Asking for something to be kept out of the news?"

"Hang on." Summer was already scrolling through tweets on her
phone. "I don't see anything, and seriously? If he hasn't said anything
yet, he probably won't."

"But is it worth asking?"

"I kind of hate to draw more attention to Maida by bringing it up. My
advice? Let sleeping bampots lie."

It was Christine's turn to snort. "Speaking from a purely personal
point of view, I can't wait for the book signing to see what happens. And
you know other people will feel the same. Whatever else she is, Daphne
will be good for business."

Gillian called shortly after Janet unlocked the door. Tallie was getting ready for the story and craft time, and Janet apologized for interrupting her.

"Let me take this in the office," she said. "I'll try to keep it short." She still hadn't thought through what she was going to say on Maida's behalf, but she needn't have worried. Gillian cut her off as soon as she heard Maida's name.

"I already heard about it from Daphne," Gillian said, "and I really didn't need this on top of everything else. Frankly, I'm surprised at Maida. *And* disappointed."

"What did Daphne tell you?"

"She thought, at first, that Maida let herself in while she was out walking the dog. As if that isn't bad enough. As far as I'm concerned, as long as Daphne's staying in that house, paid for by my grant money, it's her property and she deserves her privacy. Do you not agree, Janet?"

"I do, but—"

"But when the police arrived, she says that's when she got frightened, because things were blown out of all proportion."

"The policeman said Daphne accused Maida of attempted murder."

"Daphne says she didn't."

"Really?" Janet asked. "She actually said, 'I didn't accuse Maida of attempted murder'? Why would that even come up in her version of the story if she hadn't said it?"

Gillian didn't answer and Janet wondered if her phone had dropped the call. "Gillian?"

"Aye. Right. Well, if Maida thinks Daphne said that, then maybe the policeman exaggerated to scare her, to keep her from doing it again. But I really don't need this additional aggro, Janet. Daphne said the whole thing was a misunderstanding—all of it—and I believe her. So, tell Maida everything's fine, but no more snooping. And no real harm done, ken?"

Janet disconnected. *Gillian's probably right*, she thought. *No, not probably. She* is *right. In the great scheme of things, and compared to the sad death of Sam*

Smith, this eccentric author and whatever she's up to are a mere blip. She nodded, in firm agreement with her own thoughts, and stepped out of the office in time to hear the door jingle.

"Oh blip," she said under her breath. If it wasn't one eccentric author casting a pall over her day, it was another. "Hello, Ian."

Ian Atkinson was also an incomer to Inversgail, having lived in London most of his five or so decades. He was the author of the Single Malt Mysteries, international bestsellers and bestsellers at Yon Bonnie Books, too. Ian almost never bought anything himself when he came in the shop, though. He hadn't had a new book in several years, but as he explained it, he believed in meticulous research and never liked to rush the process. Whisky wasn't only the focus of his books, either. Ian was on the lookout for the right property in Inversgail to start a boutique distillery.

Tallie had a theory that Ian thought of himself as a replacement for the late actor Alan Rickman during his Jane Austen period. He wore his hair long enough that he had to flip it out of his eyes and he went in for languid poses. He also went in for somewhat passé author wear—turtleneck and tweed jacket with elbow patches. His trousers and shoes varied. Today, it was dark corduroys and chukka boots.

Ian was also Janet's next-door neighbor. *One living to my left and one behind me,* she thought as she returned to the sales counter. *If I'm not careful, I'll be surrounded by writers.*

"You missed a good time at the library last night, Ian," Tallie said.

"And I hated to miss it," Ian said with an artful slump. "Some writers are able to take three months at a time off, but that's not the way it works for me. You two, though, you must have had quite the wild party at home after the ceilidh last night."

"Sorry?" Janet said.

"I thought that might be why the police stopped by."

"You're such a kidder, Ian," Janet said. He was obviously fishing for information, and she didn't feel like obliging him. "Will we see you at the signing next week?"

"I'll check my schedule. See if I can fit it in."

A few families with children came in and they went with Tallie to sit on the rug in front of the fireplace for stories. Ian wandered over to listen as Tallie read one of Daphne's picture books, then he went to browse the cookery books. Janet had noticed that he often spent time looking at the cookbooks, yet he never bought one. She knew he might be "shopping" their shelves and then going online to find the books at a discount. He might also be taking pictures of the recipes he liked with his phone.

True to form, after story time was over and the children had giggled out the door, Ian wandered back to the sales counter empty-handed. "I'm assuming something," he said, his face and voice sliding into a tone of quiet confidentiality that Janet immediately doubted. "All joking about wild parties aside."

"What are you assuming, Ian?"

"That you're looking into our most recent tragic death. That *is* why Inspector Reddick called on you last night, isn't it?"

"Good lord, Ian. Is that what you think?" Christine startled Ian with a hand clapped on his shoulder. "You didn't know I have ears like an old bat, did you?" She further annoyed him by standing too close behind him. He put more space between them by moving along the counter a foot or two.

Sliding to the right, Janet thought, *like a dancer at a ceilidh. Or an oil slick.* "Why on earth would you assume that, Ian?"

Ian took a moment to adjust his dignity and the lines of his jacket. "It's meant as a compliment, you know. You have a track record."

"I'm pretty sure the police don't think of it that way," Janet said.

"They're more likely to think of it as a fluke," Tallie said. She came back behind the counter and stood next to Janet.

"Well, now, it wasn't a *complete* fluke," Janet said. "We put a lot of thought and effort into it, and we—" She stopped when Tallie's foot nudged her own. "But the answer is no, Ian."

"You write mysteries," Tallie said. "We sell them. We leave the police to solve them."

"Very nicely put," Christine said. "Both of you. We are anything but flukes, but neither are we in the detecting business. No, Ian, the reason Reddick called on the Marsh household last evening is much more interesting."

"Christine," Janet and Tallie said in unison, one voice sharp, the other appalled.

"We're all friends," Christine said, spreading her arms, her teeth making a particularly wicked smile. "And here are two delightful, intelligent, attractive, single women. What else could it have been, Ian, but a social call? I leave the rest to your imagination."

Ian's imagination didn't seem to know if it should believe Christine. She put an arm around his shoulders, started him toward the door, pulled it open, and guided him through. "Ta for now, Ian," she said. "Haste ye back." As the door closed behind him, she turned back to Tallie and Janet. "That's always a nice touch, don't you think? Oh, and here's the reason I left my tearoom lair. No need to hang back, Martin."

Martin Gunn, reporter for the *Inversgail Guardian*, stood at the end of the nearest aisle, eating a scone. It was easy to see that *his* imagination was having a field day with what he'd heard from Christine.

12

"Martin says he's planning to write a review of our business domain," Christine said.

Janet was used to seeing Martin in the lower light of Nev's, and more often from behind, throwing darts. He looked younger in the brightly lit shop and his clothes looked older, his jeans frayed at the cuffs and his wool suitcoat springing moth holes. The messenger bag slung around his shoulders and the asymmetrical cut of his hair, though, brought him into the realm of *au courant* and she figured him to be somewhere in his eager but still impecunious late twenties.

Martin popped the rest of the scone in his mouth and gave a jaunty wave. "I've just been sampling your wares."

"You've been sampling them for weeks," Christine said. "You didn't invent this review to get free baked goods from our Summer, did you?"

"Not at all." Martin looked properly shocked. "The review is Haviland's idea, but I'm all on board. I think it's brilliant."

His cheeks turned a more brilliant shade of pink to go with his enthusiasm. Janet suspected his cheeks were a mortifying flaw to him and that he cultivated the stubble on them as a remedy. Knowing that he'd been at Daphne's when Reddick spoke to her the night before, Janet was glad to see Martin wasn't making furtive notes either in a notebook or into a voice recorder. Just the same, she decided to keep an open mind about being open with him.

"I plan to work the review around a central theme," Martin said.

As opposed to a peripheral one? Janet told her thoughts to be quiet and pay attention.

"One of the central themes in Daphne's own work is impact," Martin said. "She touched on that when she presented the award to Alistair last night. So what I want to do is take the larger idea of impact, narrow its focus to Daphne and the impact she'll have on Inversgail and the students while she's here, and then make it even more specific and personal by showing how she and her books impact your business." He held his hands out as though they were holding something like a beach ball. "Layer within layer within layer," he said, moving his hands closer with each repetition of *layer*. "Until I get to the core of what Daphne Wood means for us"—he flung his hands apart again—"and what she means for the bigger picture. I'm fascinated by the idea of her having one foot in the separate and self-contained world she created in Canada and the other foot in a global environmental network. From the incredibly small to the vast and huge."

"Wow," Tallie said. "Sounds good, but"—she pointed her thumb over her shoulder—"customers. I'd better go."

"I agree with the 'wow,'" Christine said. "Definitely 'wow.' Teapots are calling, though, so I'd best get back, as well. You fill Janet in and she'll pass it along to us."

Janet watched the two hurry away. *Or are they scurrying away like*—but no, that wasn't fair. Someone had to take care of customers, and if Martin was willing to include Yon Bonnie Books in his big picture ambitions, she was willing to listen.

"I'd like to get pictures of her here with her books, and I'll get her to say something about how much she values bookshops. We can show her in the tearoom, too, and get some close-ups of shortbread or scones that will make people drool down their chins. And then the B&B. Can we get pictures of Daphne staying the night? Can *I* stay the night, to get the full experience?"

"You really get into your work, don't you?" Janet said. "Those all sound like great ideas. The bad news, although it's good for us, is that the B&B is booked solid. But it wouldn't really be necessary for either of you to stay there, would it? Why don't you talk to Summer and see if you can arrange a time to take pictures up there?"

Martin's phone buzzed in his pocket and he pulled it out with an apology. Janet didn't know if it was the interruption that made his cheeks go pink again or the suggestion he talk to Summer. He blew out a single short, sharp breath, then looked at her and blinked as though reorienting himself to the world in front of him.

"Summer. Good, I'll talk to her. Sorry about—" He trailed off and looked at his phone again, then held it up. "Police released the name of the victim. Samuel Smith, twenty-two, American, from Pennsylvania. Not much else." Martin swallowed. "But the interview and article. I will, um—"

"Do you need to get back to the office?" Janet asked.

"Sorry? Oh. I should, yeah. But I'll get back to you. Ta."

Martin was out the door so fast that Janet imagined his words still hanging in the air, not knowing quite what to do with themselves. She felt the same way. She hadn't expected to have an emotional reaction to hearing Sam Smith's name confirmed. Almost as though his soul or ghost or shade had hung in the mist behind Nev's, not knowing what had happened and not knowing what to do. But now Sam was well and truly dead, and it took having his name confirmed to bring the bleak sadness of it home to her.

Janet looked around their very pleasant space filled with books and pictured Danny finding Sam that night. Curled on the pavement, Danny had said. No question he'd been killed. *With a brick. A blunt object. An impact.*

"Go get a cup of tea," Tallie said, reappearing to give her mother a quick hug. "I've got the shop."

∽

"It was more of a shock than I thought," Janet said when Christine put one of their blue teapots on the table in front of her. "He was just a boy, really." She wasn't whispering, but she kept her voice low. She didn't want her words drifting over to disturb other tables.

Christine touched Janet's shoulder and then went to greet two women who'd come in. Summer set a cup and saucer on the table, then pulled out the chair opposite Janet and sat down.

"You must have felt that same shock when Reddick came in Tuesday morning," Janet said.

"Maybe," Summer said. "Mostly I felt bad because I didn't remember more about him. I wish I could say he reminded me of someone, but there isn't even that. And how long was I a reporter? Fifteen years? I can't even tell you how tall he was."

Summer's fingers were tented on the table in front of her as though muscle memory would have them pounding a keyboard any second. If it had been Tallie or Christine sitting across from her, Janet would have touched those tense hands to calm them. Instead, she asked a question. "Was he traveling alone?"

"He stayed here alone. Otherwise, I don't know." Summer took her phone out and brought something up on the screen. "I should get back, give Christine a hand, but I received the same tweet with the police statement that Martin did. The statement was that short, too. Name, age, where he was from." She passed her phone to Janet. "Do you see what detail is missing?"

"They didn't release a cause of death."

"That's interesting, don't you think?"

⌘

Janet kept thoughts of the missing detail at bay through the rest of the morning and into the afternoon. Saturdays brought more of the bread-and-butter tourists to town, and selling books to them and straightening shelves after they'd browsed away a rainy afternoon kept her mind well occupied. An hour before closing, Daphne came in. Janet braced herself.

"Mom," Tallie whispered. "Chill."

"Trying," Janet said between gritted teeth that didn't look as much like a welcoming smile as she thought they did. "How are you, Daphne? What can we do for you?" *And please don't say find Sam Smith's killer.*

"I'm having a get-together tomorrow and I'd like you both to come."

"What kind of get-together?" Tallie asked.

Tallie did a fine job of sounding pleasantly inquisitive. Janet thought her own effort would have ranged closer to unpleasantly suspicious.

"An icebreaker," Daphne said. "Not so much chatting over refreshments, though. In fact, not that at all, because, frankly, I'm not interested. But I thought *you* might be interested in learning about Forza—the sword work you saw me doing the other morning."

"So the get-together is more of a demonstration?" Tallie asked.

"Exercise group," Daphne corrected. "Why don't we call it that? Exercise with a sword. Extremely liberating."

"I actually liked the looks of it when I saw you," Janet said.

"Wonderful. Invite your team in the tearoom, too, will you? There'll be a few others. Six, maybe eight. Tomorrow morning, ten-ish. I'll supply the swords."

"Where?" Janet asked.

"Your back garden will be perfect," Daphne said on her way to the door. "Dress comfortably."

"Wait," Janet called after her. "What if it rains?"

"We get wet."

Janet and Tallie watched the door close behind Daphne, Janet nodding. "This will be good," she said. "She kind of got off on the wrong foot when she arrived. Two wrong feet, really. Or six, if you include the dog. But now she's reaching out. This will be good. I think we'll enjoy it."

"She can supply that many swords?" Tallie asked.

Thoughts about the missing detail had their chance to surface at the end of the day, as Janet and Tallie closed the bookshop and Christine and Summer the tearoom.

"Maybe they still have questions about the cause of death," Janet said to Tallie as they settled the cash register.

"Or there's something significant about it that they're keeping to themselves."

"Significant about the way he was hit? About the brick?"

"Or some other detail we don't know anything about," Tallie said.

"Huh." Janet planted her elbows on the counter and rested her chin on her steepled hands.

When Christine and Summer came through from shutting down the tearoom, they found Tallie working around her mother. Christine nodded at Janet. "Where's she gone?"

"Sorry." Janet straightened up, and then rubbed her hands to warm them. "I was giving myself the willies again, wondering what the police don't know, or what they don't want *us* to know."

"Martin told me something I didn't know," Summer said. "He and James stopped back at the office that night. Martin heard the fight outside Nev's."

Christine shook her head. "Danny says it wasn't anything more than an argument that he sent outside. Lads and a few fists, and the fists were out for show, not for blood."

"Martin called it a *rammy*."

"A brawl?" Christine considered that. "Danny's ex-navy, so his ideas of argument and rammy might be different from Martin's. Whichever it was, he stopped it, and he didn't think Sam Smith was part of either the celebration that brought the lads in or the argument. Of course, neither was Tom Laing, but he threw one of the punches."

"I thought Gillian took Tom home," Tallie said.

"She did. At least, that's what she said when they left," Janet said. "So that's interesting. Did she leave and he stayed? Or did he leave and come back? And if he came back, was that with or without Gillian?"

"I think I'm more interested that there are two versions of what might or might not have been a fight," Tallie said.

"At least two versions," Summer said.

"At least," Janet agreed, "and almost certainly more. And what version would Sam Smith tell us if he could?"

∽

Janet was glad to see the sun the next morning. She had mixed feelings about meeting Daphne and however many people she'd invited for the exercise group in the back garden. Learning sword moves appealed to her, but the possibility of the exercise group turning into a tea party in her living room didn't. She'd bought real cream on the way home the evening before, though, just in case. And she'd told Christine and Summer about Daphne's invitation. Summer said she'd think about it. Christine said she'd pass. To make up for Christine's defection, Janet opened the cream for her own tea at breakfast, and kept it out for a second and then a third cup.

Tallie came in the kitchen and spotted the carton on the table. "A cream-fix kind of day?"

"Yes, it is," Janet said without looking up from her crossword. "And I'll thank you to remember you're a lawyer and not a judge."

"You're harder on yourself than I would ever dream of being." Tallie gave the top of her mother's head a kiss, and then looked out the window over the sink. "I think we have future Forza fanatics lurking at the bottom of the garden."

"Already?" Janet put her pen down and drained her teacup. "I'll go on out. You're coming, aren't you?"

"Be there in a few minutes."

Janet was surprised by how much she really was looking forward to the class or whatever Daphne wanted to call it. She'd never held a sword before, and she wasn't usually attracted to weapons, but she had an idea she would be good at this. *Or at least good at making a fool of myself,* she thought. For comfort, she'd first put on her old sweats, but after looking at herself in the mirror, she'd decided presentable needed to be part of the equation and changed into blue jeans.

A small but interesting group met Janet at the bottom of the garden. Summer and Gillian were there, and the teacher Janet had met at the high school and seen dancing at the ceilidh, Hope Urquhart. Rhona from the GREAT-SCOTS was there, too, talking to Maida. Maida had her back resolutely turned to her house, as though she'd been warned against even sneaking a peek at it as long as Daphne and Rachel Carson were staying there. She looked as though she'd come from church, which was possibly as comfortable as she ever looked. Gillian, Summer, and Rhona wore jeans, yoga pants, and hiking shorts respectively. While they greeted each other and exclaimed over the sunshine and wondered where Daphne was, they heard a hullo from the top of Janet's garden, and Tallie came into view, followed by Christine.

"Seemed too good to miss," Christine said when they'd joined the others. "My inner swashbuckler got the better of me. I thought you said this started at ten."

"Ten-ish," Janet said.

"That 'ish' rather sums up my impression of Daphne," Rhona said. "A bit unpredictable."

"That's certainly a nice way of putting it," Christine said. "Especially after her rant at the library Friday night."

"She had a rough first few days, I think," Gillian said. "What with jetlag and adjusting to an urban setting, even if we're only a town and not Glasgow or even Fort William. But isn't it nice of her to invite us to learn her workout routine?"

"In Janet's garden rather than her own," Christine said. "That makes it nice-*ish*."

Their talk wandered as they waited for Daphne. Janet told them about seeing Daphne practicing Forza in the middle of Ross Street. Maida told them about seeing Daphne smoking the night she arrived. They wondered if that had been to steady her nerves after driving across from Glasgow in the dark and the fog. Hope told them Daphne was visiting her literature classes the next day, her first official day in the schools. Christine asked Hope if she was worried how Daphne would do in the classroom, after hearing her Friday night. Hope hesitated, looking thoughtful, but Gillian said she wasn't worried at all. Maida whispered to Janet that *she* would worry.

Despite the sun, hands began disappearing into pockets against the chill, and now even Maida cast occasional glances toward Daphne's house.

"So, Gillian," Christine said, "did your Tom go back to Nev's without you Monday night?"

"Sorry?" Gillian said.

"You said you were taking him home when you two said good night. I was just wondering when he decided to go back."

Janet wondered if Gillian hadn't known Tom went back. But more interesting than Gillian's apparent confusion over Christine's question was the look on Hope's face as she watched Gillian stumbling over an answer. Janet thought back to Monday afternoon at the school and the interplay between Hope and Tom. Did Gillian know how Tom looked at Hope?

"You know," Summer said, rubbing her arms and stamping her feet, "it really isn't warm out here. How long are we going to wait for Daphne?"

"That almost sounds like a philosophical question," Tallie said. "I'll go knock on her door."

They watched her fumble, briefly, with a latch on the gate at the bottom of Daphne's garden, and then trot to the back door. Tallie knocked, waited, knocked again, listened, shrugged. By the time she'd trotted back, Gillian had her phone out.

"Daphne? Oh—" Gillian took the phone away from her ear for a moment. "Voicemail."

They listened to Gillian leave a message. Janet thought she did well to keep it upbeat, although her voice sounded higher and tighter than usual, possibly with the strain of keeping it pleasant.

"Typical," Gillian said when she'd disconnected. "She almost never answers."

"Text her?" Summer said. "She might pay more attention."

Gillian tapped and sent. They waited, staring at the phone. *Like people at a séance waiting for a message from a crystal ball,* Janet thought.

Christine broke the spell. "We've been stood up and I'm not quite broken-hearted."

They all agreed and they further agreed when Christine declared it completely unnecessary for Janet to ask them in for tea. Janet thanked Christine for that. Maida and Janet were the only ones who said they hoped Daphne would reschedule.

∾

Not many minutes after Janet had poured herself another cup of cream-laden tea and stood at the kitchen window wondering why they'd been stood up and where Daphne was, the latter question was answered. Daphne, with a long and heavy-looking duffle slung over a shoulder, opened the gate at the bottom of the garden. She and Rachel Carson came through. Daphne stopped and Rachel Carson sat down. While Rachel Carson yawned, Daphne put her hands on her hips and looked around as though she expected to find people waiting. Janet put her teacup down and went back out.

And if she acts exasperated, or if Rachel Carson yips at me in my own garden, I won't be responsible for my own exasperation, Janet thought.

"I blew it, didn't I?" Daphne called when she saw Janet coming. Rachel Carson yawned again.

"We did wait quite a while," Janet said, "and called, texted, and knocked on your door."

"I'm not good at these social things. Another reason I'm better off with trees. I let the photographer talk me into going on another photo shoot."

"Tom Laing?"

"He has a high opinion of his talents." She let the duffle down onto the ground and rubbed her shoulder. "I'll do better with the newspaper interview. And a radio interview Gillian arranged for tomorrow morning. I'm supposed to mention the signing at your shop."

"When is it? I'll be sure to listen."

"No one who matters will be listening to a wee local station at half-six in the morning."

Janet was inclined to agree with her, but made a show of taking her phone out and setting an alarm. Daphne didn't seem to notice.

"Are the swords in your bag?" Janet asked. "May I see?"

Daphne unzipped the duffel and handed one of the long wooden swords to her. Janet immediately loved the sturdy feel of it. Carved from a single piece of wood, this "sword" wasn't at all thin and whippy like a fencing sword, nor would it slice like a saber. It was an inch or so thick, with a slightly curved blade, a handle but no hilt, and a blunt point at the tip. In all, it was a bit longer than a yardstick and didn't weight more than a pound or two.

"It's called a *bokken*," Daphne said. "It's a practice sword. Made of red oak."

"Cool." Janet couldn't remember the last time she'd said *cool* like that, but she meant every *oo* of it. "Where did you get them?"

"You can get anything online."

"Will you show me some of your workout?"

"Some other time."

"Would you like to come in for a cup of tea?"

"No."

Janet swished the sword from left to right.

"Why does any one person like another?" Daphne asked.

Janet stopped mid-swish and looked at Daphne. Daphne wasn't looking at her, though, and might not have been talking to her. She'd sunk onto her heels next to Rachel Carson and stroked the dog's head.

"Here's an example: Why does Gillian like me? She claims we've been friends since we were schoolgirls. But is that true? And if it's true, why is it? Because I don't know. I remember that I called her G.G. Why? I don't know that, either. For the sake of expedience? To save my breath?"

"Because you liked her initials? Or maybe it was just fun, or cute."

"I don't remember being cute." Rachel Carson rolled onto her back so Daphne could rub her belly, or possibly take a lesson in being cute.

"What did Gillian call you?" Janet asked.

"In our final year at school, I wanted to be called Laurel."

"That's a pretty name. Did Gillian call you Laurel?"

"I never asked her to. I never told anyone. It's from a Greek myth. I used to read a lot of escapist stuff and that myth was the ultimate escape. A naiad named Daphne escaped the clutches of a rapacious Apollo when her mother turned her into a laurel tree. Or her father turned her into one. It depends on which story you believe. Or which one you like better.

"Schoolwork was another escape. I was always good at it, and I've kept at it. I've studied the flora and fauna around my cabin minutely, down to what some so wrongly consider to be the most trifling of creatures. Fairyflies, for instance, which are the world's smallest flying insects. Imagine that; the world's smallest. I feel very strongly about fairyflies. Do you know what I became as a result of my studies?" She turned intense eyes on Janet, but didn't wait for her to answer. "A detective. That's why I called one of my books *The Deciduous Detective*. Studying—investigating—every aspect of nature in the woods around my cabin has kept me sane.

"That's why I'm interested in the murder of Sam Smith now. Studying it is going to help me through this. It will keep me sane during what I expect is going to be a very painful interlude. I had an academic understanding of how filled the world has become with heartless people. Now that I've witnessed the lack of outrage, the callous response to this man's death, I'm seeing that heartlessness firsthand. I honestly had no idea it would be so painful."

Daphne was still hunkered next to Rachel Carson, but she'd stopped petting the dog and brought her hands together in a fist beneath her chin.

Janet had no idea what to say. Any response—"the police are looking into it," or "people do care," or "*I'm* not heartless," or if she gave Daphne a hug or shoulder squeeze—would come across as simple and inadequate. Saying nothing wasn't adequate, either, but there was more going on with Daphne than she could fix. She started to put the sword back in the duffle.

"Keep it." Daphne said.

"You're sure?"

"Keep it."

"Thank you."

Daphne zipped the duffle and hefted it onto her shoulder. She and Rachel Carson left through the back gate without saying anything more.

Janet watched them go and thought about heartless people. *But how do you know someone's heartless? Maybe they're unaware or oblivious. Or maybe they're hurting and don't have room for sympathy or empathy.* Then Janet remembered Gillian's reaction at the ceilidh supper, when Tom said he and Daphne were going to work together on a calendar, and another thought occurred to her. *Is there such a thing as premeditated heartlessness?*

13

Janet took a few more swipes with the sword, first at the air, then at a burdock that had infiltrated her flower border. She accidentally whacked some purple asters in the process.

"Bugger." She tried to straighten the leggy things, but they were like gangly teenagers with a natural tendency to slouch. She gave up when she heard a twig snap and a snicker at the privet hedge between Ian Atkinson's garden and her own.

"That was a heartless move," Ian said. "They were so pretty, too."

He stood sideways to the hedge, and spoke over his shoulder, almost as though he'd been casually walking the boundary of his property and happened to look over at the exact moment Janet slew the poor daisies. But in the months since she'd moved in—prime gardening months—she'd never seen him puttering outside at all. She thought it more likely he'd seen the "get-together" for Daphne's workout demonstration and taken an interest in *that*. His calling her "heartless" made her wonder how long he'd been listening and how much he'd overheard.

"Any particular reason for your mad slash?" he asked.

"Hello, Ian."

"Birth, marriage, and death."

Janet waited, sure he wanted her to ask him what he was talking about, and knowing he'd continue anyway, without her prompting.

"My mother was big on plants with meanings, and she had those things you just tried to decapitate in her garden. They're associated with birth, marriage, and death. That's a lot to ask of something that falls over in the first good blow. Funny, I remember all that about them, but never bothered to find out what they're called."

"Asters. Michaelmas daisies."

"Asters?" He spread his hands and brought them together in an almost soundless clap. "Wonderful. Do you see what that means? You've reaped destruction and disaster for the purple aster. But no. Wait." He held his hands up as though framing a movie scene. "You hold the sword of justice, but wield it only in symbolic display."

Even knowing his ploy, she couldn't help it; she had to ask. "What are you talking about?"

"You crushed the symbol of death, but you're left under the crushing weight of the unresolved mystery of who killed the lad behind Nev's. *I* know that *you* know that you want to know whodunnit. So does she." He nodded toward Daphne's house. "I say repent your heartless ways. Give in to your inner sleuth before it's too late. Speaking of which, you'll love the title of the new book. I'd planned to call it *The Dirk in the Distillery*, which fits the pattern I've established for the series. But last week I had the most splendid jolt of inspiration and the dirk and the distillery flew right out the window. Or rather, I tucked it away in my file of future titles. The new title is splendid."

This time, Janet did wait. Judging by the puff of Ian's chest, the wait wouldn't be long. She was right.

"Joining *The Bludgeon in the Bothy*, *The Halberd in the Hostel*, and *The Claymore in the Cloister* on bookshop and library shelves and bedside tables worldwide next summer will be *The Shillelagh in the Shed*. A shame you got rid of yours."

They looked toward the empty corner at the bottom of Janet's garden where her shed had stood. *Curtis's shed*, she reminded herself. Her ex-husband had bought the ugly thing. She'd never liked it. And when Summer had discovered a body there shortly after they'd arrived in Inversgail, Janet had vowed to get rid of it.

"You truly are heartless," Ian said. "You should have warned me you were having it taken down and carted away so that I could have snapped a picture while I had the chance. Then I could have sent it to the cover artist and your shed would have been famous, as well as infamous."

"Shoulda, coulda, woulda," Janet said while thinking, *Bugger.* "How is the book coming along, Ian?"

"Still working out a few sticky plot points."

"Then don't let me keep you." She tucked the sword under her arm like a major general's swagger stick and stalked back to the house.

∽

That afternoon, Janet gave in and indulged herself with a stop at Paudel's Newsagent, Post Office, and Convenience. Basant Paudel, owner of the small business, had emigrated from Nepal to the UK and bought the shop so he could afford to bring his younger sisters over for schooling. He'd succeeded in that, and the girls had thrived in the Inversgail schools. One sister was now finishing a nursing course in Glasgow and the other was reading history and languages at St. Andrews in Aberdeen.

Basant stood behind the shop counter reading a book when Janet opened the door. His carefully chosen stock surrounded him, sitting on shelves on either side of him, behind him, running down both walls of the long, narrow space, and on both sides of a tall shelving fixture running down the middle of the shop.

"How are you, Mrs. Janet?" he asked.

"I'm well, Basant. How are you?"

"Very well on a beautiful day."

Janet looked back out the door. Had she really not noticed it was beautiful? Basant's eyes returned to his book. Janet went down one aisle and found a bottle of mango chutney. She came up the other aisle and

stopped for a package of naan from a refrigerated case. She took both
back to the counter and added a bar of Oban ginger and orange dark
chocolate from the display next to the cash register. The chocolate was
what she'd really come in for. She refrained from taking a second bar.

"Curry tonight," Janet said, "and a bite of chocolate for the walk
home."

"The BBC and I approve. They say curry is good for your brain
and chocolate will chase away your blues. If you'll forgive me, the
hummingbird feet at the corners of your eyes give your blues away.
Can I help?"

"Calling them hummingbird feet helps more than you might know,"
Janet said. "T. rex feet is more accurate for the way I'm feeling, but no
one with hummingbird feet can really be heartless, can she? So thank
you for that, too."

Basant's eyebrows went up. "*Heartless?* You?"

Janet nodded.

"Who says you are? I'm genuinely puzzled."

"Thank you for that, too. I've heard it twice this morning from two
different people. Actually, the first time it was more of a collective con-
demnation of all of us in Inversgail."

"Ah." Basant turned to the shelves of jars on the wall behind him.
"I've met our visiting author and her dignified wee lion," he said over
his shoulder.

Janet echoed Basant's *ah* and watched as he touched one, then
another of the jars. Each one held a different kind of old-fashioned sweet.
"Daphne's obviously been upset by the murder, which is completely
understandable," she said. "And that's on top of whatever emotions she's
feeling about being back here after however many years it's been."

"Decades of living amongst the weasels and the moose. And snacking
on them."

"You heard about that? Well, she's bound to be feeling stressed, but I
don't need to let her stress turn into mine."

"There," Basant said. "What you just said proves my point. You empathize with her. You aren't heartless." He took a jar from a shelf and put it on the counter, and then picked up the book he'd been reading. Janet saw that it was *The Sasquatch Squad*, one of Daphne's novels for children.

"Funny and exciting," he said, when he saw her interest. "I've also read some of her serious nonfiction. Her books are enjoyable." He shrugged. "In person, she's another story. But you said there were two. Who else called you heartless?"

"Ian Atkinson."

Until that moment, Janet had never heard Basant guffaw.

"But now *I'm* being heartless," he said, regaining control. "Ian writes smashing books and I enjoy talking to him about them. He's brilliant at manipulating the interpersonal relationships of his characters, but he's absolute rubbish at handling his own." Basant opened the jar he'd taken down. It was full of red and white heart-shaped candies. He scooped some into a white paper bag and handed it to Janet. "You were not heartless when you came in, and you are less so now."

⁂

Janet woke to her phone alarm the next morning. She felt groggy but virtuous when she padded down the stairs to the kitchen to hear Daphne's interview. She could have listened while lying in bed or curled in a more comfortable chair in the family room, but bolt upright in a hard kitchen chair insured that groggy wouldn't triumph over virtuous.

The station had news of the tides. They were either coming in or going out. Janet knew it was one or the other, but her eyelids were drooping, taking her Scots comprehension quotient down with them. A roads report followed a fishing report interspersed with fiddle tunes livelier than Janet. She listened to an interview with a weaver from one of the islands. She was beginning to think Daphne had gotten the time or day wrong when Tallie came downstairs.

"Coming for a run?" Tallie asked.

"Trying to avoid a snooze." Janet explained why she was up.

"Shh," Tallie said. "I just heard Daphne's name."

They listened, only to hear the announcer give his regrets and tell them that Daphne had been unavoidably delayed, and they would reschedule the interview for another day. Janet switched off the radio. Tallie started the coffee, stayed until it was ready, and poured a cup for her mother.

"It's not like we were depending on her interview to whip up enthusiasm for the signing," Janet said after a sip and a sigh for her missed sleep.

"You didn't get up just to hear her plug the shop, did you?"

"Partly." Janet took another sip. The coffee was really still too hot. "Partly as a friendly gesture. There's something sad about Daphne. Her moods flip. Have you noticed that? Up, down. Back, forth. Swash, buckle."

"Swash, buckle?"

"Like fencing," Janet said. "Maybe swash is the same as thrust and buckle is like parry. Or the other way around. Anyway, Daphne was sure no one would listen to the program, so I thought I would."

"She made sure no one listened," Tallie said.

"The friendly part of me wants to be fair and say we don't know why she missed the interview. But the unfriendly part of me tuned in and stood by, ready to start damage control, in case she said something about the murder or something unpleasant about Inversgail like she did at the ceilidh. My unfriendly part is also wondering what her excuse is this time and what flips her switch from up to down." Janet held the coffee under her chin, fogging her glasses and picturing herself getting a steam treatment with tendrils of caffeine caressing her cheeks, her brow, and every last tiny nerve ending.

"If you see her, are you going to ask her why she missed the interview?" Tallie asked.

"Probably not."

"I don't blame you. I'm heading out, but here's a useful tip, before I go. If they reschedule the interview, you don't have to crawl out of bed for it. It's a with-it kind of station; they stream their programs, so you can catch it later, when you're fully awake, with coffee or wine ready at your elbow."

"Or both?"

"Now you're thinking. Don't think so hard about Daphne that you lose your swash, though. Or your buckle. Or whichever makes you so nice to be around. See you later."

∽

Daphne was up again when she stopped by Yon Bonnie Books that afternoon. Janet, straightening the picture books in the aftermath of a three-year-old's escape from his parents, hadn't heard the door jingle.

"Do you want to bop her with a bokken, or shall I?" Daphne asked.

Being on her knees, Janet couldn't quite jump at the suddenness of the question, but her heart hurdled a rib or two to make up for it. *Too much caffeine*, she wondered, *or too much Daphne?* She got to her feet, one hand on her heart, the other on the back of her neck, which hadn't had a twinge of pain until that minute. Daphne must have come in through the tearoom.

"Sorry, Daphne, you'll have to bop her yourself. Who are we talking about, by the way?"

"As if you didn't know." Daphne chuckled.

Janet resented the conspiratorial tone of that chuckle. She was sorry, too, that there weren't any other customers in the shop so she could tell Daphne to hush. She could tell her to hush, anyway, but she was also curious. "No, really, I've been asked to kill or bop several people lately and probably ought to be keeping better track. So who's upset you?" *This time*, she wanted to add.

"Have you really been asked to kill several people? Are you more violent than you appear?" Daphne looked Janet over. "You don't look like any of the assassins I've known."

Janet told herself it was ridiculous to feel inadequate for coming up short against whatever assassins Daphne claimed to know, especially because she was exaggerating her invitations to murder. She tried to smile, and came up short there, too. "I tend to be a pacifist, Daphne."

"A peaceable bookseller, a woman after my own heart. And, of course, my request wasn't serious. I really came because I thought it would be good to touch base before the signing, if you have a few minutes."

"Of course," Janet said. "Let's go in the office."

Tallie was at the sales counter, reading and marking a restocking report, and gave a thumbs up when Janet let her know where she'd be. Janet ushered Daphne into the office behind the counter and closed the door.

The four business partners had plans to improve the office, which was currently about as appealing as a galley kitchen without windows, though the project was fairly low on their to-do list. The narrow space held two desks, one facing each long wall, and a bookcase at the far end.

Janet pulled out one of the rolling desk chairs and offered it to Daphne, taking the other herself.

"Your window display, by the way, is charming," Daphne said. She looked around the office in a way that suggested charming wasn't the word for *it*. "And I'm sure that, in its own small way, the shop will do nicely for Sunday's signing. I dare say you're working hard to keep up the tradition of Yon Bonnie Books, which is admirable from a purely historical point of view, even if the production of printed books is anachronistic in today's society and ought to stop."

Janet had been about to say, "We try," but instead found herself trying not to sputter.

"Between the two of us, though," Daphne continued, "we should be able to pull this signing together. You'll see; we'll make it an event this town will long remember. Do you have any questions?"

Janet did, but none were polite enough to ask. Instead, she counted ten imaginary bops with a bokken and then took a deep breath. "Thank you for your vote of confidence, Daphne. All four of us at Yon Bonnie Books and Cakes and Tales are working hard to make sure the signing is a success. Gillian gave me your list of suggestions—"

"Requirements. That's good, and that brings us in a neat circle back to where I came in, because it is Gillian for whom you should be breaking out your bokken and jettisoning your pacifist tendencies."

Janet counted to ten again. "Gillian is one of our favorite customers."

"*Is* she? Well, I'm a wee bit miffed with her and I blame it on the numpty masquerading as an advice columnist in the *Inversgail Guardian*."

No doubt Summer was the numpty in question. Janet felt the twinge in her neck again, this time on Summer's behalf. "Did you follow the advice?" she asked. *And if you did, who's the numpty?*

"Aye."

Question answered.

"The column was about how to reconnect meaningfully with old friends," Daphne said. "With a tip from the agony aunt about sharing old memories while creating new ones. So I called Gillian and we went hillwalking. Lovely day for it."

"And it sounds like a lovely thing to do."

"So you would think, but the agony aunt's advice put pure agony into the afternoon."

"How?" Janet asked.

"We walked. We chatted. Gillian remembered birthday parties and Guides. She thought I would remember that she got the two of us into trouble over forbidden cigarettes. I didn't, but I laughed, anyway, the way one should, and then I dredged up something *she* might not remember."

"It sounds as though you were having a good time, Daphne."

"Up until then."

"So she didn't remember?"

"She said it couldn't be true, which is a silly thing to say. We were back at our cars, by then, so I laughed and told her to forget it. She sort of threw something over her shoulder about the radio interview that led me to believe the interview wasn't that important. So when I skipped it this morning, she called, and *that* created a memory I would very much like to forget. She was downright vicious."

"She probably didn't mean to be," Janet said. "She's been juggling a lot lately. She's under a lot of stress. But vicious really doesn't sound like Gillian."

"Of course it does. I've known her for over forty years."

"But you haven't spoken in almost thirty."

"And how does that signify?" Daphne asked. "If I've learned one thing in all my years alone in the woods, it's that a tree never changes its bark."

"Right," Janet said. "Nor a leopard its spots." *Nor a bam its pot.*

"We're talking about trees. The remains of so many of which are entombed on the shelves out there in your shop."

14

That's when I took my bokken and bopped her a good one on top of her head," Janet said that evening at Nev's. "No, no, better yet, I bopped her in the snoot."

"You should have bopped her in the *behouchie*," Christine said, "so she'd have to stand when she signs books Sunday next."

"You are so right, Christine, and if I ever do any real bopping, that's exactly where I'll do it. My make-believe bopping was extremely satisfying, though. Cathartic, even." Janet raised her half pint of Selkie's Tears to celebrate her satisfaction, then took a healthy swallow. The four women were at their usual table, enjoying their weekly wind-down. Janet, who didn't ordinarily need much winding down, felt as though she was fizzing after relating her meeting with Daphne for the others.

"Just as long as you don't cross over into the realm of reality bopping," Tallie said. "As tempting as it might be."

"Sorely tempting," Summer said. "Daphne was in the tearoom this afternoon, and asked for another table because the people behind her ordered a pot of Earl Grey. That would've been fine. If she really objects to the smell of bergamot, I can understand that. But she made such a production out of it that she embarrassed the couple at the other table."

"Summer smoothed it over," Christine said. "They insisted on paying for their tea, but she gave them half a dozen scones to take away."

"To Summer's good sense," Tallie said, raising her glass.

"And swordsmanship," Christine added, raising hers. "Do you realize our daftie author has only been here a week? And look at all she's stirred up."

As though taking Christine literally, Janet looked around the pub—at the tables of twos and threes and a few solitary patrons. A hand on a shoulder there, heads close together in a booth, laughter at the next table, a snatch of song from Christine's dad and her mum gazing at him with her chin in her hand as though she'd just fallen in love again. Danny orchestrated drinks behind the bar. Janet picked out the smells of good ale, greasy chips, and wool wet from the smirr coming down outside. The one week since Daphne Wood had arrived hadn't stirred the essential picture of Nev's. *Snap a photo, right now, in black and white,* she thought, *and except for minor details and no haze of cigarette smoke, this might be any decade for the past hundred years.*

"Only a week," Summer said. "On the one hand, that's hardly a blip. On the other, that means it's been a whole week since someone killed Sam Smith."

"Not all crimes are solved quickly," Tallie reminded her.

"No, and they aren't all solved." Summer raised her glass. "In memory of Sam."

"To Sam," the others said. As they raised their glasses, James Haviland, from the paper, arrived and made his way over to their table.

"Evening, all," James said. "Celebrating?"

"Remembering," Janet said.

"Do you remember that you owe me a column?" James asked Summer.

"Do you remember that I've never been late?"

James laughed. "If only your darts were as sharp and fast. Fancy a game?" His smiling invitation took in the whole table. Summer and Tallie picked up their pints.

"Coming?" James asked Janet and Christine. Christine shook her head. He nodded amiably and followed Tallie and Summer into the darts room.

"You know, though," Janet said after he'd gone, "if Rab's in there, maybe I can corner him. What with one thing and another, we had an odd week, and he made it odder with more erratic hours than usual. Maybe I can get something like a schedule out of him. If nothing else, I'd like to get a commitment out of him for the signing."

"You might have an easier time getting a commitment from a cat," Christine said. "I'll go check on my ancient lovebirds."

Janet took her glass and went to the doorway of the darts room. She stood to one side before going in. *Not peeking in*, she told herself. *Not spying; getting the lay of the land.* Rab was there, toward the back right. Slightly surprising was Reddick's presence, standing ready for his turn to throw. Quantum, Reddick's smooth collie, sat beside him. Janet sidled into the room and over to Rab.

"How's the game?" Janet asked.

"See Reddick's dog staring at the other team?"

Janet looked and it did appear as though Quantum was staring down his long nose at each of the other players in turn.

"Psyching them out," Rab said. "That's why Ranger stays home. Unfair advantage."

"Isn't it unfair for Quantum to be here, then?"

"Ranger's more sensitive to that kind of thing."

"We didn't see much of you at the shop last week," Janet said. "Did you meet your deadlines?"

"Deadlines?"

"Yes, the ones keeping you from more regular work hours."

"Och, aye."

"Can we count on your help for Sunday?"

"For the signing?"

"Yes. In fact, can we count on you coming in, occasionally, the rest of the week, too?"

"Hmm." Rab appeared to be consulting a mental social calendar, looking off to the side, slowly tapping his cheek bone with two fingers as he sorted obligated from free times.

"Rab?"

He stopped tapping his cheek and refocused on Janet. Then, before answering, he drank some of his ale. And then he didn't really answer. "I heard something you'll want to know. She's been telling people she's joined your investigation team looking into the young man's death."

"Daphne's been saying that?"

"Aye. That you're calling yourselves SCONES."

"Oh, for—"

He nodded at her empty glass. "Can I get you the other half?"

Janet shook her head. Rab excused himself and slipped past her. She saw Reddick's dog giving her the eye. That made her wonder if Reddick had heard Daphne's ridiculous claim and what he might have to say about it. While he took his turn at the dart board, she ignored the dog's furry eyebrow, and went back to the table in the other room. By the time she realized she'd let Rab get away without committing to a schedule for the week, he'd disappeared from Nev's altogether. Christine's mum and dad were nowhere in sight, either, but Maida stood beside Christine at the bar.

"Look who I bumped into outside when I helped Mum and Dad into Rab's car," Christine said. "He offered to get them home."

Maida held her elbows close to her sides as though her strict ancestors whispered dire warnings in her ears.

"It's déjà vu all over again," Christine said. "Another Monday night, and Maida would like our help again."

"I called Rab," Maida said. "He told me you were here."

"Would you like to sit?" Christine asked. "And something to drink?"

"Water," Maida said.

"There's a booth," Janet offered. "It'll be quieter."

Christine got a glass of water from Danny and the three of them slid into the booth, Janet next to Maida so she wouldn't feel alone facing the two of them.

"Now, isn't this cozy," Christine said.

From the way Maida dithered and twisted her fingers together, they gathered she felt far from cozy.

"What can we do for you?" Janet asked.

Maida started by thanking Janet for Friday night and apologized for having to sleep over. Then she told them she'd arranged with Gillian to clean the house for Daphne once a week. "Keep it tidy, like, and keep an eye on things because of the dog. I'm not certain the wee thing is quite as housetrained as Daphne says." But Daphne had nixed the housecleaning.

"That saves you time," Christine said.

"Aye."

Janet watched Maida's fingers twist into another set of knots. "What else, Maida? It's not just the cleaning, is it?"

"Och, it's daft, I know, but it's the pots my plants were in." They were three special pots, she told them, given to her by her daughter. She wanted them back, but was afraid to go ask for them. "When you're dealing with someone who roasts weasels and serves up a houseplant salad," Maida said, "there's no telling what she'll do next."

"It's a fair guess it won't be normal," Christine said. "It's early evening yet. Why don't we pay a neighborly visit and get your pots back?"

"Would you? I'd be grateful," Maida said. "Will I wait here for you?"

"You'll come with us," Janet said. She went back to the darts room and told Tallie and Summer where they were going. She invited the younger women along, but they declined.

"Just as well they gave it a pass," Christine said as she, Janet, and Maida got into her car. "There's no need to arrive at Daphne's looking like a boarding party."

"I hope we don't look like *any* kind of vigilante gang," Janet said.

"We won't at all," Maida said. She'd taken the front seat next to Christine, no knitting of fingers evident now.

"Maida's right," Christine said. "We won't at all, at all. A social call. A judicious nudge of our noses into Maida's house to see that all is well."

From the back seat, Janet looked at Maida's profile, then Christine's. They looked oddly similar—both leaning slightly forward, eyes bright. Their voices were bright, too, and Janet recognized that as Christine's "eager" tone of voice. She was beginning to wonder if those two had something planned, and was glad Christine hadn't added, *How can that hurt?* Or, *What can possibly go wrong?*

While they'd been in Nev's, the soft smirr of rain had condensed into a moth-eaten blanket of fog—woolly in some places, patchy in others. Christine drove cautiously toward Ross Street; familiar landmarks loomed and then were lost.

"We just passed the house," Janet said. "I think."

"Safer to park off the street at your place." Christine turned the two corners taking them onto Argyll and then into Janet's driveway. "If it weren't so dangerous to drive without lights in this pea soup, I would have turned them off and crept down Daphne's street like a shadow. I've always wanted to make a silent, dark approach like that."

"Aye, stealth," Maida said.

"We're paying a neighborly visit," said Janet. "There's no need for stealth."

"Try not to slam your doors when you get out," Maida whispered.

"Oh, for pity's sake." But Janet got out and closed her door softly, anyway. "I hope you noticed that her rental car was gone."

"Shh," Christine and Maida both hissed.

"The Land Rover being gone doesn't mean anything," Christine said. "She might have realized she doesn't need a vehicle that size and turned it in for something more sensible."

"Well, that's certainly possible." Janet nodded. "Or Gillian might have told her the grant wouldn't cover that kind of expense."

"That thing she chose is one of the most expensive vehicles to rent," Christine said, "and completely unnecessary. Inversgail isn't as wee as a village, but we're hardly Oban or Inverness."

"Right then. Let's go see if Daphne's home." Janet glanced around. "Where's Maida?"

They heard the creak of a gate, and through the patchy fog saw Maida at the bottom of the garden. She'd opened the gate just enough to slide through like a curl of mist. Light shone from the kitchen windows of Daphne's house—Maida's house—cozier and more beckoning because of the fog. Maida stood with one hand on the gate looking toward them. Then they saw her skitter across Daphne's garden to a rowan tree. It was hardly big enough to hide her from anyone looking out the windows.

"A tiny Mata Hari," Janet said. She and Christine stifled giggles. Then they jumped at the sound of a throat clearing directly behind them.

15

During the split second Janet was airborne, she knew that if she were a braver person, or more practiced at sneaking and skulking, she would be able to turn upon landing, greet the throat clearer with a confident smile, and say something pleasant or disarming. Instead, she witnessed one of Christine's transformations. Elizabeth II turned with a frosty look to quell any further coughs directed toward them. It fell with full force on Janet's neighbor, Ian Atkinson.

"Ian." Janet patted her heart back into place. "You shouldn't sneak up on people that way."

"Nice evening," Ian said, taking a step back. "For clandestine casing, I mean." He'd met Christine's eyes and quickly looked away, but Janet saw them shift again, and now he was looking over her shoulder. "There go Christine and Maida."

"What?" Janet whipped back around to see both of them creeping in the most obvious way possible up Daphne's back steps. "Oh, for— Christine!" Janet didn't call her name nearly loud enough to be heard.

"It's all right," Ian said. "Daphne isn't home. She left quarter of an hour ago with her dog and a young fellow in her expedition vehicle. Do you suppose she's planning a quest of some sort? And what are *they* looking for?" He nodded toward Christine and Maida.

Daphne isn't home. Those three words gave Janet strength. The strength to lie. "I think they just didn't want to startle the dog, Ian. We decided to stop by to, you know, see how Daphne and Rachel Carson are settling in. Let them know where the fuse box is, that kind of thing." Janet smiled and wondered if such a thing as a fuse box existed in Maida's house.

Ian winked.

Janet looked back toward the house. Christine and Maida crowded the stoop, faces pressed to the window in the back door.

"Oh, gosh, wouldn't you know it? The doorbell must be on the fritz," Janet said quickly. "I'll go let them know Daphne isn't home after all. Thanks for stopping by, Ian. See you."

Janet smiled again, but only until she'd turned her back on Ian, then she tried her best not to run down her garden path and up Daphne's. Christine was now stretching up, trying to get a look in another window.

"Just a little higher, Christine," Maida was saying.

"Christine, stop it," Janet said. "For heaven's sake, we have a witness. Maida, stop encouraging her. Do you both want to spend the night in jail?"

"Nothing illegal about fresh air exercises, Janet," Maida said.

At this, Christine turned around and did half a dozen jumping jacks and then bent to touch her toes. Janet closed her eyes.

"You can open your eyes now. He's gone," Maida said. "Yon *glaikit* lump."

"Maida!" Janet said, surprised to hear her speak so rudely about Ian, for whom she occasionally worked. Maida might have been surprised, too. She coughed until Christine gave her a few thumps between her shoulder blades.

"Ian's a . . . a good neighbor," Janet said.

"A neighbor of some sort, anyway," Christine said.

"A neighbor who was kind enough to overlook your suspicious behavior." At least Janet *thought* he was overlooking it.

Maida wrinkled her nose. "I've gone off him since that business with your last murder investigation."

Christine made a noise that managed to sound both rude and in agreement with Maida.

"Ian also told me that Daphne and Rachel Carson left in the Rover before we got here," Janet said. "So there's nothing to see here, nothing to do, and let's please not give him a reason to call the police—like breaking and entering, which you have already been warned about. Put your key away, Maida. We're not going in there. I'll come over tomorrow, when Daphne is home, and knock on the door like a civilized person, and get the pots, and that's the end of it. Okay?"

"You're a wee bit tense, Janet."

"You could be right, Maida. I'm going home now."

"We'll come with you," Christine said.

"I'd rather you didn't."

"Och, I don't see why not." Christine put an arm around Maida's shoulders. "We could all use a glass of your restorative sherry and will sleep better for it."

Janet looked up into the twilit sky and sighed. "All right."

Christine's arm dropped from Maida's shoulder and she started for Janet's house.

"Come along, Janet," Maida said, taking her arm. "And *dinnae fash yersel* about Ian calling the police. I've got something on him."

"What are you talking about?"

"He's a Peeping Tom."

∞

Maida refused to say anything more about Ian Atkinson being a Peeping Tom. Even after Janet poured three small glasses of sherry and they were sitting comfortably, companionably, in the living room, no amount of reasoning or cajoling would convince her. Janet knew from personal experience that Christine was an excellent cajoler, but even she failed to pry the details from Maida.

"If I tell what I know," Maida said, "then I won't be able to hold it over his head."

"Why would you need to hold anything over Ian's head?" Christine asked.

Maida took a small sip of her sherry and set the glass on the end table beside her. "It's true, the occasion may never arise. Nevertheless."

"You've trusted us this far," Christine said. "You trusted us to sneak over there to Daphne's this evening. You must know you can trust us with the rest of what you know."

But Maida wouldn't budge. She said goodbye, and when Christine offered to give her a lift, she said she'd walk home. She left without finishing her glass of sherry, which Janet thought was just as well, as she didn't seem to have a head for alcohol.

"I shouldn't have used the word 'sneak,'" Christine said when Janet came back from walking Maida to the door. "Did you see her backbone straighten when I did? Do you think what she says is true?"

Janet pulled the curtains before sitting back down. "I should have done that as soon as we came in. Does that answer your question?" She told Christine about Ian overhearing her conversation with Daphne in the back garden after the missed sword class. "It's unnerving to think he might've been peeping all this time. I don't always pull the curtains, but you can bet I will now. Do you think Maida's told anyone else?"

"Possibly not. It isn't a topic of conversation that fits easily into the usual pleasantries. *'Lovely day, isn't it, Maida?' 'Yes, it is. It stopped raining for five whole minutes and the cat's had kittens again, bless her furry wee heart. Speaking of which, did you know Ian Atkinson is a Peeping Tom? The great glaikit lump.'* It doesn't quite work, does it?"

"Not quite, so you're probably right. And she did say she might want to hold it over his head someday."

Christine drained her sherry. "She probably regrets telling *us*."

∽

After seeing Christine off, Janet thought the social part of her evening was over. It wasn't. She heard from two people she hadn't expected to.

First came an electronic postcard from Sharon-the-librarian, with a photograph of bookstalls along the Seine:

> Bonjour, Janet,
>   I'm sitting in a café, drinking wine, eating petite madeleines, and putting thoughts of visiting authors far behind me. The bookstalls are everything I hoped they'd be. I've already spent my book allowance for the foreseeable future.
>   Au revoir,
>   Sharon

Paris wasn't a warm, sunny beach, and spending her money at the Parisian bookstalls might mean Sharon had less to spend at Yon Bonnie Books when she returned. But if books and a café in Paris brought her stress levels down, Janet was happy for her.

She took the sherry glasses out to the kitchen and realized she'd never put a curtain or shade on the window over the sink. She washed the glasses, thumbed her nose at anyone rude enough to be staring in, and went back to the living room to curl up with a book and bring her own stress levels down.

Her phone rang a short time later, but she'd fallen asleep. The ringing phone became part of a dream, morphing into an alarm bell alerting the world that Christine, Maida, and Ian Atkinson were breaking out of jail. In the dream, Janet couldn't decide if she wanted to admit knowing them, but finally realized the alarm bell was more obnoxious than they were and she tried to muffle it with African violet leaves and an unruffled Rachel Carson, plus three dozen of her fellow Pekingese. Surfacing into reality, Janet fumbled the phone to her ear.

"Norman Hobbs, here, Mrs. Marsh."

Janet's phone slipped from her hand into her lap and from her lap down the side of the seat cushion. She fished it out and put it back to her ear. "Hello?"

"Norman Hobbs, here, Mrs. Marsh."

"Where?"

"I'm so sorry. Did I wake you?"

"I certainly hope so. Where did you say you are?" She heard laughing and snatches of music in the background.

Hobbs belched quietly in her ear. "I beg your pardon."

"Have you been drinking?"

"What?"

"Are you in a pub? Are you inebriated?"

"No, I'm in Tulliallan." He belched again. "Pardon me. I've been eating falafel. Did Reddick not tell you?"

Hobbs told Janet he was at the Scottish Police College in Tulliallan for a professional development immersion course introducing him to multiple cultures, languages, and religions. Janet said she thought that sounded smart. Hobbs agreed, though he realized others on the force weren't as keen.

"That's why courses like the one you're on are so important," Janet said. "And Reddick was being considerate of your privacy. I'm sure that's why he didn't tell us where you are."

"No doubt." Then Hobbs told her why he'd called. "Sam Smith."

"Did you know him?"

He hadn't, but he'd heard about the murder. "The Major Crime Team hasn't found it necessary to consult with me, and as I'm not in Inversgail, I lack information."

"Are they purposely keeping you in the dark?" Janet asked.

"I wouldn't say precisely that."

"You could ask Reddick to fill you in."

"I like Reddick," Hobbs said, "and I wouldn't want to put him in an uncomfortable position."

"May I interpret that to mean you don't want whoever's in charge to know you're interested in the case?" Janet asked. "And should I be pleased that you think I can fill you in or worry that you think I'm overly interested in the case? I've seen Reddick a time or two, but now that I think about it, I don't know who's in charge."

"Why don't you tell me what you do know?"

"Is it that officious man who was here in the spring?"

"Quite possibly."

Janet told Hobbs the little they knew about Sam Smith and the sequence of events leading up to his death, then asked, "Do you know Tom Laing?"

"Teaches at the high school?"

"Yes. Danny said he threw a punch or two, though he hadn't seemed to be part of the party group, either. Here's the thing about Tom being there, though. Earlier, we saw him leave with Gillian Bennett. She took him home because he'd had a bit too much. We don't know why, how, or when he went back. We left before he did, anyway, and before Sam Smith or the party arrived, so all I have is secondhand information. How am I doing?"

"*We* being you and Mrs. Robertson?"

"And Tallie and Summer. Rab was there, too, and left when we did. We had a situation to attend to for the visiting author. You knew about her coming, right? Oh."

"Mrs. Marsh?"

"You'll want to know this. Daphne Wood, the author, is . . ." Janet trailed off as she tried to think of an efficient way to sum up Daphne.

"She's what?"

"So many things."

"And at least one of those things sounds troubling to you."

Janet was quiet for a moment. Was she telling on Daphne? *No*, she thought. *Daphne made it clear in her presentation at the library.* "Basically, she doesn't think enough is being done to find Sam Smith's killer.

She wanted us—Christine, Tallie, Summer, and me—to investigate. She wanted to join us in investigating. I told her no. Rab says she's telling people that she *is* working with us."

Now Hobbs was quiet, although Janet heard something that sounded like a hand rubbing the bristles of a five o'clock shadow.

"If it makes the situation any better," she said, "or if it makes you feel better, Christine says Daphne is a bampot."

"It's difficult to see why that information should make the situation better," Hobbs said. "Are you investi—"

"No. Do you know who else has mentioned investigating, though?"

Hobbs didn't answer.

"Are you there, Norman?"

"Sorry, yes. I was just praying you wouldn't say Ian Atkinson."

"Prayers are tricky. They aren't always answered right away or the way we want. Maybe Ian won't be interested in the next case, but he's been flitting around this one. Norman, are there any Peeping Toms in town?"

"None that I've heard about. Why?"

"Curiosity and precaution."

"I like the word 'precaution,' Mrs. Marsh."

"Norman, why haven't the police released the cause of death? Danny was fairly certain the blow from the brick did it."

"They could have held onto that information for several reasons. They might be keeping certain details out of the public forum while they locate and speak to the lads involved in the party."

"And to Tom, too, I suppose. Do you want me to find out when and why Tom went back to Nev's?"

"No, Mrs. Marsh. I do not."

"Because you don't trust him or because you don't trust me?" Janet immediately apologized for the questions and her tone of voice. "That was uncalled for, Norman."

"But not unexpected. You have a streak of curiosity wider than most cats. That's merely an observation, Mrs. Marsh, not a criticism."

And it nicely glides over the fact that I'm quick to take offense, Janet thought, *and maybe quicker to see a challenge.* "Did you know Daphne Wood when she lived here?"

Hobbs had grown up in Inversgail and would be about the right age to be in school when Daphne and Gillian were. "I didn't know her well," he said. "I participated in a youth hillwalking group organized by Gillian's father. Gillian and Daphne came along with us a few times. Why has Mrs. Robertson diagnosed her as a bampot?"

"Mood swings, for one thing," Janet said. "If that's what they are. Daphne's mood swings, I mean, not Christine's." She heard a muffled snort in her ear. "Daphne's a mixed bag. For someone who claims to prefer solitude and trees and the company of her dog, she's occasionally, amazingly social. And then she's not. She flips on, then off. When are you coming back?"

"At the weekend."

"She's doing a book signing at Yon Bonnie Books Sunday afternoon. Four o'clock. You should come and see her for yourself."

"I might."

"We're expecting a good turnout, if for no other reason than people will want to see what she does next. She's added an odd zest to life in Inversgail in more ways than one. And some of that zest was literal, if you consider the salad she made out of Maida's houseplants. Tom will probably be there. He and Daphne have gone out on a couple of photo shoots that Gillian didn't seem to know about."

"I'll give it some thought."

"Maida might be there, too, even though Daphne accused her of attempted murder. Did I tell you that Daphne knows how to use a Samurai sword?"

"I'll be there."

"Good. Refreshments will be served."

16

Janet had the coffee ready and waiting when Tallie came downstairs for her run the next morning.

"What?" Tallie sat down across from her mother. "I know it's something, because early isn't you, and two days in a row, plus making the coffee, makes the person sitting in front of me practically an alien."

"Do you remember the pact the four of us made when we were looking into Una's murder? The buddy system. That we wouldn't take chances by going places alone."

"It'd be hard *not* to remember it. Why?"

"A couple of reasons, precaution being one." Janet told Tallie about Hobbs's phone call. "It was one of those conversations that lets you fall asleep but starts poking at you and asking questions at four in the morning. I finally got up when I realized that for people who aren't investigating a murder, we have a lot of information, a few trails we could follow, and a couple of people either encouraging us to investigate, convinced we *are* investigating, and—"

"Norman Hobbs isn't one of them, is he?"

"No."

"Good."

Janet held up a finger. "And we've got Daphne telling people that she's working with us and we're all investigating the murder together."

Tallie sat back and crossed her arms. "No wonder you woke up. That isn't just annoying or disturbing, it's alarming. If Sam Smith's killer is here and hears Daphne or any of that, he might think we're on his trail. Or she might."

"I don't want you out running by yourself."

"*Might* think we're on the trail," Tallie repeated. "I know I just said it was alarming, but logically, is it *that* alarming? We don't have a reputation for being super sleuths. The killer's going to be more worried about the police."

"It's alarming to me. We don't know who killed Sam Smith, or why, but we know that person is violent—*suddenly* violent, too. Think about it, Tallie. Who kills someone with a brick to the head? Sam's death might have been premeditated, but it might not. You might say we don't know enough about this person—"

"But we do. We know he or she's a killer."

"I don't want you running alone."

Tallie nodded.

"Oh, and there's one more thing. Maida says Ian's a Peeping Tom."

"Gah!"

"I know, I know. Norman said he hasn't heard any reports of Peeping Toms recently, though, so Maida could be wrong. Then again, she probably didn't report him. She said she's waiting to hold it over his head someday."

"That is a *such* bad idea."

"Again, I know. Here's a good idea, though." Janet raised one of her feet so Tallie could see her running shoe. "We can run together."

৵৹

"It was *not* a good idea," Janet whispered to Christine at noon. She looked guiltily over her shoulder hoping Tallie wasn't within earshot. She'd promised she would stop complaining about the morning run after her seventh heartfelt groan before they'd unlocked the bookshop's door for the day. The "run" had turned into a jog, then a fast walk punctuated by frequent stops for breath, then a limping walk back to the house, a short collapse, and a long shower.

"You have me on speed dial," Christine said. "Next time you feel the urge to self-destruct, use it. I'll talk you down off the ledge. I agree we should all be careful, though."

"I'd like it better if we knew who we need to be careful of."

"If we knew, we wouldn't have to worry. We'd tell Reddick and that would be the end of it."

"True."

"Why don't we come up with the most likely suspects and invite Reddick to come round? We'll tell him it's for tea, scones, and a list of scoundrels."

"Because unless he arrested the entire list, it wouldn't solve our problem," Janet said. "Besides, who would we put on it? Where would we start? With everyone in or near Nev's that night?"

"Logic," Christine said with dripping derision. "The downfall of many a would-be amateur sleuth."

∞

Rab was like the shoemaker's elves, Janet decided. They saw little of him in person in the days before the signing, but he assured her in a text that his work would be done, and it was. The floors were swept, the books were straightened, and the tearoom was spotless and shining every morning. Janet did get a commitment from him for the signing on Sunday and counted that as a victory. Another victory was hearing from Tallie that she'd found a running partner who could keep up with her.

"Anyone I know?" Janet asked.

"I was in Paudel's and mentioned something about our 'run' the other morning."

"Air quotes and all?"

"It's all right, Mom. You know Basant would never laugh at you. He said he'd been thinking about getting back into running, anyway, and early mornings are the best time for him to get away."

"You're running with Basant? That's a very neat solution. I forgive you for spreading true stories about how out of shape I am."

Martin Gunn was in and out of the bookshop and tearoom the first half of the week, asking questions for his article on Daphne and review of their business. The joy he took in his job and the tearoom's scones charmed Janet. Summer and Tallie gave him a tour of the B and B. Given the plans he'd initially shared with them for the project, they were surprised that Daphne wasn't in and out with Martin.

"Not that we'll look the gift of an absent bampot in the mouth," Christine said in an aside to Janet. To Martin she said, "Won't it be difficult to gauge Daphne's full impact on the business, with all those layers within layers you were talking about, if she isn't here?"

"I've been getting a series of mini interviews," Martin said. "Haviland's idea. Daphne with some of the teachers and students at the school, walking in the glen with the GREAT-SCOTS, round at her place. She has quite a busy schedule, and I've been trying to disrupt it as little as possible."

"Adding a few layers, as it were," Christine said. "Will all those lovely layers be in this week's paper?"

"Aye. Well, with Haviland's approval," Martin said with a glance at Summer. "Very hands-on, is our James."

"It's good of you to be so accommodating to Daphne," Janet said.

Martin looked starstruck. "She's flat-out brilliant."

Another electronic postcard arrived from Sharon, shorter than the first, but just as enthusiastic. She'd left Paris and moved on to Germany:

> *Guten abend!* I'm in Heidelberg, staying in a *gasthaus* so near
> the zoo I heard the lions roaring at dusk. The schnitzel is out
> of this world.
>   *Auf wiedersehen,*
>   Sharon

∾

Gillian arranged for the same high school culinary class that catered the library event to cater part of the food for the book signing. She didn't have the details of the menu, but she told Janet the students would tip their toques to Canada and Scotland.

"Their families will all show up," Gillian said, "though I can't guarantee they'll buy books."

"Not a problem," Janet said. "A crowd of happy people mingling does a lot for a book signing."

The tearoom was handling drinks and Summer planned to debut the new scones they'd taste-tested for her. She confirmed Janet's guess they were orange almond scones, and identified the elusive spice Janet hadn't been able to put her finger on—cardamom. With their part of the menu set, Summer and Tallie enjoyed wondering what the culinary class might be whipping up for the signing.

"Representing Scotland, the ever popular haggis balls," Summer said.

"Representing Canada, moose jerky," Tallie said.

"Scotland—smoked salmon."

"Canada—bear haunch, roasted rare, sliced thin, and served with a cranberry glaze on planks of birch bark." Tallie kissed her fingertips.

"Are the ingredients coming from Gillian's grant budget?" Christine asked. "Except for the haggis, you might be going kind of pricey."

"Besides," Janet said, "Daphne says she and Rachel Carson are vegetarians."

"Bite-sized wild blueberry tarts from Canada, then," Summer said.

"And a herd of little lemon Jell-O moose," said Tallie. "Because we need moose in there somewhere."

"Shortbread moose," Summer said. "Jell-O isn't vegetarian."

"I'm not so sure Daphne and Rachel Carson are, either," Janet said. "I saw her grab a dozen haggis balls after the ceilidh and put them in her backpack."

"She is too strange for words," Summer said. "It makes you wonder how she's earned the reputation she has without earning a poison toadstool or two along the way."

"Or without poisoning someone else," Christine said, "given her peculiar taste in food."

"Speaking of which, Mom, you never fetched Maida's flower pots, did you?"

"Darn it, no. I completely forgot."

"If Maida hasn't brought it up again, don't worry about," Christine said.

"What if she goes over there and causes another scene?"

Christine put her arm around Janet's shoulders. "Your heart's in the right place, and I don't say this to offend you, but here's another old adage that still rings true: Not your Maida, not your bampot."

∞

Janet opened the *Inversgail Guardian* Saturday morning, eager to see what Martin had written about the bookshop, tearoom, and B and B. There were articles on the front page about an expected rise in planning fees and a call for action on a proposed roundabout. Also on the front page was a beautiful photograph, taken by Tom Laing, of the harbor in the mist. Janet flipped pages, scanning the headlines. She stopped and read "Ask Auntie," Summer's advice column on page three. "Auntie" Summer had answered a question from "Afraid to Take the Plunge" about starting a workplace romance and another from "Scunnered," who was fed up with a relative who'd turned into a bridezilla. Janet found a brief mention of the book signing on the local events page, but no article, no review, and no glowing words about the brilliant Daphne.

"Auntie, I'm disappointed," Janet said when she was able to catch Summer between customers. "Do you suppose James didn't okay Martin's article?"

"I was kind of surprised not to see it," Summer said. She held up her phone. "I just texted him. I'll let you know what I hear."

Janet was busy with another customer when she realized she didn't know which "him" Summer had texted with her question.

"You'll find out soon enough." Tallie said when Janet mentioned it to her. "Does it matter?"

"Nosy information more than necessary. I was just wondering who she thought to ask first, Martin or James." Her phone tweedled with a text alert and she pulled it from her pocket. "And now we'll know." She swiped and tapped her phone. "The winner is James, and his answer is 'ran into difficulties.'"

"In other words," Tallie said, "his answer is less than enlightening."

17

Sunday was the kind of Scottish day when the sun changed its mind as often as a cat on one side of a closed door. It came out, it went in, came out, went in. Janet knew that it didn't really matter what the sun finally decided to do. A little rain, or a lot of rain, or a full blown torrent of sunshine might all happen during the next few hours and none of them would keep people from getting on with their plans.

"When does the bampot author plan to arrive?" Christine asked as she and Janet watched Rab and Tallie rearranging the comfy chairs to make space for the signing near the fireplace.

"You can't go around calling her that," Janet said.

They'd debated whether or not to turn on the gas logs for a cozy atmosphere, and have Daphne sit at a table beside it. Daphne had nixed that when Janet mentioned it to her, pointing out that if she sat to the side, the fireplace would remain the visual focal point and she refused to play second fiddle to the conspicuous consumption of nonrenewable energy. She'd also nixed live music. James Haviland had offered to play suitable background music on his fiddle, perhaps in the tearoom where the refreshments would be laid out, but Daphne hadn't wanted to play second fiddle to him, either. She countered with a request for standard classical fare on the sound system.

Tallie and Rab moved past Janet and Christine with a folding table and set it up in front of the fireplace. Rab moved one of the chairs from the tearoom behind it and Tallie draped it with a dark green damask tablecloth.

"Perfect," Janet said. "Those are probably famous last words, though, aren't they?" She ran her fingers up the back of her head, giving herself a ridge of gray spikes. She patted her hair back in place and looked at her to-do list. "The culinary class should be here no later than three. I asked Daphne to be here by half-three. Does Summer need more help in the tearoom before the kids from the class get here?"

"The tearoom is so under control that Summer has the teapots doing synchronized calisthenics," Christine said. She then assured Janet that she wouldn't utter the word *bampot* again that afternoon, and further assured her that she hadn't let her mother hear her referring to Daphne that way. "Mum would have far too much fun with that to keep it to herself. Now, Janet, remember to breathe. Or do your meditation thing, if that helps. We all need you to be the calm and collected one this afternoon, in case the rest of us are driven to the point of lunacy by the author-who-shall-not-be-called-bampot. I'm sure none of us will snap, though, and it's going to be a really lovely signing."

Although Janet hadn't worried about the weather keeping people away from the signing, she did worry that Daphne's own behavior might. A needless worry, as it turned out. Daphne and Rachel Carson were there on time, Daphne in slacks and an embroidered tunic top, Rachel Carson with a sprig of heather in her collar. People started arriving before the advertised start time of four, but Daphne and Rachel Carson stood at the door greeting them as they came in, until the shop and the tearoom were pleasantly full of mingling, chatting guests. If Janet noticed more people gravitating toward the tearoom and the refreshments, and not making it all the way back to the signing area, she forgave them. The culinary class had brought an array of delicious savory and sweet finger foods, and Summer's orange almond scones were a definite hit.

Daphne inched the signing table a few inches one direction and the chair a few in the other. Then she and Rachel Carson took their places,

Rachel Carson stopping first to sniff suspiciously at the chair that Ranger so often sat in. Janet stood ready to open books for Daphne and to hand Post-it notes to people waiting so Daphne wouldn't have to ask for correct spellings of names.

Rhona of the GREAT-SCOTS was first in line for a signature, followed by Alistair. Janet reached for Rhona's book. Daphne reached faster.

"You appear to be the hovering type," she said, waving Janet away. "I've decided I don't need an assistant. I'll pop my own soda cans. Come by every so often with a refill of hot tea for me and fresh water for Rachel Carson, and that will be sufficient."

"Would either of you like a plate of refreshments?" Janet asked.

"No."

Janet refrained from snapping a salute and went to join Tallie and Rab at the sales counter, telling herself to walk, not stalk.

"That works out well for us," Tallie said when Janet told them of the change in plans. "Now we can take turns circulating. You can go first, if you like. Oh, and guess who came in and headed straight for the tearoom?"

"Norman Hobbs," Rab said.

"That wasn't fair," said Tallie. "You saw him come in."

"Aye, but telling saves time. In case he doesn't stay."

"Good point," said Janet. "If you two are all right here, I'll go through and say hello."

Janet tried, but wasn't able to make a beeline to the tearoom. She met Gillian and Tom in the photography section along the way, ran into James Haviland, and said hello to several others she knew or recognized before reaching her goal. When she got to the tearoom, Hobbs wasn't there.

"Didn't you see him?" Christine asked when Janet told her why she'd clucked her tongue and looked disappointed. "He filled a plate and went back into the bookshop before I could tell him not to take more than his share of sausage rolls." She stepped to the door of the tearoom. "There he is. At the corner of the picture book nook."

"The sausage rolls are good?" Janet tried not to be obvious in casting a longing look toward the refreshment tables.

"The sausage rolls are excellent. So are the stuffed mushrooms, the haggis balls, cream buns, tea bread, and macaroon bars. The students cook and behave like professionals. Watch this." Christine turned and raised a finger as a signal for one of the students, then turned back to Janet. "Something else about the students—they've been getting Summer to laugh. Ah, here you go."

A student wearing a chef's toque and white apron appeared at Janet's elbow. She handed Janet a plate and napkin and gave a shallow bow.

"Thank you so much," Janet said.

"You're welcome," the girl said, then repeated it in Gaelic, "'S e ur beatha."

"That was adorable," Janet said when the girl was gone. She nodded toward Hobbs, who hadn't moved from where he stood just outside the picture book area. "I'll go see what's gluing him to that spot."

Janet had never seen Constable Norman Hobbs out of uniform. Or if she had, she hadn't recognized him. She wondered if his grandmother had knitted his jumper. Or Jess? No, closer up, the sweater was comfortably worn at the elbows, which would have taken more time than he and Jess had been a rumored item. Janet wondered if it meant anything that she didn't see Jess now.

"Hello, Norman."

Hobbs didn't quite jump, but he twitched. She knew she hadn't been fair, approaching him quietly while he was engrossed in—what? Certainly not the copy of *Wee Granny's Magic Bag* he was pretending to read.

"What are you up to?" she asked.

Hobbs tucked the book under his arm, took his plate from a shelf, and moved around Janet into the alcove where they shelved children's picture books. Janet followed.

"Good afternoon, Mrs. Marsh," Hobbs said, and took a bite of sausage roll.

"Please don't take another bite and use those innocent sausage rolls as a way to stall your answer."

Hobbs chewed, swallowed, and pulled the book from under his arm. "I've been looking for a present for my niece."

"It's a good choice, Norman, but you weren't turning the pages while you were standing there. Were you even looking at them?"

"I've read the book before." Hobbs stepped out of the alcove, looked left, then right, then stepped back in. "While I was flipping through it, refreshing my memory, I discovered something you might not be aware of. If you don't mind, go to the spot where I was a moment ago. Stand facing the shelves and listen. I'll hold your plate, if you like."

"I'll keep my plate, thank you." For all Janet knew, this was an elaborate ploy on his part to get her sausage rolls and macaroons. She went and stood as he directed.

"A step closer to the shelves," Hobbs said.

Janet shot him a look and he retreated into the picture book alcove. She moved closer to the shelf and listened—to the pleasant rise and fall of voices around her, to laughter somewhere near the front door, to the closing strains of a lovely guitar version of "Farewell to Stromness" coming over the sound system. She ate a sausage roll, which was every bit as excellent as Christine had said they were, and waited, but heard nothing at all unexpected.

"What am I—oh. Hello, Ian."

Ian Atkinson, leaning an elbow on a shelf next to *Curious George*, smiled at her. "If you're looking for Constable Hobbs, he's gone into the tearoom. Shall I give your existential question a try?"

"I wasn't really—"

"Don't burst my bubble by telling me what you were really doing. Fiction is more exciting. So, what *are* you?" Ian took his elbow from the bookshelf and crossed his arms. He gave her an assessing look, head slowly tilting to the side.

Janet felt her own head following his. She straightened and popped a macaroon in her mouth.

"You're brave," he said. He brushed at something on his tweed sleeve. "And now I'll be brave and go introduce myself."

"To Daphne? Haven't you met her yet?" Janet was sure he would have found a way to run into her or an excuse to knock on her door before now.

"A small secret," he said, moving closer and talking near her ear without making eye contact. "I write books for a reason. Writing is safer." He brushed at the sleeve again, tugged on both, and headed for the signing area.

Janet decided Hobbs could find her, if he wanted to explain the experiment she'd just failed. She went back to the sales counter, chewing her last sausage roll, and found Hobbs anyway, standing with with Tallie and Rab. As she approached, Hobbs said something that caused the usually imperturbable Rab to react in a way that Janet hadn't seen before; his eyes widened. Hobbs nodded and Rab left the sales counter.

"Rab's gone to try it," Hobbs said when Janet raised her own eyebrows.

"He thinks he found an acoustic anomaly," Tallie said. "A spot where it's easy to pick up on conversations from several directions at once."

"It didn't work for me," Janet said.

"Height must make a difference," Hobbs said. "I was quite startled. There I was, flipping through *Wee Granny's Magic Bag*, when I heard Ms. Wood chatting with some of her admirers. It was rather interesting."

"What they were saying or the phenomenon?" Janet asked.

"Both. Wonderful refreshments, by the way. I'll go give my compliments."

"They're chatting in a public space, with no expectation of privacy," Tallie said when he was gone. "In case you were wondering about the ethics of eavesdropping via anomaly."

"I was." Janet was also annoyed that she wasn't tall enough to have heard anything herself.

"And we can try it standing on a chair, after everyone's gone," Tallie added.

"Good."

A burst of laughter came from the signing area. Janet saw Daphne put her hand on Ian's shoulder and lean on him as though helpless. Her voice was plenty strong, though, and as people came to see what was going on, it rose.

"I'm using him," she said, "but at least I'm honest about it. He wants to show off, I want to get away from pavements and roads for a few hours. It's a win-win. But what he's been saying . . . !" Her words dissolved into another gust of laughter. It was contagious and had others laughing, too. "That we're going to work on a calendar together. It's just too funny. I couldn't. Could *not*. Could not *possibly*."

"Ouch," Tallie said to Janet. "That's Tom she's talking about. And he didn't need an acoustical sweet spot to hear it."

"She wanted him to hear it," Janet said. "She had to have seen him come over and stand there."

"Shh," Tallie said. "Here he comes."

As Tom passed the sales counter, he handed Janet one of Daphne's books.

"Sorry," he said, heading for the door, "I dinnae want it after all." He turned as he pulled the door open. "Oh, her wee dog. Female or male?"

"Female," Tallie said.

"A bitch. That's what I thought."

18

That was quite a show," Martin Gunn said, pointing first at the door closing behind Tom, then into the signing area where Daphne and Ian were still talking.

"Not for the paper, I hope?" Tallie asked.

"Probably not."

In a moment of panic, Janet let a small "eep" escape.

"No, no, Mrs. Marsh. Don't worry." Martin put both his hands on the counter, the pink of his cheeks now looking earnest and sincere. "It would only be a human interest story, and not a nice one. More of a human misery story. Not the kind we go in for."

"Thank you."

"Besides." He grinned and pointed toward the signing area again. "You heard her flay Tom. I wouldn't want to get on the wrong side of that. Or the wee one kipping under her chair."

"I was sorry not to see your article and review in the paper this week," Janet said.

"Not the first time I've been disappointed," he said, "and I'm a firm believer in creating rather than complaining. Get right back to it and eventually you'll get somewhere."

"That's a good attitude, Martin. I'm sure it'll take you far."

∞

Sales of Daphne's books came in dribs and drabs, not enough to keep two of them tied to the cash register. Rab hadn't returned yet, but Janet told Tallie to go ahead and take her turn circulating.

"I'll see if Daphne or Rachel Carson needs anything, while I'm at it," Tallie said.

"No need." Gillian, followed by Ian, came from the signing area. "She's going to fetch it herself. Stretch her legs. *Their* legs. She suddenly wanted someone to take the dog for a walk."

Ian threw his hands up in mock horror. "Not I, said I."

"She should have put 'dog walker' in her list of demands," Tallie said. "Maybe I should circulate my way into the tearoom, first."

"Thanks," Gillian said, then crooked a finger, beckoning Janet closer. Ian leaned in, too. "I'll tell you why she's been living alone in the woods. It's got nothing to do with Thoreau or St. Pekingese or anyone else she quoted the other night. It's self-defense."

"She's terribly funny and clever, though," Ian said. "Do you know, she recognized my name and acted as though I'd made an arduous trek to see her this afternoon, from whatever more cosmopolitan metropolis she thought I must live in, and she congratulated me on not being tied to so provincial an area. And then she said being stuck in a bookshop for the afternoon is like being in a forest full of dead trees."

Janet didn't quite see the humor, but Ian, apparently as helpless to mirth as Daphne, threw an arm around Gillian and rocked with laughter. In a slick move, Gillian slipped out from under, leaving Ian unbalanced so that he had to catch himself against the counter. He had decent reflexes, though, and immediately righted himself, straightened his jacket, and disappeared down the nearest aisle of shelves.

"Honestly," Gillian said when he was gone, "the only thing that's gone smoothly from the beginning of this grant was writing and winning it. The rest has been one thing after another."

"I'm sure Tom agrees at this point," Janet said. "I sort of wondered if you'd leave with him."

"Och, he'll be all right."

"She wasn't very kind."

"I warned him about her, though, and that's why he wouldn't thank me for following him out. Too much like 'I told you so.'"

Not more than five minutes later, Daphne and Rachel Carson returned from the tearoom. "I'm thinking of calling it a successful signing," she said, "and then calling it a day."

"Sorry?" Janet said.

"It's been a long day."

"You've only been here half an hour," Gillian said.

"It feels like so much longer. I must be operating in dog years. Very well, we'll stay, although between you and me, the book-buying public seems more interested in scones and haggis balls than having books signed."

As if on cue, one of the culinary students, in her toque and white apron, approached them with a tray on one arm and a stack of small plates in her opposite hand. Janet thanked her and took a scone and a haggis ball—not because she particularly wanted either, but because she was feeling petty. She smiled at Daphne and ate the scone. The scone was delicious, but the pettiness was wasted. Daphne was watching another student offering a tray to Gillian's father near the front window.

"'A thing of beauty is a joy forever,' isn't it?" Daphne said.

Gillian gave Daphne a quick look, also wasted, and went to join her father. She tucked her arm into Alistair's and said something that made the student smile. She took a macaroon and a scone, and then pointed to a couple browsing down the aisle from them. The student made a shallow curtsey and moved on. Alistair kissed Gillian goodbye and left.

"Didn't Alistair look taken with that charming creature?" Daphne said. "And isn't he lucky to have a daughter like Gillian."

"He is. That was a really nice thing to say, Daphne."

"Well, I hope you know that I didn't say that thing about beauty. That was someone else, and I'd be willing to debate the issue."

Janet turned away so Daphne wouldn't see how hard it was for her to keep from rolling her eyes. Happily, she saw several people waiting patiently at the table near the fireplace. "Good news, Daphne. Fans are lining up for your signature."

"Lovely!"

Daphne and Rachel Carson returned to the signing area, and almost immediately Rab reappeared behind the counter. When Janet looked back toward the display window, she saw Christine there talking to Gillian.

"Take over for a few minutes, will you?" Janet asked Rab. He nodded and she joined Christine and Gillian.

"I really like that wombat," Gillian was saying. "I don't care what Daphne says."

"She doesn't like it?" Christine asked.

"I don't care. I do. It's a good wombat. It reminds me of Tom. It's something subtle around the eyes. And the smile."

"Hmm." Janet took a closer at the small animal. "Maybe you're right."

"If you ask me," Christine said, "it looks more like Rab. And the way it looks as though it's about to disappear from sight around that stack of books, that's typical Rab MacGregor behavior."

"Oh," Janet said, looking over at the sales counter. "He was just there. Where's he gone?"

"Exactly," said Christine.

"He's probably helping—there he is."

Rab appeared from the next aisle with a stack of paperback novels, followed by a giddy-looking elderly woman who barely came up to his elbow.

"Mystery solved," Gillian said. "It pays to keep tall help. I'll go keep Daphne company so she doesn't get bored or antsy, or at least so she stays as long as we agreed she would."

"Hang in there, Gillian," Christine said, and then to Janet, "That was brilliant advice, don't you think? If Summer ever gives up the advice column, I might apply. Here's a further example of my keen insight. Assume someone has written a letter asking how to deal with a bampot author, giving details of said author's behavior." Christine posed, elbows out, hands lightly clasped at her midsection. "Dear Befuddled, it appears your author is less of a mystery and more of a mind-boggler."

They heard a soft laugh behind them and turned to see James Haviland. He bowed to Christine.

"Masterful," he said. "The job is yours if Summer decides to quit."

"Good to hear," Christine said. "And good of you to come, even if you weren't allowed to fiddle around. Did you enjoy the afternoon anyway?"

"You mean, 'Apart from that, Mrs. Lincoln, how did you like the play?'"

"I hope you didn't feel *that* badly about it," Janet said.

"No, no, not at all. I'll tell you something I don't like, though," he said. "It's the way that wombat is looking at me. Cheers."

After the door jingled shut behind him, Janet asked, "*Is* Summer thinking about quitting the column?"

"I've no idea," Christine said, "but here come Maida and Ian, and neither of them look happy."

"Oh, dear," Janet said.

"This might be another chance for me to practice giving advice."

"Oh, dear," Janet said again. "Hello, Maida, Ian. Is there something we can do for you?"

Maida told them she hadn't come to get a book signed, but to ask Daphne about her plant pots. "And do you know what she said? She said, 'Houseplants are like caged animals in a zoo.' Then she hissed at me."

"Oh, Maida, I'm sorry," Janet said. "I told you I'd get the pots for you, and I didn't. But where's Gillian? I thought she was over there with Daphne."

Maida pulled her cardigan tighter around her. "If she had been, I would have told her I want out of this house agreement—*out* of the agreement and yon hissing bisom *out* of my house."

"Why don't we take this into the office," Christine suggested. She looked at Janet, who nodded.

"No need for that," Maida said. "I'm leaving." But she made no move to leave. Instead, she replanted her feet and crossed her arms so firmly she set the purse hanging from her forearm to swinging.

"I'm concerned about Ms. Wood," Ian said quietly. "I mean to say, she's not—"He stopped, thought, and started again. "She's in the business of using words." He stopped again.

"And?" Christine prompted.

"Her words to Maida were disturbing. I honestly think she's not quite right."

"Ah, well, we're ahead of you there, Ian." Christine slapped him on the back, something Janet knew she enjoyed doing because he never seemed to expect it.

"Christine," Janet warned.

Christine glanced toward the signing area and lowered her voice. "Let's think of her as eccentric. We might go as far as *exceptionally* eccentric. She was rude to you just now, Maida. She was rude to the GREAT-SCOTs, Alistair, and the whole town at the ceilidh. And, don't forget, she accused you of attempted murder. So, no, she's not your garden variety former Inversgailian, but we have the power to render her harmless. She uses her words like weapons, but as long as we know that, then we can protect ourselves against their sting."

Ian looked impressed.

"Rubbish," Maida said, possibly biting back a more colorful word. "But all right, if we can't say her words are disturbing, then I'll say this: *She's* disturbing. I feel it in my heart and in my bones."

Ian's loyalties shifted. "I feel I have to agree with Maida. She has a sense for this sort of thing, you know. She proved herself by using it to bring—" He shuddered. "To bring that villain to justice a few months ago."

"She used a frying pan to bring that villain to justice," Christine said. "It was a combination of luck and violence."

"Exactly. Violence," Ian said. "And that's what I feel now."

"Do you really think she's violent?" Janet asked.

Ian thought about that then asked, "At this point, who are we talking about? Maida or Ms. Wood?"

∞

When she heard about Daphne's confrontation with Maida, Gillian found Janet and apologized. Tallie was with her.

"*She* didn't want tea, but I needed some," Gillian said. "I shouldn't have left her alone, though."

"She shouldn't need a babysitter," Tallie said.

Janet looked at the time on her phone. "We said this would go two hours. Do you think we can make it? Can *she*?"

"Let's not ask her to," Gillian said. "The kids are doing a fine job. You have more customers chatting in the tearoom and browsing than lining up to see Daphne. Let's tell her that her part is over and be done with it."

"Will she mind?" Tallie asked.

"*I* won't mind." Janet immediately clapped a hand to her mouth.

"Right," Gillian said. "Care to come help her gather her things, Tallie?"

"Delighted."

Daphne was delighted, too. She insisted on making a "farewell tour" of the bookshop and tearoom, thanking people for coming to see her. Tallie and Gillian accompanied her. Janet stayed at the sales counter, imagining the atmosphere, like a fog, lightening and lifting with each minute Daphne drew closer to being gone.

"She thanked the students when we got to the tearoom," Tallie told Janet back at the sales counter. "Really, she was very sweet. Then she took a thermos and bag from her backpack, filled the thermos with tea, and picked half the scones off a couple of trays and put them in the bag. All of that went back into the backpack and then she left. Gillian left with

her. She said something about going all the way home with her, just to
make sure she doesn't come back."

The rest of the afternoon passed quickly. The students did all the
cleaning up in the tearoom and checked the bookshop for stray plates,
cups, and napkins left on shelves. Norman Hobbs helped Rab fold the
signing table and stow it, and then move the chairs back into their accustomed positions near the fireplace. Hobbs then came to the register to
buy *Wee Granny's Magic Bag* for his niece.

"Thank you for helping, Norman. I hadn't realized you were still
here."

Hobbs blushed above his brush of a mustache. "I sat down in the comfy
chair, there with the picture books and, I'm sorry to say, fell asleep."

"I imagine they worked you hard on your course," Janet said.

"You have a kind imagination."

"How's Jess?" she asked. "We haven't seen much of her lately."

"Neither have I," Hobbs said.

"Well—" Her imagination thought quickly for something kind to say.
"You've been away."

"Aye." He handed the book to her.

"Did you pick up any intel from the acoustic anomaly?" Tallie asked.

"It's more of a party trick than useful," he said.

"Or more of a technique for amateur sleuths than professionals?"

"Only for amateurs who depend on flukes," Hobbs said.

Christine, coming from the tearoom with Summer, overheard him.
"And as we all know, amateurs who depend on flukes aren't worth their
weight in liver. What kind of amateurs are we talking about?"

"Sleuths," Janet said.

"Have you told Norman about Daftie Daphne's idea of us teaming up
together to solve Sam Smith's murder?"

"His murder isn't a joke," Summer said.

"Amen," Christine said. "I mean that in all seriousness, Summer.
Norman is our constable, though, and now that he's back, he needs to

be aware of what's been going on. I don't know how focused Daphne is on actually investigating, Norman."

"Since returning, I've been hearing reports."

"I'm not surprised," Janet said. "She's given us a name. I think I left that out when you called. She says we should call ourselves the SCONES— the Shadow Constabulary of Nosy, Eavesdropping Snoops."

Hobbs's lips disappeared for a moment, and then he said, more mildly than Janet expected, "I see. How long has Ms. Wood been in Inversgail?"

"A week," Janet said. "Since Monday night."

"I see."

"What do you see, Norman?" Christine asked.

"That Ms. Wood has been busy." Hobbs saluted with *Wee Granny* and headed for the door. Tallie went with him and turned the deadbolt after he'd gone.

"You know, Mom," she said, coming back to the group, "you left out SCONES when you talked to Constable Hobbs earlier, and no one can blame you for that. But now we've left something else out. You told him Daphne's been here since Monday night."

"She has." Janet looked at Christine, then Summer, then Rab. They each nodded.

"It only seems like longer because Norman's right," Christine said. "She's been busy and she's irritated a lot of people in one short week."

"What did we leave out?" Summer asked.

"A few words that might be important," Tallie said. "She's been here since Monday night—as far as we know."

19

Before Janet had a chance to do more than draw her eyebrows together and decide whether to say *yow, yeesh,* or *bugger,* Christine's phone rang. It was Danny, asking how the signing had gone. Christine gave him what Janet called afterward an unnecessarily florid rendition of the afternoon.

"But it broke the tension, didn't it?" Christine said. "And his suggestion that we drop by for a round on the house to decompress was generous."

"And welcome and, frankly, necessary," Janet said. "So, thank you, Christine."

"I do my best. Nev's in an hour, then? You'll join us, Rab?"

"Aye. I'll propose a toast."

Janet moved past her indecision over *yow, yeesh,* or *bugger* on the walk to Nev's that evening. She settled on the reasonable assumption that Reddick would have already checked the details of Daphne's arrival.

"If he thought there was any need to check," Tallie said.

"Mm. And just because he did check, if he did, doesn't mean there aren't implications or ramifications if she did arrive earlier. Do you really think someone wouldn't have noticed her? Or Rachel Carson?"

"*What?*" Tallie said, feigning shock. "In a tourist town like this? You think she sticks out?"

"Like a wombat in the West Highlands."

"Or a loon at the library ceilidh," Tallie said. "But so what if someone did see her?"

"I don't know," Janet said. "I'll let you know if I think of something."

Christine and Summer were at Nev's ahead of them. Christine's parents had declined her invitation to join them and Summer was on the phone to her own mother.

"She says hi and wonders how much time we spend in bars," Summer said after disconnecting. "She says she's beginning to recognize voices in the background."

"Next time tell her this isn't a bar, per se," Christine said. "It's a public house, a place for people to gather, exchange news and views, unwind, and feel a sense of community."

"Is she worried?" Janet asked.

"Jealous," Summer said.

Janet and Christine went to help Danny bring drinks. Rab and Ranger came back to the table with them.

"I have a toast," Tallie said. "To a successful afternoon, a decent turnout, and to Summer, Christine, and the students. You did a great job."

"Mostly the students," Summer said. "They were a lot of fun."

They clinked pints, and everyone but Janet drank.

"A toast to Summer's scones," Janet said.

"To Summer's scones," the others echoed.

"I can't help but notice that we aren't drinking to bampots," Christine said. "And that you're not drinking at all, Janet. Feeling all right?"

"Yes, fine. *Well chuffed*, in fact, but I want to keep a clear head through the decompression portion of the evening. Isn't that why we're here?"

"I thought the pints *were* the decompression," Summer said. "Salute the signing with Selkie's Tears and then go off and play darts, or something."

"Our Summer has a point," Christine said. "We did our bit with the bampot. And if you don't mind, I'm going to continue referring to the person in question as the bampot so that we don't have to worry about being overheard. So yes, we did our bit with the bampot today, and from here on out, she's the problem of Gillian and the school."

"You do realize that if you're going to say 'she' and then connect her to Gillian and the school that you might as well use her name, right?" Tallie asked. "Speaking as the anal attorney of this group."

"Duly noted, counselor. I doubt I'll stop calling her the bampot, though."

"Suits me," Tallie said.

"Calling her a bampot isn't kind." Janet stared at her glass as she moved it in circles on the table. "But it's better than Tom's thinly veiled insult this afternoon. And I'm glad our part is over, but I'm beginning to worry that she's a bigger problem than Gillian can handle. I'm not sure I can really explain why I think that, though."

"Undercurrents," Rab said.

"That works. That's part of it. Thank you, Rab. Didn't you say you had a toast, too?" Janet asked.

"It'll keep."

"Sure? Okay, so, yes. Undercurrents and nebulous stuff and a whole Pandora's box of 'what if's that Tallie let loose this afternoon by saying 'as far as we know.' There's an awful lot we don't know about *her*, and I want to hear what you've noticed or heard or overheard. Maybe that'll give my thoughts some direction. Or some peace. Decompression, anyway. Okay?"

"Wait," Summer said, "is this just from this afternoon, or—?"

"From any point this week." Janet took a notebook and pen from her purse.

"You're going to write it down?" Summer asked.

"Is that a problem?"

"No, but why don't you record it on your phone? That way you can concentrate on listening and you'll have all the details."

"The girl's a genius," Tallie said. "And you go first, Mom, to give us an idea of what you're looking for."

"It's going to sound like gossip, but I don't mean it that way."

"If what you're looking for is awareness and understanding, then there isn't so much wrong with gossip," Christine said. "Don't think of it as the blather of nosy neighbors; think of it as an earful of empathy."

"That actually makes sense to me," Janet said. "Should I worry about *that* now?"

"No," Tallie said. "You should never worry about anything Christine says, because she's a genius, too. Now, tell them about Tom's insult."

"It's what came before the insult, too." Janet told them about Tom taking Daphne on photo shoots without mentioning the trips to Gillian, and about Tom's excitement at the ceilidh when he told them he and Daphne were going to work on a calendar. "Here's where it gets murky, though, and it's more about Daphne's behavior than Tom's. Friday night, at the ceilidh, I got the feeling Daphne enjoyed seeing Gillian's reaction when she heard about the calendar project. That's an impression, though, not a fact."

"You said Daphne had a predatory smile," Christine reminded her.

"Still, it's only my impression. Here's a fact, though. This afternoon, Daphne was laughing and told Ian she's only using Tom to get out of town and that she couldn't possibly work with him on a calendar. Tom heard her, and I'm almost positive she knew he was there."

"It sounded to me as though she raised her voice to make sure he heard," Tallie said. "She was laughing, but it was pretty vicious."

"Tom left then," Janet said. "On his way out, he called Rachel Carson a bitch, but—this is an impression, again—he wasn't talking about her. I would say I'm surprised he had that much self-control, but I don't really know him."

"I'm surprised Maida hasn't clocked her one," Christine said. "The bampot has been rude about the house from the beginning."

"Not to mention serving up Maida's houseplants in a salad," Janet said.

Christine told the others about the confrontation between Maida and Daphne that afternoon. "It was either 'The Case of the Missing Plant

Pots' or 'The Case of the Hissing Bampot'; take your pick. Ian was there
for that episode, too, and even he said he doesn't think she's quite right."

"Those were his words?" Summer asked.

"Close, if not exact."

"I guess I didn't tell you that she asked if we could put her up in the
B and B," Summer said. "But there's no reason for me to tell you every
time I have to turn someone away. It happens frequently enough, so yay
us. Her request went a bit beyond the usual, though. She complained
about the house, said it's too Spartan. Complained about Maida, too
nosy. She wanted to know when the next room would be available. And
then she wanted me to *make* a room open up."

"When was that?" Tallie asked.

"I don't know. Tuesday, Wednesday?"

"Interesting," Tallie said. "Thursday she didn't say anything about
the house or Maida, but said she wanted to spend a night or two in the
B and B so she could get the full Inversgail experience."

"Baloney," Christine said. "We haven't been open long enough to be
part of the Inversgail experience."

"And those are two different stories," Janet said. "Is that an example
of her eccentricity?"

"You're asking us to draw a conclusion on too little information,"
Tallie said.

"It sounds like she's rude, mean, or trying to manipulate people,"
Summer said. "Or all three."

"Or is she a social klutz?" Janet asked. "That's part of what I don't
know." She told them about Daphne's despondent musings when she
arrived late for the sword demonstration. "She seemed genuinely confused about the how and why of friendship. She said she wanted to be
called Laurel, but she never told anyone. Did you know her when she
lived here, Rab?"

Rab shook his head. "There's another reason she wants to stay at the
B and B," he said quietly. "She says she's sensitive to energy and spirits.

Auras, too. She says she can learn something about Sam Smith if she spends the night where he slept."

"She told you that?" Christine asked. "Utter baloney."

"She heard I read tea leaves and reckons I'll understand her gift. She asked me to help her get access to the B and B."

"What did you tell her?" Janet asked.

"What Alistair said to her at the ceilidh. It didn't bother her the first time round."

"What *was* that bit of Gaelic?" Christine asked.

"The gist—"

"Let's have the full translation this time," Janet said.

Rab cleared his throat. "'You are stupid and unpleasant. Welcome to Inversgail. Walk carefully.'" He took a large swallow from his pint. "More poetic in the Gaelic, but."

"Do you think she really believes she has this gift?" Janet asked.

"Aye, I reckon she does, and that's the honest reason she wants to get into the B and B. But does she *have* such a gift? That's about as likely as finding answers in the dregs at the bottom of a teacup."

Summer stared at him. "You realize what you just said, don't you? You admitted you're a fraud. You're saying that when you sit in the tearoom and read peoples' tea leaves you're just making sh—you're making stuff up."

"A wee bit of blather, is all," Rab said mildly. "But I've never said it was anything different. People like to believe what they see." He sat back with his pint and scratched Ranger between the ears.

Not knowing how Summer would react to Rab's blithe admission, but seeing that she continued to stare at him, Janet slipped in a two-part question of her own. "What kind of 'aura' does she expect to get from the B and B? Wouldn't it make more sense for her to try her mumbo jumbo here where the poor soul died?"

"She seems to tailor her message for the audience," Christine said. "She's irritated Danny a time or two this past week. I'll go see if the man himself can come tell you what she's said. Another round for anyone while

I'm up?" She had no takers, so she went to see if Danny could spare a few minutes.

"Maybe she gathers auras and whatnot the way you're gathering information, Mom," Tallie said. "You don't know what you're looking for, so you're listening broadly at the outset, with plans to refine your focus as you go."

"You make my method sound almost scientific. Here come James and Martin."

"Evening, all," James said. "You look glum. I hope nothing's amiss. The signing turned out well, didn't it?"

"It did," Janet said.

"Good to hear. Fancy a game, then, Summer? Cheer you up?"

"Sure." Summer scraped her chair back. "See you guys tomorrow."

"Tallie?" Martin asked. "Anyone else?"

"I'll be along in a few," Tallie said.

When Summer had gone, Janet put her fingers on Tallie's arm. "She really did look glum. Is she all right?"

Tallie leaned closer to her mother and whispered, "Mom, dear? Your mom-ness is beginning to glow."

Janet patted Tallie's arm and looked up as Danny came back to the table with Christine. The two of them sat, Danny moving a chair so he could keep an eye on the bar.

"Chrissy says you want to know what I think of your author," he said. "I'll tell you what I told Chrissy. I don't like spreading stories about my customers."

Janet sat up a little straighter.

"That's not to say I don't like listening to them," Danny said. "But what I hear stops with me. You can call me Saint Danny, if you like. The person in question is not one of my customers, though, so I'm happy to spill anything and everything she's told me."

Daphne had stopped by Nev's twice. The first time she'd come in through the front door. "Like a normal person," Danny said. She'd introduced herself and then told him she was championing the dead man. She'd asked the staff questions. She'd sat down, uninvited, with other patrons, and asked them questions, too. "I suggested she move on from the subject, or move on, full stop. She chose the full stop version, after some choice words."

"Oh, dear," Janet said.

"A wee bit closer to the gutter than 'oh, dear,' Janet. But my ears and most of the rest of me belonged to the navy for more years than I care to remember, and they've heard worse. I'm sure I sounded cold and uncaring when I told her I wished her man hadn't ended up dead just here."

"She came back, though?" Tallie asked.

"I found her out back *greeting*."

"Crying," Christine whispered to Tallie and Janet, "not practicing for a job at Walmart."

"Ta, Chrissy," Danny said. "Crocodile tears, I thought, but she said she knew the boy's mum and her family."

"Did she?" Janet asked.

"You never told me," Christine said.

"Because it isn't true. With a name like Smith? And the lad being American?" Danny shook his head. "She created a whole story for him. How he came to Nev's because it's next door to Smith Funerals. She knows he was related to those Smiths because she 'felt' it in the 'energy' he left behind. His 'energy' told her who his mother was, too—one of the daughters. She claims she knew her."

"That would be easy enough to check," Tallie said. "Well, apart from the ghostie and ghoulie aspects. But maybe he was here looking up family."

"Maybe he was," Danny said. "But her story is only a story."

A group of half a dozen people came in, stopping just inside the door to marvel and remark. The words "quaint" and "authentic" seemed to hit Danny's ears hardest. He muttered about tourists and becoming known as the "murder pub."

"I'm needed," he said, getting up. "They might be blood thirsty, but thirsty's all that matters."

"One more quick question?" Janet asked.

"Aye?"

Janet touched her ear. "A quiet one."

Danny put a hand on the back of her chair and one on Christine's and bent his head between them.

"The police still haven't released a cause of death," Janet said. "Could there have been other injuries?"

Danny sighed. "The lad was neatly dressed when he came in, shirt still tucked when he died. But a blow like that to the head makes a fair mess, ken, and I didn't study him in great detail."

"Sorry, Danny."

"*Dinnae fash*. I'm not blessed with a photographic memory. Chrissy, tell them about Smith's." He touched her shoulder and went back to the bar.

"There hasn't ever been a Smith family at Smith's," Christine said. "Do the De Vuyst's still own it, Rab?"

"Aye, Morag and her son."

"Belgian refugees at the start of World War One," Christine said. "They named it Smith Funerals so the business didn't look so foreign."

"But they didn't change their own name?" Tallie asked.

"There's business sense on the one hand," Christine said, "and family pride on the other."

"But why is Daphne spouting nonsense like that?" Janet asked. "Not just nonsense, but lies. She can't possibly think people won't know or find out. Look how many people she's annoyed or upset in one short week. It doesn't stop."

"Will you be drinking that?" Rab pointed to Janet's untouched pint.

"Do you want it? It's been sitting."

"For my toast." He lifted the glass. "To the stoops, the steps, and the low walls in our lives, where we can stop to take off a shoe and tip out the wee stone that's been irritating and won't let up."

"Is that a traditional toast?" Janet asked.

"Just something I've been working on," Rab said.

"It works for me," Christine said. "Our bampot has become the stone in a lot of shoes."

"And that worries me," Janet said. "It's a legitimate worry, too, so don't any of you start in on me. She's been spreading it around that she's working with us to find Sam Smith's killer. That means to whoever did it, we might be a stone in the shoe, too, and that person might try to tip us out."

"She's less of a wee stone, then," Christine said, "and more of a blister."

20

Before she left Nev's that evening, Janet decided to let her momness shine through. Tallie had joined the darts game. Janet went to find her and told her she was leaving the car for her.

"I'll get a lift from Christine. You take Summer home. Do you hear that, Summer?"

Tallie gave her a thumb's up. Summer didn't look as aggrieved as Janet thought she might. Rab assured her Ranger wasn't afraid to use the sharp end of his teeth.

As they walked to the car, Christine asked, "Did any of that, back there, help your thinking? Give it direction? Provide decompression? We depend on your brains for simple things like planning cockamamie life-changing adventures, so we need to keep them from exploding."

"Direction? Possibly. Increasing the murk of nebulous worries and fears? Definitely. Decompression? Definitely not."

"There's nothing silly about healthy fear."

"Good, then I won't feel silly asking you to come into the house with me while I make sure no bampots are lurking or hiding."

Neighbors were home with lights on when they pulled into Janet's driveway. She saw Ian appear and disappear in his upstairs window. He was checking to see who'd arrived, no doubt, and she realized his nosiness was a comfort. The kitchen light was on at Daphne's, too, and Janet pictured her and Rachel Carson gobbling the bounty of scones

she'd stuffed in her backpack. Christine insisted on checking around
the outside of the house before they went inside to do the same. They
found no bampots, and a few of Janet's worries and fears dissipated like
tendrils of mist. Christine waved when she was back in her car with the
door locked, and Janet locked up behind her. She went into the family
room and sat, shoulders and arms relaxed, eyes closed—and mind back
on overdrive.

Decompression hadn't come at Nev's. The atmosphere that Janet
had felt lighten when Daphne left the shop that afternoon now felt like
wet wool. She took out her phone and listened to the recording they'd
made. The quality was better than she'd expected. It was just too bad
the clarity of the recording didn't make anything else clearer. She got
out her laptop and listened a second time, pausing it every so often to
make notes in a new document. She played it a third time, letting it
run in the background, and added notes about other incidents no one
had mentioned:

Tom at the school, interaction with Hope, the way he watched her
  walk away
Her comments about Alistair. Odd chemistry with him? With Gillian?
She knows how to use a sword
She doesn't remember details of childhood friendship with Gillian?
But she remembered something Gillian didn't?
She doesn't like bookstores or houseplants, but she has a pet lapdog?
She hasn't been in contact with anyone in Inversgail since she left?

Tallie arrived home as the recording ended for the fourth time. She
came into the family room and flopped into a chair.

Janet saved the document, but didn't close the laptop. "Good game?"

"Fun more than championship quality. Summer's getting good. I kind
of hoped I'd find you in bed."

"Did you want to be alone down here? I can—"

"No, no, sit down," Tallie said. "If you'd gone up, it would've meant you thought you could sleep, that's all. I don't like seeing you so worried."

"I'm just clearing my head."

"How's that working for you?"

"I'm fine. You're a good daughter."

"Could you use some company?" Tallie asked. "Do you *want* company?"

"Not really. You're welcome to stay up, but no, I don't need company."

"Music?"

"Music would be nice."

Tallie got up and went to their old CD player. "What do you want to hear?"

"Miles Davis. *In a Silent Way.*"

"That kind of night, huh?"

"Oh, yeah."

Janet listened to the upstairs sounds of Tallie getting ready for bed and the jazz musicians feeling their way toward genius. Then she started typing again, using Tallie's logic and adding her qualifying phrase to the end of statements they thought or assumed were true:

Daphne went to Nev's twice—as far as we know

Daphne hasn't communicated with anyone in town since she left—as far as we know

Sam Smith was killed with a brick—as far as we know

Daphne arrived in town Monday night—as far as we know

Daphne didn't know Sam Smith—as far as we know

Daphne has no interest in Tom—as far as we know

Daphne doesn't use a real sword—as far as we know

Daphne knows how to kill animals in the wild—as far as we know

Sam Smith wasn't curled on the ground hiding a stab wound—as far as we know

There's no evidence to suggest Daphne killed Sam Smith—as far as we know

Janet reread the document and decided her notes were as loose and open-ended as Miles Davis's composition. But her notes might not even make as much sense as trying to dance a tango to his music.

Now it was late. She was tired. If she deleted the notes, it might be like clearing her mind, and she'd be able to sleep. She hesitated over the delete key, then hit save, closed the laptop, and set it aside. She nestled her head into the cushiony back of the chair and listened to the final cut on the CD, her thoughts improvising with the musicians.

Daphne could have killed Sam Smith. I'll tell the others tomorrow. The SCONES. They won't be convinced—about the name or her guilt. There's no proof. I'll talk them into calling Norman, anyway. And if Daphne's guilty, Gillian and Tom can teach happily ever after. No more bampot.

Janet was almost asleep, listening to Miles wail on his trumpet, when she realized there was something else wailing. But not on the CD. Not in the house. She got up and lowered the volume, then turned it off and went to the back door. Tallie padded down the stairs as she opened it.

"Howling," Janet said. "Is it Rachel Carson?"

"Do you have Daphne's phone number?"

"No. How long has that been going on?"

"Way too long."

Tallie ran upstairs to dress, taking the steps two at a time, up and back down again, Janet sure she'd break her neck.

"And then I'd have to go out there by myself to face who knows what," she said.

"After first calling an ambulance for me and my poor neck, I hope," Tallie said, alighting on the bottom step and snarling her shoelaces by tying them too quickly.

"You know I would." Janet pulled on a jacket and got a flashlight from the kitchen. "This feels urgent, but let's go carefully."

"Aye," Tallie said.

"That sounded very natural, dear." As they crossed the small deck behind the house, Janet took Tallie's arm. "That poor little thing is howling like a banshee. It's going right down my spine."

"Banshees do that, I think. Generally speaking, they aren't a good sign. Ian's watching from his window up there."

"The least he could do is turn the light off and be less obvious about it."

Using the flashlight, they followed the footpath to the bottom of the garden, through the gate, and into Daphne's garden. Rachel Carson's howls didn't just rise and fall, they also seemed to ebb and flow.

"It sounds like she's going back and forth between the front door and the back," Tallie said. "Poor little thing is going to be hoarse."

"The neighbors on either side must be better sleepers, or you'd think they'd be out here."

"Or better at waiting to see if someone else will traipse around in the dark first."

When they reached the back door, they heard Rachel Carson's howl receding toward the front. Janet rang the bell and Rachel Carson came howling back at a run and threw herself at the door. Janet tried cooing to her. That sent her into a frenzy of barking.

"I don't know why I bothered with the bell," Janet said. "If Daphne's in there, she wouldn't be putting up with that noise."

Tallie pounded on the door anyway. "For show," she said. "So anyone watching will see that we've made a good effort to raise her."

Janet saw that lights had come on in some of the other houses. "Pound again."

While Tallie pounded and Rachel Carson alternated between howling and barking, Janet went around the side of the house and saw Daphne's Land Rover parked on the street in front.

"She might have gone out with someone," Janet said. "And just because it's—what time *is* it?"

Tallie checked her phone. "One-twenty. She is Daphne, though. Daftie Daphne. She might be out and maybe Rachel Carson just ran out of kibble. The bampot and the banshee. But I tell you what, I'm going to call Constable Hobbs."

"If something's wrong, time matters. You call and I'll try getting in." Janet tried the door. "Oh. It isn't locked."

"Do *not* go in," Tallie said. "And do not touch anything else."

"She's right, Mrs. Marsh," Norman Hobbs said, coming around the corner of the house.

Tallie looked at the phone in her hand. "ESP, Constable?"

"Ian Atkinson and one or two other community-minded neighbors." Hobbs scanned the houses he could see. "All of whom took the precaution of staying out of harm's way. Ah, except for Mr. Atkinson. Here he comes now, bristling with indignation. And curiosity. Please don't ever repeat that."

"Constable Hobbs," Ian said, slightly out of breath from trotting through the gardens. "Good of you to come so quickly. I couldn't be sure who was pounding on the door—oh, hello, Janet, Tallie."

"What do you mean you couldn't be sure?" Janet said. "You were in your window and saw us coming over here." She moved past Ian and pointed toward his window, in case he was so unsure, he didn't remember where he lived—and she saw a familiar figure coming through the dark. "Maida?"

Maida picked her way gingerly across the grass. "I got here as fast as I could." She glared at Ian. "You said there was an emergency at my house and you'd wait for me in front of *your* house, and what do I see when I arrive but you leaving me alone to walk through the dark and who knows what dog mess she's left in my back garden." Maida wasn't out of breath at all.

"I was interested to see which of you would get here first," Ian said.

"Tcha," Maida said and turned away. "Her wee dog is off its head in there. What's going on?"

At that point, Gillian came into view around the corner of the house. "Maida called me," she said. "What's going on? Has anyone called Daphne? *No* one?" The others waited while she tapped her phone with the same vigor Tallie had used when she'd pounded the door. She got no answer.

"I don't believe she went anywhere," Ian offered.

"And the door's unlocked," Janet said. She reached for the knob.

"Ah-ah," Tallie said.

"I'll go on in, then," Hobbs said.

Rachel Carson barked on the other side of the door, and in an ominous turn for Hobbs, she started snarling and growling.

"Pekes are moody and malevolent," Hobbs said, nowhere nearer the door than he had been.

"Would you like me to try calling her? Or go in first?" Janet asked.

"They're famous for pretending not to hear when you call," Hobbs said, "and for biting."

"It might be best if we all go in at once to confuse her," Ian said, moving forward. Rachel Carson chose that moment to throw herself at the door again. Ian backed away.

"Right," Maida said. Before anyone could stop her, she opened the door, shouted, "*Wheesht*," and within moments was back outside with Rachel Carson on a leash. "It's all yours, Norman," she said, and walked the dog away to stand under a tree.

Hobbs cautioned the others not to follow him, went inside, and closed the door.

"I honestly couldn't be sure who had crept up to her door and started pounding on it," Ian said.

"*Wheesht*," Tallie and Janet said.

Gillian stood off to the side, biting her nails until Hobbs returned. When he did, he gave them the solemn news that Daphne was dead.

Janet felt slack with shock. No one said anything. Maida put a hand to her heart. Ian bowed his head. Janet watched Tallie taking note of those reactions. Norman was doing the same. Then she saw that Gillian's eyes were streaming, unchecked, as she stared at the back of the house. She knew she should go to her, offer her a tissue, a shoulder, or put an arm around her. She didn't. *When in doubt, or trouble, or confusion, or especially in anger—ask questions.*

"What happened, Norman? And when?"

"I can't be sure."

"Was it her heart?"

"I can't be sure, Mrs. Marsh. At a guess, if we had arrived sooner, it would have made no difference. Thank you for your concern and for alerting me. I've called headquarters and I'm to stay here until they arrive. At this point, I would ask you all to cooperate and go home. There will be nothing more to see or know tonight."

"The dog?" Maida asked.

Hobbs's otherwise professional eyebrows rose.

"I can't take her," Maida said.

"I'll take her," Gillian said, but she made no move toward Maida to take the leash. Maida stayed where she was, holding tightly to the leash, seemingly stuck to the ground.

"Maida, Gillian," Tallie said, "come back to the house with us. We'll have tea and warm up a little."

"Please do," Janet said. "That's a good idea." Before she followed them, Janet turned back to Hobbs. "When you're ready to leave, Norman, if you see lights on, please know you're also welcome to stop by for a cup of tea."

"Thank you, Mrs. Marsh."

"Do you think that might be sooner rather than later?"

"Thank you, Mrs. Marsh. Good night."

Janet gave herself points for trying. Then, mindful of one of the reasons Maida had been so angry with Ian, she used the flashlight to make her way without misstep through Daphne's back garden to her own footpath and on to her house. There she found Ian sitting in her favorite chair in the family room and Rachel Carson enjoying a bowl of lentil soup in the kitchen.

"I could hardly slam the door in either of their faces," Tallie whispered when Janet growled at her.

"Let's just make sure he leaves when they do and that Gillian doesn't leave the poor dog behind."

The electric kettle whistled. Tallie poured it into the waiting teapot and took it on a tray with cream and sugar into the family room. Janet followed with a tray of cups, saucers, and spoons. Tallie poured and Janet handed the cups around.

"How delightful this is," Ian said.

"No, Ian," Janet said. "Delightful really isn't the right word for this occasion." She was too tired to feel bad about being rude to him. *And something else*, she thought. *Sad? No.*

"Thank you," Gillian said when Janet handed her a cup. It was the first thing she'd said since telling them she'd take Rachel Carson, and once started, she seemed unable to stop. "It's so hard to believe. She was gone for so many years, cut herself out of our lives. But she came back. And now she's gone and *willnae* ever come back." She put a hand over her mouth and shook her head. When she took her hand away again, she said, "We should have a memorial event of some kind for her. I don't know what. But something."

"I'll help you organize it," Janet said, but she wasn't sure Gillian heard her.

"So many things to think about," Gillian was saying. "I'll have to find out how to do it all. The grant—what happens to it? And the programs. There'll be huge holes in the class schedules."

"You don't have to do anything about any of it right now," Tallie said. "None of it needs to be solved tonight."

"And none of it matters, now. It just doesn't." Gillian shook her head. "I've spent the last five years developing the literature enrichment program for the school. And my favorite part, the pet project I worked on for two years, was the author-in-residence program. I found the grant money. I recruited the selection committee. They researched a raft of authors, approached half a dozen, interviewed them, and chose Daphne. I couldn't have been prouder or more excited. Do you know, the entire committee cheered when she accepted? And all of that means nothing now, because she's gone. I hadn't seen her in so many years, and now she's gone and I'll never see her again."

Janet was beginning to plan for another unexpected overnight guest when Ian spoke up.

"Gillian, you might be interested in a theory I've come up with. Would you like to hear it?"

Gillian looked at Ian as though she wasn't sure why he was there.

"My theory is that this woman we've all been feting, the one you brought to town, is not the real Daphne Wood. What you just said about not seeing Daphne for so many years lends credence to the theory. Up until now, I only had anecdotal evidence, that being that she didn't know I live in Inversgail. The real Daphne Wood, world-renowned as she is, would almost certainly have done her homework before washing up on our shore again. She would have looked for other writers living in the area. She would have sought me out. This woman did not. Ergo, as they say, ipso facto."

Janet stood up before Ian finished speaking, ready to tackle him in whatever way might be necessary. "Fascinating, Ian. Thank you for stopping by."

Maida, with a wink to Janet, helped Ian take the hint. "I'll walk out with you, Ian. Gillian, my sincere condolences on the loss of your dear friend. I'll say a prayer for her and for you. Ian, after you."

Ian stopped at the door. "Point of interest, Janet. A remark I overheard the other day, about the tone of the neighborhood."

"What about the tone, Ian?"

"That it's been going down since the American invasion. I wouldn't lose any sleep over it, though. Just some neighborhood wag, I'm sure. Thanks for the tea."

"Pay him no mind," Maida said after he'd gone. "He made that remark himself."

Gillian came to the door with Tallie and a docile Rachel Carson.

"Are you sure you're all right for getting home?" Tallie asked.

"Aye. Thank you. I know I was off my head a bit earlier, like this wee lass, here, was. Ian's blather cleared all that away, but."

"Nice to know it was good for something," Janet said. "Call when you're ready to think about a memorial. Call any time."

∽

There were too few hours of sleep that night. While Janet was using caffeine to prop her eyes open the next morning, another postcard arrived from Sharon Davis. She was in Lucerne, Switzerland. This card only had seven words and two exclamation points. They were oddly apropos: *The cheese! Died and gone to heaven!*

22

Reddick and the Major Investigation Team knocked on the door of the tearoom shortly before they opened that morning.

"No, there have not been other reports of people falling ill after consuming food or drink at your business," the detective superintendent with the Major Investigation Team said in answer to Christine's question.

"By 'falling ill,' you mean dying, do you not?" Christine, at her frosty Elizabeth II best, asked. "Which begs my next question: What leads you to believe Daphne Wood's death can be attributed to Cakes and Tales?"

Reddick stepped forward smartly. "May I, sir?"

The detective superintendent appeared to struggle with his answer, but in the end only spit out the words, "You may."

Reddick inclined his head for Christine and the others to follow him from the tearoom into the bookshop. Janet was tempted to match his step, which was close to a march. She suspected Christine might be tempted, too, and didn't dare look at her. Laughing now would be as inappropriate and embarrassing as laughing at a funeral. Janet bit her cheek and kept her eyes on Summer's face, still pale with shock.

Reddick halted their procession a dozen or so feet into the bookshop and cast a glance toward the tearoom. Apparently satisfied, his posture relaxed a fraction.

"This information is not to be shared. May I have your word on that?" The four women nodded. "Early indications are that Ms. Wood ingested a poisonous substance. It's unknown, as yet, what that substance was or what transpired."

"If you don't know, then why are you here?" Summer asked.

"We had a report of Ms. Wood carrying home tea and scones from an event here yesterday. It's possible the substance was in one or both of them."

Summer had started shaking her head as soon as Reddick mentioned the tea and scones. "It isn't possible. It absolutely isn't. Other people were drinking from the same batch of tea and eating scones from the same trays, including Constable Hobbs." Summer's eyes narrowed. "He's the one who told you she took them, isn't he?"

Tallie put her hand on Summer's shoulder. "I don't think we really have anything to worry about, Summer. Am I right?"

"We're in the process of eliminating possibilities as much as looking for the source. We won't inconvenience you for long."

⁓

Janet waited until Reddick had returned to the tearoom and closed the door, then she looked at the others. "Fireplace? For a few minutes before we open the bookshop, anyway, so we can wrap our minds around this."

They sat in the comfy chairs, first looking at each other, then off into their own thoughts. Janet felt guilty for having imagined Daphne and Rachel Carson greedily gobbling scones the night before. While she'd been picturing that, Daphne had already been dead or dying.

She looked at each of the others again. Tallie was watching Summer. Summer wasn't relaxing into the soft chair. Christine looked ready to bite.

"An accident," Christine snapped. "The woman was lunatic enough to serve up houseplants. Who knows what she's been foraging in other people's gardens? It could have been an accident."

"The dog is fine?" Summer asked.

"She was freaked out," Tallie said. "Hungry, though. I wasn't sure what to feed her and ended up giving her a bowl of lentil soup. Kind of weird, but she ate it."

"Do you think the dog was bright enough not to touch the poisoned food?" Christine asked.

"Or snooty enough," Tallie said.

"An accident could make sense," Janet said. "Maybe something she ate interacted with a medication? Or could it have been suicide? Everyone has down times, but she seemed to have a switch that flipped more dramatically than others."

"Suicide is always a possibility, even for people we think we know," Christine said. "And we certainly didn't know her."

"But we do know she irritated a lot of people in a short amount of time," Tallie said, "and made some angry."

Summer sat forward. "It's that short time span that interests me. It seems *too* short. I'd ask who kills over insults and contrary opinions, but hothead crime is in the news all the time. But poison takes planning. A hothead might cool off before getting past step one."

"You think this might be someone who's been smoldering?" Janet asked.

"If they find poisoned scones at her place, then they weren't my scones," Summer said. "And that means someone not only planned, but also went to the trouble of baking."

"Of all the bloody nerve," Christine said. "Smoldering and then scheming with our scones."

◊

The police didn't stay long. The detective superintendent didn't communicate anything beyond letting them know they could open the tearoom and resume business. Reddick, apparently, had already left. Summer and Christine immediately went to see what damage had been done to their domain, Summer rolling up her sleeves, Christine fussing like a hen disturbed from her nest.

Rab and Ranger arrived as Janet unlocked the bookshop door. First things first, they went to Ranger's chair and Rab spread a bath towel on it.

"That's new," Janet said, nodding at the bath towel Ranger was walking circles on before settling.

"Second best," Rab said. "He prefers the Rangers tea towel. It's in the wash."

"Nice to have you back, Ranger," Tallie said. The dog yawned and Tallie turned to Rab. "You heard the news about Daphne?"

"Aye. Sad, that. I was afraid I might have to quit while she was here, but."

"You pretty much did," Janet said.

"Ranger didn't take to her. I was afraid she'd be stopping in here all hours and I didn't like to upset the lad."

"He didn't mind you coming in without him yesterday?" Tallie asked.

"Special circumstances. He wouldn't like being on his own too often. Bottom shelves need dusting. I'll just go—" A nod toward the far corner of the store finished the sentence.

Janet watched Rab drift off with a duster and thought, not for the first time, that his easy-oasy way of dealing with life's wobbles and peccadilloes might be healthier than most.

Their business came from tourists more than locals that morning. Janet told Tallie she was just as glad. Although repeated exchanges of wonder over the sudden death might add incremental layers to eventually cushion the shock, they were also exhausting. But without those layers laid down, she wasn't as prepared as she might have been when the door jingled and Martin Gunn came in. The bounce in his step had gone and his cheeks looked as though they might never glow pink again.

"Martin, hi, how are you?"

He flicked a half-smile at her, one that quickly sank.

"Shocking news," she said.

"Aye." He seemed to cast around for something else to say, and she couldn't blame him for coming up short. Then he stuck his arm out and waved vaguely in the direction of the tearoom. "The police were here?" He looked as though he couldn't bear to say more.

"All's well," Tallie said, coming to his rescue. "Eliminating possibilities, they said. Go on through. It's business as usual."

"Summer will be glad to see you," Janet added.

His cheeks did color slightly at that, but it wasn't the happy pink Janet had seen the morning after the ceilidh. He took himself off to the tearoom before she could study his mood further. Tallie excused herself to run inventory reports in the office. Janet, alone for the time being, practiced the syllable Martin and Rab shared in common, saying "aye" quietly to herself, trying it with various stolid, reserved, and unresolved emotions. It didn't seem to come naturally to her, though, and she wondered if the addition of a sigh would help.

"Are you all right?" Rab asked, suddenly there and looking at her with concerned eyebrows.

Janet put a hand to her chest. "Fine, yes. Startled, but fine."

He looked only slightly skeptical. "Have you got a wee moment?" He held up his phone. "There's something you might like to see. A blog post on one of Daphne's websites." He handed the phone across the counter to her.

"She had more than one site?"

"Modern communication."

"How did she have any?"

"She thanks her public library," Rab said.

"She had rude things to say about librarians." Feeling a scowl coming on, Janet took a calming breath and read the blog's headline and the first paragraph. "Well, good Lord, she doesn't pull any punches, does she? This is—" She didn't want to say what it was before reading through to the end. She handed the phone back to Rab. "Send me the address, will

you? I definitely want to read this, but I don't want to tie up your phone."
And she didn't want to spit invective all over it. "If you have her other
site addresses handy, send them, too, will you?"

Rab did some dexterous thumb work and slipped the phone into a
pocket.

"Do you think anyone at the paper has read that?" Janet asked.

"Could be. It's dated Saturday morning." He took a duster from
another pocket and stuffed it in the bag of others below the counter.

"Finished with the bottom shelves? Thank you."

"I'll finish tomorrow."

"Oh."

"I'll wash those dusters, too. Thought I'd see if they need me in the
tearoom just now."

"Oh." Janet knew few people would fault her for being annoyed that he
hadn't finished dusting, Christine among them. But she forgave him this
morning because he'd just helped her realize she had her own "aye" for
which she needed no practice. She took out her phone, navigated to the
web address Rab had sent, and with an "oh" expressing several emotions,
settled on the stool behind the counter.

Reading the blog post between customers helped Janet digest it.
Daphne was in rare, ranting form throughout, and smaller portions of
her vitriol were easier to take. She railed against reporters, editors, newspapers in general, and print newspapers, in particular. She framed her
rant by choosing the *Inversgail Guardian* as her prime example. She made
it specific by calling out James Haviland, and made it personal by calling
him names Janet had heard references to but never read or heard with
her own ears. When Tallie came out of the office, Janet sent her back in
to read it on the computer.

"Maybe reading it on the small screen intensified the vileness of it,"
Janet said. "See what you think."

What Tallie thought took longer to find out than Janet expected.

"Time suck," Tallie said when she came out of the office again. "Sorry about that. I read some of her other posts and took a look at her other sites. I'm not surprised by any of it, really. We heard the same kind of thing at the ceilidh. She definitely had her own slant. That's what a blog's good for, though. It's a personal soapbox, and you can skew things any way you want."

"She didn't just skew with the post about James and the *Guardian*, she skewered. Anyone at the paper who read it would be furious. I take it there's more like that?"

"She spread the wealth," Tallie said. "To put it politely and mildly, she was a committed environmentalist. I wonder if any of her targets found out she would be in Inversgail."

"And dropped in to see her? In that case, if we thought retracing her steps in Inversgail might help us figure out what happened—"

"It might not help at all. Her blog let her step on people all over the globe."

"It seems unlikely someone would come any great distance to kill her," Janet said. "But say someone flew in and then flew out again, how would we ever know? Check car rentals or hotel registries? We wouldn't know what we were looking for. That would be a dead end."

"And that's a bad term."

Early in the afternoon, Rab and Ranger called it a day. Rab gave a soft, short whistle. Ranger hopped down from his chair, took hold of the bath towel in his teeth, and followed Rab to the door. Rab took the towel from the dog and folded it. They left as Constable Hobbs entered, the dog and both men nodding as they passed.

Hobbs disappointed Janet by having no new information about Daphne's death, explaining that the Major Crime Team was still collecting and sifting information. She thought he might be buttering them up when he told her he would most likely get more and better information from them than he would from the specialists.

"Even from Reddick?" Janet asked. "That's disappointing. Do they have a working theory? I feel like we're in the dark and it's not a good feeling."

"They might be in the dark, as well," Hobbs said. "The DS wasn't interested in hearing that Ms. Wood was interested in Sam Smith's death."

"The DS?"

"The one you might refer to as 'the officious person in charge,' the detective superintendent."

"Dopey and shortsighted is more like it," Janet said. "Reddick knows she was asking questions, but if the DS isn't listening, he probably won't consider that we might be in danger, too."

"And that's why I'd like you to pass along any information you come across. I see that as a good way to avoid another homicide."

∽

"Jolly Norman," Christine said at the end of the day when Janet told her about his visit. "How comforting."

"It'll be a way for him to beat the specialists, too," Janet said. "And by him, I mean we. We did it last time and bloody well can again." She pounded a fist on the counter.

"I hadn't realized what a competitive streak you have," Christine said.

"It's for the greater good. We're really all on the same side."

"And now you sound like a politician."

"Heaven forbid. How did it go in the tearoom today? Any fallout from the search?"

"One or two comments about opening late," Christine said, "but no one mentioned police and neither did we."

"Martin did," Summer said, "but discreetly. And he shared a draft of his revamped article with me."

"Are they going to run it?" Janet asked. "I mean, as is, or rewrite it again? How sad and awkward."

"They could run it as is with a special note under the headline," Summer said. "Martin was in the dumps to begin with because he said James turned the article into a fluff piece. He got pretty emotional about it this morning. He'd spent a lot of time with Daphne, and felt as though he'd really gotten to know her. He said the cuts, especially now, feel like they're cutting away at her, personally."

"That's interesting," Tallie said.

"He said she talked a lot about honesty and truth and that resonated with him. *Resonated* is one of his favorite words, judging by how often he used it."

"Did you ask him if anything she said about honesty and truth resonated in particular?" Christine asked.

"She told him she lived in the woods because they're honest. More honest than cities or towns or the people in them. She also said her dog is more honest than most people."

"A Pekingese trimmed to look like a lion?" Janet asked.

"Her ideas of truth and honesty were interesting, to say the least," Christine said.

"And irritating," said Janet. "Depending on *who* they irritated, and how much, I wonder if they provide motives?"

"That's why I asked Martin if he'd share the *original* article with me," Summer said. "It might prove educational. He said he'd get it to me."

"You're brilliant," Janet said.

"And his notes. He said he'd get them to me, too."

❦

Ian Atkinson knocked on Janet's door that evening, bearing a package of dark chocolate digestive biscuits. Both were a surprise, the biscuits more pleasant than Ian. He told her he'd just met a deadline and he was coming up for air and thought he'd make the neighborly call he should have when she first arrived. Janet, though not fond of him, saw no point in being rude. She supposed the circumstances of the previous night's visit meant it hadn't counted as a neighborly welcome. Now, his timing was good. The kettle she'd put on started to whistle. She invited him in, accepted the biscuits with thanks, and after showing him to the living room, went to put the tea things on a tray. When she went back to the living room, he was standing at the back window.

"Tell me those aren't binoculars you have trained on Daphne's house," Janet said.

Startled, Ian whirled around. The binoculars were on a strap around his neck or he might have flung them like a discus.

"You can't use my living room for a stakeout, Ian. For goodness sake."

"You snuck up on me."

"I did not. Why do you even have binoculars with you, if this is your long-postponed social call? And don't tell me you've taken up birdwatching. What do you even hope to see?" She really did want to know and wondered if she'd already blown the chance to find out by scolding him.

"Not what. Who."

"What?"

"Who," Ian repeated. "And no, I haven't taken up birdwatching."

"Someone's in the house?" Janet couldn't help herself and went to the window. She couldn't see anything and first wondered if he was pulling her leg, then wondered if she still had the old binoculars her children had used to look for seals and pirate ships. "Is it the police?"

"No-o-o." Ian drew the word out as though they were playing a guessing game. "They finished their activities there this afternoon."

"Then it's Maida and she has every right to be there without being spied on."

"Nor is it Maida."

"Really? If it's someone who shouldn't be there, we should call Norman Hobbs."

Ian patted the binoculars and, with another of his insufferable smiles, pushed past Janet. "I knew you'd be interested," he said on his way to the door.

"Ian, who is it?"

Nose in the air, he said nothing and kept walking.

Janet hated herself for it, but she followed him. "Ian!"

He let himself out, but before closing the door poked his head back in. "No, dear neighbor, no. I will not tell."

After he closed the door, Janet gave it a good kick. Then she remembered she still had the digestives. Reveling in that minor victory, she poured the tea and put three biscuits on her saucer. She'd just made herself comfortable, when her phone rang. It was Gillian, sounding as though she was calling from the bottom of a deep well.

"I can hardly hear you, Gillian. What is it?"

"Tom. It's Tom. He's gone missing."

23

Gillian's voice crawled back up from whatever depth it had sunk to, and now came through clearly in the short, staccato bursts of someone close to panic. She said she'd rung Tom after leaving Janet's the night before and he hadn't answered. She'd left a message, assuming he'd return the call or that they'd talk in the morning before school.

"But he didn't ring back. He didn't answer this morning, either. I went by his house. His car was gone. I thought he'd gone on to school. I wasn't overly worried. It's not like we're in each other's pockets. But he wasn't at school. I asked in the office if they'd had a message. They hadn't. Then I went to *his* office. The message light was blinking on his phone. I listened. It was Daphne. It was like listening to a ghost. A nasty, malevolent ghost."

Daphne's message had been demeaning and rude, completely rejecting Tom's suggestion that they work together on a calendar or any other project.

"But working together was *her* idea. Not his," Gillian said. "And then, just before she disconnected, there was something in the background. A noise. Knocking. I don't know what. And she said, 'So *that's* why you're not answering. What a waste of good invective.'"

"She had a nasty streak," Janet said. "I've tried to think of it as tone-deaf, but in the end, it doesn't matter why she said things like that. If you were on the receiving end, it was nasty. What did you do after hearing the message?"

"I lied. I told the office he was home sick and needed a substitute. No one questioned it."

Gillian's biggest worry was that Tom had reacted by taking himself off on a photo shoot that turned into a drinking binge, that he'd had an accident and lay somewhere in the wilderness needing help. Janet thought that was either a sweet and touching worry, or a naïve one. *Or maybe I'm projecting,* she thought. *But with Daphne dead, the author program ruined, and Tom missing, shouldn't her biggest worry be that Tom killed Daphne and ran?*

"Gillian," Janet said, "you need to call Norman Hobbs."

∞

"Tom Laing," Christine said the next morning, after Janet told her business partners about Ian's visit and Gillian's call. "We need to know who Ian saw. I bet it was Tom Laing."

"Why?" Janet asked.

"Retrieving incriminating evidence."

"Surely the police have someone watching Daphne's house in case something like that happens."

"They might not for any number of reasons. Limited manpower? Limited imagination?"

"Or they have a pretty good idea about what happened, and we haven't heard yet," Tallie said. "Why was Ian spying from our living room, anyway? He could've done it from the backyard or sneaked over and looked through the windows."

"He was showing off," Janet said. "He's a silly man and he wants us to think he's up to something."

"Like trying to solve the crime himself?" Summer asked.

"Lord love a duck," Janet said. "A sense of doom is settling over me."

"That's exactly why we need to know who Ian saw," Christine said.

"If he saw anyone at all," Janet said. "But I'm not asking him. He annoys the hel—the haggis out of me."

"Maybe he'll fall for the same kind of malarkey you did last night," Tallie said, "with a phony, neighborly story. We must have some of his books that he hasn't scrawled in yet. Let's ask him to come in and sign stock."

"I don't fall for malarkey," Janet said. She wanted to stamp her foot, but had the feeling that would only further convince them that she did.

"Catch up to us, Janet," Christine said. "You had information within reach yesterday and lost it—"

"Through no fault of my own."

"Absolutely right," Christine said. "Entirely through the fault of the conniving horse's arse next door, and now we're making plans to recover that information."

"Lure him with books and soften him up with tea?" Summer asked.

"What do you think, Mom?"

"It'll get him in the shop, but I'm not sure he'll answer our questions."

"Not *our* questions," Summer said. "Mine. You lure and leave the rest to me." She took her tablet from her purse and poised her fingers. "You want to know who he saw. Anything else, while I'm at it?"

"He said he saw a man leaving with Daphne in her truck last Monday night," Janet said.

"That might have been Martin." Summer entered notes on the tablet without looking up. "He spent a lot of time with her when he was working on the interview."

"Or was it Tom?" Tallie asked. "Poor Gillian."

"Speaking of Tom, or Toms," Christine said, "there might be another explanation for Ian's behavior. Perhaps he did stop by to be neighborly, but only thought of it on his way home from using his binoculars some-where else. Maybe he's found his true calling as a Peeping Tom."

"We don't know he is one," Janet said. "It seems like an odd thing for Maida to know."

"Odd people know odd things," Christine said.

"True. I guess it's nice to know she's good at keeping secrets," Janet said. "Half-secrets, anyway."

"Nonsense," Christine said. "Half a secret is as bad, or worse, than finding half a worm in an apple. They breed distrust and could lead to paranoia. And not knowing for sure that Ian is a Peeping Tom is all the harder for *us*, because we're so firmly on the side of all that is good. It means we can't ask everyone we meet if they know what Ian has done to be labeled a Peeping Tom. Talk about worms; that could open a can of the worst. It wouldn't do at all."

"It wouldn't," Janet said. "That's why I didn't ask Norman about Ian specifically when I asked about Peeping Toms. But that pest seems to know an awful lot about the comings and goings at Daphne's house."

"Here's a new theory, then," Christine said. "There might have been an evolution to this hobby of his. As a writer, he probably stared out his window a great deal. Being observant, he might have developed a habit of watching the neighborhood go by. He showed up on Janet's doorstep to kick it up a notch."

"Or he's just plain nosy," Summer said. "I'll see what I can find out."

"And if it works," Tallie said, "then we can try the same thing with Maida and find out how she knows what she knows."

෴

"We did it," Tallie said, nudging Janet later that morning. "Here he comes."

Janet looked up from the review journal she was reading. The door jingled and Ian stepped in. Janet took it as a good sign that he'd worn another of his "author outfits." Today, it was a dark turtleneck, black jeans, and his chukkas—author casual. Tallie went to meet him.

"Thanks for coming in, Ian," Tallie said, putting her arm through his. "Why don't we take the books into the café, where you can be comfortable? Maybe Summer can give you a cup of tea."

Janet thought taking the arm might be going a tad far, but Ian seemed pleased. The suggestion of tea pleased him further, so good. Also by plan, Tallie stayed in the tearoom to help Christine with customers, so Summer could take tea and a plate of scones to Ian and then "help" by handing him books to sign one by one.

While the plot unfolded in the other room, a man approached Janet at the sales counter. "I wish to lodge a complaint."

Drawing on her years of dealing with the public, Janet met the man's supercilious eyebrows with a calm, steady gaze. She smiled, but felt her cheeks grow warm with the effort not to laugh. The man, unusually tall and wearing a tan trench coat, looked and sounded so much like John Cleese, she half-expected him to plunk a birdcage with a dead parrot in it on the counter.

"How may I be of assistance?" she asked. And now she was talking like someone out of a BBC sitcom. Her cheeks grew warmer.

"Was that a scone from the tearoom you were eating a moment ago?" the man asked. "If it was, then I think you're taking unfair advantage by flaunting baked goods in the faces of your customers."

A woman came over and put her arm through his. When he opened his mouth to say more, she pulled his arm firmly to her side. "Sorry," she said. "I hope you'll excuse my husband. He thinks he's funny and he's just been put on a diet. Not the best combination."

Her husband harrumphed, but reached over and patted her hand.

"Do you have any of those coloring books for grownups?" the woman asked.

"The *Highlands and Islands Colouring Book* is popular," Janet said.

"Something like that might take his mind off the diet." She put her free hand up in a mock aside and whispered, "Or mine."

"Something like a good single malt would do it faster," her husband said.

Janet led them to the arts and crafts section, but along the way they passed too tantalizingly close to the local guide books. These included several on the history and making of whisky.

"We've found my alley," the man said, slowing down. "And the books right up it." He stopped in front of an oversized photographic history of the whiskies of Islay. Leaning toward it, he drew in a breath with his mouth slightly open. "The proper way to nose whisky," he said. "Nosing allows you to actually taste the aroma."

"We're cutting back in this area, too," his wife said with an apologetic smile for Janet. She tugged on the elbow still tucked in hers, got her husband moving again, and towed him along in her wake.

When they reached the display of coloring books, Janet pointed out their bestsellers, the markers, and a new line of colored pencils they were trying. The man was clearly not interested. He wanted to know why they'd come at all if so much of the Highland experience was off limits. His wife shushed him.

"Do you like crime novels?" Janet asked in a moment of inspiration. "Let me show you a series by a local writer that should also be right up your alley. Have you heard of Ian Atkinson and his Single Malt Mysteries?"

Half an hour later, the couple came back to the counter to pay. The woman had two coloring books, a set of markers, and one of Daphne Wood's books. The man had a full set of the Single Malt Mysteries.

"A stroke of luck arriving while this fellow was having tea here," the man said, "and jolly nice of him to sign them and chat with us for as long as he did. I told him that if I can't have my dram, I'll bloody well read about it. He said he might use that line in the next book."

"Wonderful," Janet said. She hoped the pleasant encounter had further softened Ian up for Summer's questions. She slipped a Yon Bonnie bookmark into one of the mysteries.

"Free?" the man asked. Janet smiled and nodded. "One for each then, if you don't mind." He helped himself from the stack next to the register.

"He's big on free souvenirs," the woman said.

"How nice." Janet wondered whether the woman was apologizing or bragging.

Summer appeared shortly after the couple left, and she was definitely apologizing.

"He knew exactly what we were doing," she said. She'd opened all the books for him. Then, he'd made a huge production out of talking to his "newest number one fan." He'd had the nerve to ask for more scones, and then she hadn't gotten beyond asking him who he'd seen the night before when he hit her with a counterproposal: "He'll tell us who he saw, if we tell him what we know about a secret whisky society."

Janet felt slack-jawed. "What?"

"I told him that *huh?* is the sum total of what we know. I could tell he didn't believe me. He played along with it, though, and then said that we can just tell him what we find out. Sorry, Janet."

"Don't even think about apologizing for something that horse's—" Janet stopped when she remembered there were children in the bookshop. "You told Christine and Tallie?"

"Christine finished what you were just about to say. Quietly, but with feeling."

Not long after that, Janet had a chance to hear Christine say it herself, and shushed her.

"He's just so incredibly irritating," Christine said.

"I hear you. But here's something to take your mind off him. I got another postcard from Sharon."

"I had no idea you two were such great pen pals," Christine said.

"It's news to me, too."

"Where is she now?"

"In Amsterdam. She says she's being delightfully shocked by the red light district."

"That's what I've always said about you, too."

"You've said what?" Janet asked.

"That librarians know how to get wild." Christine held out her hand. "Or maybe they don't, and that's why she's shocked. May I see it? I haven't been to Amsterdam in decades."

"Hang on, I'll bring it back up." Janet handed her phone to Christine.

"*Electronic*? This isn't nearly as much fun as getting a picture of the red light district through the post and picturing the postie going goggle-eyed. Besides, I thought she was going someplace warm and sunny."

"Maybe the girls in the red light district have sun lamps," Janet said.

∞

Gillian called while they were closing for the day and reported that Rachel Carson wasn't eating. "I think she's in mourning, like Greyfriars Bobby," she said, and then she burst into tears.

Janet hushed rather than shushed her, and Gillian eventually calmed. Janet asked if she'd heard from Tom, and though tears threatened to erupt again, Gillian said no. She also hadn't called Norman Hobbs.

"Gillian, you must," Janet said.

"I know. I will."

"Please don't put it off. What are you going to do about Rachel Carson?"

"I don't know. Can you—"

Janet jumped in before Gillian finished. "I'll see if I can find someone else to take her, Gillian. In the meantime, see if she'll eat lentil soup. Or haggis balls."

"Problems with the dog?" Christine asked after Janet disconnected. "Why don't you take her? She'd be a companion for you."

"She'd be a dog," Janet said. "I want a cat." It was the first time she'd said it aloud and she suddenly realized it was true. "I always had a cat back home. But the last dear old guy died right before my marriage did, and it's taken this long for me to want to commit to another."

Summer, on her way to the office, did a double-take. "I know you didn't, but for a second there, for a nanosecond, I thought you said, 'It's taken this long for me to want to commit murder.'"

Tallie had been counting down the cash drawer during Gillian's phone call. She chuckled with the others over Summer's mistake. When

she finished counting, she asked Janet what the rest of Gillian's call had
been about.

"She hasn't heard from Tom and she hasn't called Norman. I told her
she needed to."

"Good," Tallie said. "And if she doesn't, we need to."

"Agreed," Christine said.

"My thinking, too," Janet said. "I'll call him when I get home. I'll tell
him I told her to call, and see what he says."

That evening, Tallie and Summer went to a talk at the library about
supernatural water creatures in Scottish folklore. They invited Janet
to go with them, and another time she would have been happy to, but
the problems of encountering water kelpies seemed less pressing than
her more immediate worries. Finding another home for Rachel Carson
didn't make the grade, either. Calling Norman Hobbs came first, and
she did that after waving Tallie off.

"Thank you, Mrs. Marsh," Hobbs said when she told him why she'd
called. "Ms. Bennett told me you encouraged her to contact me."

"She told you about Tom?"

"I'm sure you know our conversation was confidential, but you should
also know that Tom Laing is now officially missing." Hobbs hesitated.
"This next information is not yet official; Tom Laing is a suspect in the
death of Daphne Wood. I'm advising you and your business partners to
be careful, Mrs. Marsh. We don't know where he is, but he knows where
you are. If her death is connected to her supposed investigation, he might
have heard of your supposed involvement."

They were both silent for a moment.

"Mrs. Marsh?"

"How long before it'll be official that he's a suspect?"

"I don't have that information, but I shouldn't think long."

"There are a couple of things I should tell you, Norman. The first
is that Ian Atkinson says he saw someone in Daphne's house last night.
He wouldn't say who it was. I told him he should call you. *I* should have

called you, but he treated it like a game and there's no knowing what that infuriating man is ever really up to, or if what he says is true. The second is something I hadn't thought important before, but now I wonder."

"If someone was in Ms. Wood's house, that information was also important."

"Which goes to show that you think like the professional you are, and I think like a retired librarian turned bookseller."

"Who channels Miss Marple."

"Please don't stoop to sarcasm, Norman. Do you know how many people read mysteries? The mystery genre is second only to romance in sales and readership, and every one of those mystery readers is an amateur sleuth. We are legion in number. Many of us are bright and good at solving puzzles and also ready and willing to help the professionals. But we have feelings, so when we make mistakes, we would appreciate some understanding. Do I need to remind you that you make mistakes, too?" She felt a twinge of guilt for bringing up the unusual stopgap and very sneaky housing plan Hobbs had hatched shortly after she and the others arrived in Inversgail.

"No."

"Good." She shook off the twinge. "Now, to make up for my earlier lapse, let me tell you about this other thing, and then I'll let you go.

"When Reddick came into the shop, immediately after Sam Smith's death, one of the questions he asked, almost as an afterthought, was if we knew anything about a whisky society. None of us did. The way he asked, his question might have been totally unrelated to the case. Then, today, Ian asked what we know about a secret whisky society. When we said we didn't know anything at all, he offered an information exchange. He would tell us who he saw last night if we tell him what we can find out about the society. Summer thinks he could be trying to solve the case—or, at this point, cases—himself. But what that has to do with a whisky society, I have no idea." Janet laughed lightly at that, thinking it sounded fairly preposterous. "Do *you* know anything about a secret whisky society, Norman?"

"I have to ring off, now, Mrs. Marsh," Hobbs said, and he was gone.

24

J anet opened her laptop and then a blank document and typed a
summary of her conversation with Hobbs, including the way he'd
ended the call. She'd gotten the distinct impression that he'd rung
off so abruptly in reaction to her information and question about the
whisky society. So what was this society? If it was secret, how had Reddick
and Ian both heard about it? And, perhaps more intriguing, why did Ian
need their help to find out about it? She glanced at the time—later than
she'd expected—and started a new document.

∽

The next morning, the four women stood in their accustomed spots for
their before-hours meeting in the communicating doorway between the
two shops. Janet liked to think of that space as being between a teapot
and a bookcase. Before going to bed the previous night, she'd saved her
new documents and the transcription of their conversation in Nev's to a
cloud account, and then let the others know the documents were there.

Tallie and Summer had created the account for their first (and only
other) "investigation." Janet put mental quotation marks around the
word, not because it didn't accurately describe what they'd done, but
because it was a label. Labels had a way of making things, whether they
were concrete or abstract, more real, like "divorce" and "my husband,

Curtis-the-rat." Janet, being a librarian, liked labels, but in her experience, they needed to be assigned carefully. Not only did they make things more real, but they tended to freight them with consequences. That was why a question from Christine startled her.

"The way you laid things out is quite logical," Christine said. "But before we go further, shall we vote on calling ourselves the SCONES? Private use only. Show of hands for aye?" She raised a hand. So did Tallie and Summer.

"I only included it so we'd have an accurate record of our interactions with Daphne," Janet said. No hands came down. "I don't think she was being complimentary." she added. "There *is* something about it, though."

"It's lightly snarky, over a layer of accuracy, with a dash of subterfuge," Summer said.

"Plus, it's baked goods," Christine said. "If anyone overhears us, it'll be free advertising."

Janet shrugged and put her hand up, too.

"You do all realize that Mom's second document can be seen more as a series of rationalizations than as a list of appropriate and justified actions, don't you?" Tallie asked.

"Don't you think we have a good reason to make ourselves as aware of the evolving situation as possible?" Janet asked.

"I do, absolutely," Tallie said. "I'm just offering a lawyerly perspective."

"The devil's perspective, as it were," Christine said, "but it's good to be aware of that, too."

Summer had the second document open on her tablet, and tapped a finger on her lips as she read it again. "This question. 'Should we warn Ian that Tom is a suspect?'"

"A moral dilemma," Christine said.

"Kind of a hedgehog's dilemma," Summer said. "Get too close to him, and it can be trouble."

"But I think it isn't *our* dilemma," Janet said. "We've done our duty by letting Norman know Ian might have seen someone."

"Passing the torch of responsibility on to Norman," Tallie said.

"Norman warned us," Janet said. "I think we can trust him to warn Ian. He told us to be careful, and the best way to do that is to have as much information as possible, be fully aware, alert at all times."

"We sound like a troop of meerkats," Tallie said, and then at a slightly aggrieved look from her mother, "but it's better than being a quartet of ostriches. I wonder how wombats react to danger?"

"Dive into their holes and plug them with their rumps," Summer said without glancing up from her tablet. "Wombat Wisdom 101."

Tallie intercepted another look from Janet. "Let's not mix zoology with baked goods. SCONES it is. What's our first step?"

"We know Ian plays games," Janet said. "We don't know if he's playing one now. If he is, though, then the best way to keep from getting mixed up in it is to refuse to play along. We'll let Norman handle the question of who Ian saw in the house. But it might be interesting to find out about this whisky society, and important to know more about Tom Laing."

"Speaking of subterfuge, a wee bit of judicious pressure on Norman might yield results on this society," Christine said. "He still owes you for not exposing his own subterfuge, doesn't he? The Hobbs housing scheme for innocent and unsuspecting grannies." She rubbed her hands, looking conspiratorial and slightly wicked.

Janet felt like rubbing her own hands and saying, "Excellent." Instead, she said, "Let's see what we can find out on our own, first. I'm happy to take advantage of Norman, but just because Ian hasn't had any luck finding out about a whisky society doesn't mean we won't. People might not tell Ian on general principle."

Ian, an incomer from Slough, near London, had arrived in Inversgail a decade earlier. As far as Janet could tell, he hadn't developed a circle of friends, and she wasn't sure if that was entirely by design. He talked about falling in love with Inversgail and the Highlands when he'd come north to research the background for his Single Malt Mysteries. He also sighed and excused his "antisocial ways" as being the lot of a successful writer. He wasn't as blunt, or rude, as Daphne had been, but Janet noticed he often seemed to be on the wrong footing with the people around him. To look on the positive side, she thought the tensions and conflicts he created might provide inspiration for his work.

"Finding out more about Tom is probably our first priority," Janet said.

"Did Norman say he's a suspect in both deaths?" Tallie asked.

"He didn't, and I didn't ask." Janet made an irritated noise. "I should have."

"If you had, he might not have told you," Tallie said. "There's been very little obvious activity and very little said about Sam Smith's death, either by the police or around town. It feels to me as though the specialists think they already have a case, but they're waiting for something. Final pieces to confirm it, maybe. Cause of death might be one of those."

"Tom's disappearance might be another," Summer said. "Not that they were waiting for him to disappear. It puts egg on their faces if he turns out to be guilty, though, doesn't it? I'll see what James can tell me about Tom. He knows him through his photography."

"I'll ask Basant," Tallie said. "If he knows Tom at all, he might know quite a lot."

"Basant the font," Christine said. "I'll go to my own font of information."

"Danny?" Tallie asked.

"Danny, too, but I was thinking of Mum and Dad. It might take time to break through the fog of memory, but what they don't know from their years as district nurse and head teacher, or haven't heard since in their years of good works and going down the pub, wouldn't fill a saucer. What's your plan, Janet?"

"I told Gillian I'd help her organize a memorial for Daphne. I'll use that as an excuse to contact people at the high school and in the GREAT-SCOTS."

"While we're at it, shall we ask about the whisky society, too?" Tallie asked.

"Yes." Janet looked at each of the others. "But we all need to be careful—about the questions we ask and the places we go. That was the point of Norman's warning."

"It's also the point of asking the questions," Summer said. "But don't worry." She held up her tablet. "Texts are a great way to travel when you have a business to run. We can stay right here, armed to the teeth with our books and our teapots."

∽

"We have another font of information," Tallie said, after she and Janet opened the shop for the day. She nudged her mother and nodded with her chin at Rab, arranging Ranger's second-best towel on his chair.

Janet answered with a distracted, "Mm."

"Or we could discuss things with the wombat in the window."

"Mm." Janet looked at her daughter. "What?"

"What are you stewing about?"

"Oh. I just wish Summer hadn't said 'armed to the teeth.' It gave me a small case of the heebie-jeebies."

"I've never known you to be superstitious."

"A dash. Not even a whole dash. A half-dash, at most. Or a sprinkle."

Tallie turned Janet to face her and put a hand on each shoulder. "You might very well have that half-dash or sprinkle, but what you're feeling today is worry and healthy fear. It's why Norman warned you and why you reminded us to be careful. And you've been thinking about this since you talked to him last night, so you're ahead of the rest of us on the worry and fear curve, which you tend to be ahead on, anyway. Why don't we practice a few careful questions on Rab, and then you can go in the office and start calling people about the memorial? You need more action, Mom, and less stewing."

"Right." Janet turned to look for Rab and almost jumped. He and his easy half-smile stood patiently on the other side of the counter. "Good morning, Rab. We're wondering if you've heard that Tom Laing is missing."

"Aye."

"From what I know of him, it seems out of character."

"Aye."

Janet didn't look at Tallie, but imagined she was about to sputter or laugh out loud at her "practice" questions and Rab's responses. She decided to switch topics and tactics. "Have you ever heard of a secret whisky society in Inversgail?"

Rab's half-smile drifted toward uneasy. "Och, well, I've just remembered—" But rather than say what he'd remembered, he whistled for Ranger. The dog took the towel in his teeth and brought it to Rab. "I'll be back this afternoon," he said as he folded the towel. "Might be tomorrow." And man and dog were gone.

"The biggest conversation-stopper in Inversgail," Janet said. "Curiouser and curiouser."

"Let's make a note and be sure to tell the others: if we want to ask more than one question, don't start with the whisky society."

∞

Janet took Tallie's advice and spent time in the office that morning. Rather than make phone calls about a memorial for Daphne, though, she started another document, labeled it "Theories," and gave free rein to the possibilities stewing in her head.

THEORIES: Tom killed Sam Smith for whatever reason. Daphne found out. She was going to tell the police. Tom killed her, panicked, and ran.

OR: They were in it together. Daphne arrived in town earlier than we thought. She killed Sam Smith for whatever reason.

With her sword because she said she'd try anything once? (Does she have a real sword?) (Was she that nutty?) The sword didn't kill him immediately, so Tom hit him with the brick. But what if she actually had a motive? Did she know Smith? She claimed to know his family. Did she know anyone at the party that night at Nev's?

BUT: The end is the same for both theories. Tom killed Daphne because she was going to talk. Then he panicked and ran. Evidence? Slim. He was at Nev's that night. He threw punches. He and Daphne went on photo shoots together. Then she turned on him.

QUESTION: Why would Tom be cool about the first murder and panic over the second?

OR: Daphne didn't mellow over time. She sharpened. The rough edges of her personality weren't rubbed off by constant contact with other people. She didn't live out in the wilds all those years because she was an ardent environmentalist or some kind of modern me-Jane heroine. She was there because, if she wasn't, someone, somewhere would want to kill her. Is that what happened?

OR: Was there anyone, besides Gillian, responsible for bringing Daphne to Inversgail? Gillian said she found the grant money, and put the committee together, but did someone else have input? Who suggested Daphne as the author? Was her invitation above board or was it orchestrated? Maybe the person who killed her had no way of getting to her in Canada. What's the motive? An old wound that festered? Or reopened? Something Daphne did? How? When? Through social media? What if someone wanted her here for a confrontation, but it turned into murder?

Janet sat back after pounding her keys. *Stream of consciousness sleuthing*, she thought. *But where did it get me?* She saved the document to the cloud and went back out front to spend time with the things she understood and trusted—books, family, and friends.

"How'd it go?" Tallie asked.

Janet told her about her theories document. "It's a somewhat-organized stew," she said. "Possibilities, with overtones of *hmmm*. I'm sure there's a pinch of *hoo-boy* in it, too. And I didn't make calls to organize the memorial, because I haven't heard from Gillian to know what she has in mind."

"I wonder how she's holding up."

"I wonder if she knows Tom's a sus—" Janet stopped herself, not knowing if there were customers within earshot.

"You're fine," Tallie said. "Quiet morning here. In the tearoom, too. Summer had time to ask James a few questions about Tom."

"What did she find out?"

"How hard it is to start a casual text conversation with a newspaper editor and ask questions about someone under suspicion without raising suspicions. She ended up telling him text-time was over and teatime was in full swing, but she wasn't real happy lying about it."

"Did you get a chance to text Basant?"

"Yes, but I didn't, because I was going to have the same problem as Summer."

"What a thoroughly modern pickle to be in," Janet said.

"With an easy, old-fashioned solution that it took our genius Christine to point out."

25

"To the synergy that is Nev's," Christine said that evening, lifting a half pint. "The mutually advantageous conjunction of neighbors, news, and a comfortable place to share them."

To the casual listener, Christine's toast was a pleasant tribute to her local. To the SCONES, it described the workings of their information hub. Janet, Tallie, and Summer raised their glasses to the toast, then got down to business. Tallie and Summer went through to the darts room. Christine joined her parents and a few of their neighbors at a table near the door, where they liked to sit so they could see and comment on who came and went. Janet took her glass to the far end of the room and sat down with Gillian, Hope, and Rhona.

"This was a good idea, Janet," Gillian said. "Gets us out, gets us together." She sat with her elbows on the table, hands clasped below her chin. "It's been such a shock." She bent her head to rest her cheek on her hands.

"Aye, thanks," Rhona said. "A memorial's the right thing to do, and I'm happy to be part of it. I wasn't sure I liked Daphne. I certainly didn't like her remarks at the ceilidh about the GREAT-SCOTS, but I've learned the value of digging deeper and looking beneath the surface. I wish I'd had the chance to know her better."

"And you'd like the chance to take her place as visiting author," Hope said without looking up from her glass. "I saw your note offering to fill in now she's gone. You might not know, but I was on Gillian's author selection committee. Daphne was by far the best candidate. What have you written? Articles for a newsletter? Not exactly literature."

"It's still considered writing, last I heard," Rhona said.

"And I asked her to write the note offering to fill in," Gillian said. "It's an easy fix to the problem and we need to move forward. For the sake of the students."

"I hadn't realized there was an application process for choosing the author," Janet said. "I thought you said the selection committee approached the candidates."

"For the sake of the students, is it?" Hope said, as though Janet hadn't spoken.

"Someone has to fill in," Gillian said mildly, then turned to Janet. "The author selection committee identified and approached some candidates and also took applications. They did a great job, but ultimately, I'm in charge of the grant. We need to move forward."

Rhona crossed her arms over her chest, her shoulders rising slightly. But the argument, if it was one, didn't bother Gillian enough for her to lift her cheek from her knitted hands. Janet didn't know if the tension between the women was old chemistry or fallout from the shock of Daphne's death. It might be a mixture of both, but whatever tensions or emotions were stirring at the table, she was fairly certain Gillian still didn't know the police considered Tom a suspect. Otherwise, how could she sit so calmly? And then she wondered why *no one* seemed to know he was a suspect.

Janet took out her phone and sent a group text to the SCONES. "if tom is missing & a suspect why no hue & cry to find him from police?" When she looked up from her phone, she knew she'd missed something.

"No," Gillian said. Her back was straight, her forearms on the table, the fingers of each hand curled. The look in her eye offered a challenge to Rhona. "He can't make it."

"Are we talking about Tom?" Janet asked.

"What?" Gillian turned the challenge toward her.

"I asked about her dad," Rhona explained to Janet. "I asked if Alistair is coming along tonight."

"But what about Tom?" Hope asked. "Why aren't we talking about him?"

"Photo shoot," Gillian said, her hands going to her lap. "He's on a photo shoot."

"Where? And missing classes?" Hope hadn't once looked up from her glass and couldn't have seen, as Janet did, how each question made Gillian look more miserable. "He didn't say anything about being away. He's not answering his mobile. He always takes my calls. Is he taking yours, Gillian?"

"Can't you leave it?" Gillian said. "He's on a photo shoot and he'll be back soon enough. End of story."

"You don't expect anyone to believe that at this point, do you?" Hope asked. Now she did look at Gillian, and Janet could see that Hope's eyebrows certainly didn't believe it.

∞

Janet went to join Christine and her parents at their table near the door. "Is the memorial well and thoroughly planned?" Christine asked when Janet dropped into the chair beside her.

"We tabled the idea for the evening," Janet said. "I'll tell you about it later." She greeted Christine's parents, Helen and David. David introduced her to the other couple at the table and they all made polite noises at each other.

"When it comes time to plan my memorial," Helen said, "I hope you'll remember . . ." She turned to David. "What was it I want remembered?"

"Next time you think of it, we'll write it down," David said.

"And forget where we've written it, like as not," said Helen.

While Helen, David, and the other couple laughed, Janet quietly asked Christine if she had read the text she'd sent. "No one answered," she said.

"I was beginning to wonder—" Her phone buzzed and she pulled it out. "Here's Tallie. She says, 'good question.'"

"You often ask brilliant questions," Christine said. "I look forward to hearing the answer to that one. In the meantime, I asked my own."

Janet looked at her phone again. "I don't think I got it."

"Something I asked Danny, and he said yes."

Janet put a hand to her chest.

"Good Lord, no," Christine said. "You should know better than that. No, when he gets a chance, he'll take us out back to see where he found Sam Smith."

Janet mouthed a silent, "Oh."

"Here he is now," Christine said, nudging Janet's elbow.

While Christine told her parents they'd be back shortly, Janet sent a text letting Tallie and Summer know where they were going. Then they followed Danny behind the bar and through the kitchen, where a lank young man with an enormous pair of tongs conjured the warm smell of fish from a bubbling deep fat fryer. They passed through a small office, a back room, and on out the back door. Janet didn't ask why they were going to see where Sam Smith had died, but she doubted Christine was hunting for auras.

"Can this be called a wynd?" Janet asked when they stepped outside into what she would call an alley. It was wide enough for a single vehicle.

"A wynd? A bit posh, but you could call it that, if you like," Danny said. "After finding that poor lad, and after finding Daftie Daphne back here gawking, acting like she might sell tickets to the tourists, I was ready to call it a pain in the arse. There's where he was."

They stared at an unremarkable patch of ground near the back door. Janet did feel something, but unless she'd suddenly gained supernatural senses, she knew it was just the unutterable sadness of Sam's death.

"We saw Tom leave with Gillian that night," Christine said. "So he must have come back. Did she come back with him?"

"I didn't see her," Danny said.

"Did Tom know anyone in the party? Did he join them?" Janet asked.

"I'll tell you what I told the police. He joined them with a fist or two, after they'd gone outside, and that's the first I noticed he had anything to do with them. Do I know what the argument was about? No."

"Have you seen anyone from the party here since then?" Christine asked.

"Except that they'd be young men who aren't regulars, I wouldn't recognize them."

"Could Daphne have been here that night?" Christine asked.

"I don't think she could slip in anywhere unnoticed. The dog certainly couldn't."

Janet walked to the corner of the building, where a space narrower than her own front path separated Nev's from the newspaper building. "He could've walked down the alley or come through this passage. But why? Was he chased? When you broke up the fight—"

"High spirits gone awry, is all," Danny said. "It was hardly started when I sent them outside, and over before anyone bloodied a nose or blackened an eye."

Janet started down the passage toward the street. Danny and Christine followed.

"James and Martin said they heard the noise next door," Christine said. "Sound and fury?"

"And came to naught," said Danny. "It didn't take more than threatening to call the police and they were gone. That's what I thought, anyway, until I found the poor bugger. Then I thought one or two of the lads had gone too far."

"But the police have cleared them," Janet said. "As far as we know."

Heading toward the lit street, the passage wasn't a frightening place. There was a minor amount of litter, unidentifiable bits of urban detritus. They passed a window and a door in the *Guardian*'s wall, the window long-since bricked up.

"Where did the brick come from?" Janet asked as they emerged onto the pavement in front of the businesses.

"There's always been some back there," Danny said. "Leftovers from this and that. The sort of thing you hang onto, if it isn't in the way, because you never know."

They stood on the pavement looking back at the passage. From this end, with the streetlight only reaching so far, it wasn't an appealing space. *The sort of space I wouldn't enter at night, if I didn't have a very good reason,* Janet thought, *because you never know.*

"What happened when you broke up the argument?" Christine asked.

"They took off running."

Janet tried to picture the chaotic scene. "Did Tom run?"

"I've never known Tom to run from anything. He stood, just there, and laughed."

"Just where?" Janet asked.

Danny moved to the mouth of the passage. "Here."

"Evening, all," James Haviland greeted them. "You gave us a start, popping out from between that way." He stepped away from the front of Nev's, and Janet saw that Martin was with him. She hadn't noticed them, but she'd been focused on the passageway.

"Did I hear you mention Tom?" James asked. "Have you seen him?"

"Sunday," Janet said. "At the signing." She wondered about the intent of his question. *The idle curiosity of a friend? The sniff of a newshound?*

"Sunday. Aye." James craned his head to look past Danny, who hadn't moved from the opening of the dark passage. "He's a good man. I count on his photographs." He straightened. "Well, if you see him, tell him we're on deadline."

∽

Before rejoining Helen and David, Janet and Christine went to catch up with Tallie and Summer in a corner of the darts room. "Officially missing, but the press doesn't know?" Janet asked. "How can that be?"

"I'm willing to bet James knows," Summer said. "We danced around each other with the same kinds of questions, but we didn't ask and we didn't tell. I think Martin caught onto that. Maybe if I went over and caught James alone in his office—"

"Not alone and not tonight, please," Janet said.

"Which I was about to say."

"Good."

"We do have to trust some people, though, Mom," Tallie said.

"Trust can be a slippery devil." Christine put an arm around Tallie's shoulders. "And hope a false prophet. I'm not sure I believe that, but where did I hear it recently?"

"Rab," Summer said. "He read it in someone's tea leaves yesterday."

Tallie and Summer quit the darts room when Janet and Christine did. The other couple at Helen and David's table had gone home, but Rab and Ranger had joined them. Rab got up to pull another chair over and they all listened as Helen reminisced about a dog.

"Whose dog are we getting all soppy about?" Christine asked Rab.

"Wee dog you had when you were a lass. Saved Danny's life when he fell in the harbor."

"I saved Danny's life," Christine said. "I've never had a dog."

"Shame," Rab said. "From the sound of him, Pogo would have been a champion."

"Danny might like that version of the story better, too. Pogo wouldn't have pushed him off the wall in the first place."

Danny came from behind the bar with a half pint, and pulled another chair over to the table. "Pogo didn't just save my life, ken. He taught me to dog paddle, first, then pulled me out. I owe my naval career to him. God, I loved that dog."

"He and Chrissy were inseparable," Helen said. "A lass and her pup."

"Mum, while you're remembering days gone by, do you remember Daphne Wood? Did you know her as a child?"

"I nursed a lot of lasses like her. Lasses who don't like getting paste or paint on their hands and cry over skinned knees. You weren't like that, Christine. I was aye proud of you. Who were we talking about?"

"Daphne Wood."

"She was . . . I can't think of the word."

"She must have gotten over her fear of *ick*," Janet said. "Judging from her books and the years she spent in the wild. She was hardly out there skinning the animals she trapped with a clothespin on her nose. But she had definite ideas about what she wanted or needed while she was here."

"People change," Summer said. "Some."

"Some do." Danny nodded. "Or somewhat."

"Not all changes are happy ones," Helen said. She held her hands out, turning them over, and gazing at their backs as though wondering who the old things belonged to. "Some change is just change and some shouldn't be allowed to happen."

Heads nodded. David took one of Helen's old hands, kissed it, and held it between both of his.

"But like it or not, change is necessary," Summer said.

"Aye," Danny said. "Still, necessary or not, it's not for everyone. Some folk find a comfortable harbor and anchor themselves for the duration. Ride it out, like." He and Rab raised their glasses half an inch toward each other.

"*Pernickety*," Helen said. "That's the word I was looking for. I knew she was that pernickety, and that's why I was surprised."

"Why were you surprised, Mum? What surprised you?"

"You'll have to ask her. It's not for me to say."

"She's gone, Mum. It won't matter now."

"I ken that well enough. The pernickety thing took herself off to Canada."

"Is that what surprised you, Helen?" Janet asked. "That she went to Canada?"

"No, I had an idea she'd want to get away. They often do and come back later. Glasgow or Edinburgh is usually far enough, though. But now I can't be sure. It's been a long time. Too long." Helen started to get up.

"Where are you going, Mum?"

"To find the loo. It's been too long."

∽

"We need to talk to Gillian," Janet said later, once Christine had settled Helen and David in the car.

"We do," Christine said, "although if this happened, depending on with whom it happened, it might still be a delicate situation."

"Or Gillian might not know anything about it," Tallie said. "But we've all had experience asking careful questions, so if the situation is at all delicate, then between the four of us, or just a couple of us, we should be able to manage it."

"And when do we tell Norman Hobbs and let him deal with it?" Summer asked.

"When we know it won't be wasting his time because Mum was talking about another Daphne, another lass, or someone with a dog named Pogo and fairy wings, as well," Christine said. "I'll see if she remembers more in the morning."

"Or your dad?" Tallie asked.

"I'll see what I can do."

Janet's phone buzzed with a text. By the time she pulled it out and read it, Christine was waving and driving off. Janet raised a hand and started to call after her, but stopped.

"What?" Tallie asked.

"We need—" Janet dropped her hand to her mouth, then shook her head. "Not us. Tom. And Gillian. They need our prayers. Hillwalkers found his body."

26

J anet waited until she was home to call Constable Hobbs. "Thank you for the text, Norman, but do *you* believe it was suicide?"

"There was a note."

Tom Laing had taken himself to a lonely part of Glen Sgail with a packet of scones, a flask of tea laced with whisky and something else, and a bottle of whisky besides, apparently intending to do himself in in style. A note found with the body apologized to Gillian and confirmed for the specialists that he'd killed Daphne and then taken his own life. At a guess, he'd been dead several days.

"This is appalling, Norman, and it has to be utterly devastating for Gillian. But saying there was a note and saying you *believe* the note are two different things. What kind of scones and tea? Are they what Daphne had? Will the Major Crime Team have to come sniffing around Cakes and Tales again?"

"Nothing has been confirmed, but there was the same odor of almonds present."

"Summer's scones for the signing were orange almond, but the orange scent is stronger. Wait—are you saying it was cyanide?"

"No. Tom helped them out there, too. They found a book on poisonous plants in his rucksack. He used a piece of cherry laurel as a bookmark. All parts of the cherry laurel are highly toxic and smell strongly of almonds. Reddick tells me that Nero poisoned the wells of his enemy with laurel water, and during the eighteenth century, there was a habit of using laurel water in baking for the almond scent and flavor. But a wee bit of laurel goes a long way, and that practice led to accidental—and perhaps not-so-accidental—poisonings."

"Where did he get it?"

"The hedge round the old Farquhar garden at the school would do. It's quite common. The specialists will run tests, but they're confident they know the answers to all three deaths."

"Sam. That's why his cause of death hasn't been released."

"Aye. It was a complicated death. There was evidence suggesting he'd ingested something toxic, though not a lethal dose. The almond smell gave them possibilities to test for in the first two deaths. Now with Tom's death, and the new evidence at that scene, they very likely have the answer, although the precise cause of death, in each case, will be withheld, pending a toxicology report."

"What was that you said—the note confirmed for the specialists that he killed Daphne? Confirmed how? Did he actually *say* he killed Daphne? Did he say anything at all about Sam?"

"No."

"Is that what's bothering you about it?"

"That, and his choice of whisky."

❧

"That's when I blew it," Janet said after repeating the conversation to Tallie. "I had to go and say the words 'whisky society,' and suddenly he had another call."

"He really might have had another call," Tallie said. "What kind of whisky did Tom have?"

"I didn't quite catch what Norman said. It sounded like 'aardvark,' but I'm almost positive that wasn't it."

"Although that might be *why* Norman was surprised by Tom's choice. Can't you hear the slogan? 'Drink Aardvark Vat Forty-nine, so braw it lays you on your spine.'"

"I can't be laughing at a time like this. I'm going to bed."

∽

Janet and Christine stopped by Gillian's the next morning, fairly certain she wouldn't have gone in to teach. She hadn't. She didn't cry while they were there. She also didn't believe what Norman had told her.

"It was good of him to come tell you," Christine said. "Our Norman is a decent chap."

"Not if he believes Tom was a murderer," Gillian said. "Not if he believes he killed himself. Tom is the last person I'd ever imagine killing someone. He was a contradictory sort, aye, and sometimes he drank too much. Who doesnae? But he had everything going for him. He could have gone pro with his photos. He was *planning* to. He worked hard. He took care of himself. He did yoga." She stopped, breathing hard, and then choked back a sob. "He gave kilted yoga a try, after seeing a clip on telly. Made me laugh."

She didn't laugh now. There were no more choked sobs.

In the silence, they heard the *click-click-click* of nails on the bare floor. Rachel Carson came from another room and looked at them.

"Will you take her?" Gillian asked. "Please? She won't eat. I'm at my wit's end and I'm not sure I'll ever get them back."

∽

"Gillian has a point about Tom and his plans," Christine said, casting a glance at Rachel Carson sitting on the back seat of the Vauxhall. "But if he'd killed two people, he might think he'd buggered those plans. With good reason."

"He showed a lot of self-control at the signing when Daphne was laughing and berating his talents," Janet said.

"That might show he was capable of being a stone-cold killer."

"I think it backs up what Gillian was saying about him. He took care of himself and believed in himself. I didn't like him, partly because he *was* so sure of himself, but I didn't have to like him to think there's something awfully convenient about his death."

Christine glanced in the back seat again. "This dog is awfully *incon-*venient. For me, that is, with my oldies to look after. But she's bonny. You should keep her."

"I can't. I'm looking for a cat."

"I didn't know you'd made up your mind."

Janet hadn't known, either.

∽

Tallie disconnected from a phone call and shook her head, first at Janet, then at Rachel Carson, then at Rab and Ranger. Janet thought Ranger might have rolled his eyes.

"Sorry, guys," Tallie said. "Basant politely declines. He says it's best to be wary of feeding a captive lion."

That time Janet knew she saw an eye-roll, except the eyes were Rab's. "Only until we find someone else, Rab," she said. "But if anyone can get her to eat, I'm sure you and Ranger can."

After Rab and Ranger left with their houseguest, Tallie asked her mother, "What makes you so sure they can get her to eat?"

"A better chance he'd take her if I said it."

∽

The rest of that day and the next, they heard from shaken and disbelieving friends and acquaintances of Tom Laing. *Their stories come like plypes of rain and patches of mirk*, Janet thought.

Gillian called Janet that afternoon. "I've thought it over," she said, "and I think the police are right, after all."

"You do?"

"About it being murder and suicide, aye, but they have it backward. It was Daphne. She poisoned Tom's scones and tea and let him go off on his photo shoot. Then she killed herself. He's been out there, dead, all this time, and she's the one who did it." That was followed by a string of colorful Scottish oaths involving body parts Janet hadn't ever pictured in the particular combinations Gillian suggested.

"Why would she kill him?" Janet asked when Gillian ran out of imagery.

"She was mentally ill. She had to be. You saw that."

"It's clear she had issues."

Gillian repeated one of her oaths.

"Mentally ill or not, she loved Rachel Carson. Would she abandon her like that?"

"She knew someone would hear the howls and take her in. Tom was *not* a killer."

After they disconnected, Janet added Gillian's theory to her page in the cloud.

Summer told them about calls she had from James and Martin. She appreciated the camaraderie they showed by keeping her in the news loop. James, like Gillian, didn't believe Tom would kill anyone. "He said the idea that Tom killed Daphne and then himself made no sense, if you knew the man. Tom loved teaching and he loved photography. He's sure Tom could have made a go of it professionally, and he's sure Tom was working toward doing that. 'Very focused, forgive the pun,' he said."

"How well did Martin know Tom?" Janet asked.

"A bit through the paper and darts at Nev's. He's shocked, of course. He asked if I still want to see his article and interview notes."

"I hope you told him yes."

"I had to promise it was curiosity only and that I'm not planning to write my own article."

"Did he say when he'd get them to you?"

"Sorry, I didn't ask. I didn't want to sound like I was in a hurry."

The most surprising call came from Maida on Saturday, six days after Daphne's death and three after Tom was found. She'd just heard from Norman Hobbs that her house—Daphne's house—had been broken into.

"He's been keeping an eye on the house since receiving a tip. I'm meeting him there now. I'll ring you up later with the details."

Instead, she stopped by the bookshop.

"Reporting in," she said. "I thought it would be better in person. For the nuances."

There were no customers nearby to hear Maida's odd statement. But Tallie, collecting stray books, heard. She came to the sales counter and shooed Janet and Maida to the office. They settled in chairs facing each other, knees almost touching. Maida looked unimpressed by the cramped space.

"You don't really need to call it reporting in, Maida," Janet said.

"You are looking into the murders, though, aren't you?"

Janet thought Maida made more of the rolled *R*s in murders than she needed to. When she didn't answer right away, Maida nodded.

"You're not satisfied they've got the right end of this, either. So then, my report. Nothing of mine is missing, but why would it be? I put nothing fancy over there. Someone might have gone through Daphne's things. Bit of disarray."

"Why are her things still there?"

"What are they supposed to do with it all?" Maida asked. "The police took her papers and electronics. They haven't found a relative, so I suppose it'll be up to me to pack up the rest and send it to a jumble."

"How did they get in?"

"The locks are that flimsy."

"What did Norman say?"

"Crime of opportunity, he called it. Happens all the time."

"But would anyone know if something of Daphne's is missing?"

"Aye, there's a nuance for you," Maida said. "Here's another. How would anyone know if it's the villain returning or louts taking advantage of an empty house?"

An empty house that might hold a secret or be a ghoulish attraction too exciting for louts to pass up.

"End of report. I'll let you know if I hear anything else." Maida was up and out the office door almost before Janet realized.

"Thanks for taking the time to come in," Janet said, catching up to her. "You know, you're taking this awfully well, Maida." She lowered her voice. "Starting with your plants, and then Daphne's death; you would hope *that* was the end of it, but now *this.*"

"Tears never solved anything," Maida said, with probably several dozen of her ancestors nodding prim agreement. "As well, a bit of notoriety might bring attention to the house and help sell it." The several dozen ancestors might not have approved of that thought, but it put a lift in Maida's step as she left the bookshop.

"Nuances?" Tallie asked when she'd gone.

"Mm. Let me—" Janet ran her fingers over an invisible keyboard.

"Sure."

Janet went back into the office. Far easier to type on a keyboard than thumb-fumble notes into her phone. She opened another document, called it "Nuances," and entered the questions she'd thought of that she hadn't mentioned to Maida.

The killer returning or a crime of opportunity?

Why take a chance on returning to the scene of the crime?

Looking for what?

Why didn't s/he look for it immediately? Before the body was discovered?

Because of Rachel Carson?

OR: S/he wasn't *returning* to the scene, because s/he wasn't there when Daphne died.

BUT AGAIN: Looking for what?

"Did sending your nuances to the cloud help?" Tallie asked when Janet left the office again.

"I don't know, but it gave me a big, fat—" Janet swirled her hands around her head.

"Headache?"

"No. A question I'm not sure I want to ask."

Tallie raised her eyebrows. A couple had browsed closer to the desk, so she scribbled something on a scrap of paper and handed it to her mother: *Did Maida kill Daphne?*

Janet's eyes goggled. She crushed the note into a ball and threw it away. "That honestly never occurred to me. You aren't seriously suggesting it, are you?"

"No, but it's obviously a question you don't want to ask."

"Janet!" Elizabeth II had left the tearoom and bore down on them. "I've had an inspiration. Office."

Janet looked at Tallie and swirled her hands around her head again, before going back into the office and closing the door. Christine, too inspired to sit, paced the length of the office. Janet stood with her back to the door to give her room.

"I read your latest bit of rambling in the clouds."

"That was fast."

"Don't interrupt. This is what occurred to me. If the killer is still out there, and if Norman *isn't* right about the break-in at Daphne's being a crime of opportunity, what about Tom's place?"

Janet's hands were swirling again. "That's exactly what I was thinking!"

"And?"

Janet's hands dropped to her side. "That's as far as I got."

"Ha! Then I'm that far ahead of you. I made a phone call and we have an appointment for a spot of breaking and entering."

✥

"It's only entering," Rab said that evening. "I have a key. But I'm not sure this is a good idea."

Rab, Janet, and Christine stood on the pavement in front of Tom Laing's house. Rachel Carson sat on her haunches beside Rab, looking at the house, too. Janet wasn't sure bringing the dog along had been a good idea. *What if she starts howling?* Aloud, she asked, "Won't Ranger feel left out?"

"This one thinks she owns the universe," Rab said. "Left the lad at home. He needed a break."

"Has she started eating for you?"

"Like a horse. It won't do."

"So, what's our plan of attack?" Christine asked, rubbing her hands.

"I called Norman. Told him Tom would ask me to feed his moggie when he's away. He said it's all right to go in."

"You've taken some of the fun out of it," Christine said.

"I didn't tell him you'd be here."

"Better."

"But this is *appalling*!" Janet said. "The poor cat! Has it been alone all this time? For almost a week?"

"No, no," Rab said. "It's all fine. The cat died last year. Come on. Back door."

He led the way around the side of the house. Elizabeth II, the owner of the universe, and Janet followed. And there, sitting on the back stoop, they startled a desolate-looking Gillian. *As though she's haunting the place,* thought Janet.

"What are you all doing here?" Gillian asked, shrinking against the door.

"A good man, Gillian," Rab said softly. "I'm sorry for your loss. We've come to check on the house, make sure no one's gotten in who shouldn't."

Rab showed her the key and she moved aside to let him unlock the door. When he opened it, she pushed past him and went in, Christine on her heels.

Janet hung back. "This really doesn't seem like a good idea, does it?" she said to Rab.

"Let's see what we see."

Tom's house was a modern four-room detached bungalow. They entered through the kitchen, which also served as the eating area. The other rooms were a lounge, a bedroom, and a second bedroom he'd turned into a darkroom. Janet left Rab and Rachel Carson in the kitchen. She found Gillian and Christine in the lounge, Gillian with her arms wrapped around herself, hands tucked in her armpits.

"I didn't own him," Gillian was saying. "He had an eye for a pretty bit, the land or a lass. He always said that. Couldn't be helped. But we had good times."

"Is this how he kept house?" Janet asked.

"More or less."

Janet glanced around the lounge. Books on a shelf tipped like dominoes. More books sat in a haphazard pile next to it. She moved on to the bedroom and bath. The door to the medicine cabinet wasn't quite shut. A drawer in the bedroom stood half-open. The darkroom—she couldn't begin to guess what might be missing or moved.

"The floors are tracked up," Christine pointed out, "but that might be from the police or Tom himself. There's no sign of forced entry."

"But someone's been here," Gillian said. She continued to hug herself in the middle of the lounge. "The windows don't all latch properly. Some of Tom's students knew that. Anyone at Nev's might. He let himself in that way, a time or two, when he'd left his keys."

"What makes you think someone's been here?" Janet asked.

"The smell," Gillian said. "Like a cologne. Tom never wore scent."

"The police have been here," Janet reminded her. She sniffed.

"That would've been a day or two ago, at least," Christine said. "If they wore something that lingered this long, couldn't they be accused of contaminating a crime scene?"

"Do you smell it?" Janet asked.

Christine shook her head.

"Patchouli," Rab said from the door.

"Aye," Gillian said. "That's the scent. Faint, but."

"We should go," said Rab.

As if to encourage them, Rachel Carson whined. They left through the kitchen door and walked around to the street. Christine asked Gillian if she needed a ride home.

"No, my car's along there. Will you tell Norman someone's been in the house?"

"We will," Janet said. "This must all be so hard for you, Gillian."

"They say God only gives us as much as we can handle, but I'm beginning to wonder if He hasn't mistaken me for someone else."

"Gillian, do you remember telling me that Daphne went through a difficult patch during your last year in school?"

Gillian took a step back, tucking her chin like a turtle. Without another word, she turned on her heel and disappeared down the street.

Janet and Christine looked at each other. Rachel Carson whined again. They looked at her and then at Rab.

"Norman's right," Rab said. "Tom's choice of whisky was wrong."

N orman fancies himself a writer," Rab said, "but he has no poetry."

"If he has no sense of smell, he won't believe anyone doused in patchouli was in Tom's house," Christine said.

"Here he is," Rab said. "I'll let him in."

Hobbs, in civilian clothes that did nothing to disguise his profession, preceded Rab into Janet's living room. The men sat. Rachel Carson turned her back on the room and stared toward the kitchen.

"You went to Tom's house?" Christine asked.

"I did. I found no evidence of a break-in."

"Tcha."

"I'm sorry, Mrs. Robertson. I do appreciate your civic-mindedness."

"Tcha."

"So, Norman, Rab," Janet said, hoping to move past Christine's irritation and on to the reason the men were sitting in her living room past a hoped-for early bedtime. "My daughter is out at a film and the curtains are drawn against nosy neighbors. Of course, with your cars in front—"

"Mine's round the corner," Rab said.

"And mine's two streets over," Hobbs said.

"But why the secrecy?" Janet asked.

"Tradition," they both said.

"Why are you telling us, then?" Christine asked.

"A secret told is safer than one ferreted out," said Rab.

Janet thought she heard a slight sniff from Hobbs. "Then, by all means, tell us."

"I'm the current historian of the Deoch-an-doris Society," Hobbs said, with the residue of the sniff in his voice.

"The have-a-drink-for-the-road society?" Janet asked, trying not to sound incredulous.

"Close enough," Hobbs agreed.

"From the Gaelic," Rab said. "'Drink of the door' is more accurate."

Hobbs cleared his throat with authority. "I'll give you a summary of our history. The Deoch-an-doris Society is the oldest organization in Inversgail, its beginnings lost in the mists of the nineteenth century, when thwarting excisemen was a way of life."

"Survival for some," Rab said.

"However," Hobbs harrumphed, "we aren't a society given to drunken bacchanals. Although, judging by the historian's notes from the turn of the last century, something like that might have gone on in the past. Usually during the dark winter months. Or perhaps there's some other reason for the deterioration of the historian's handwriting."

"And spelling," Rab added.

"Membership was originally limited to men," Hobbs continued. "That changed shortly before the start of World War One."

"That change following closely on the bacchanal period, no doubt," Christine said.

"Quite possibly," Hobbs agreed. "Memberships are handed down within families, but because membership has dwindled over the years, due to deaths and people leaving the area, there are other ways to join. For instance, memberships can be transferred. Membership is ecumenical. The society isn't so much secret as not talked about—part of the tradition of thwarting the gaugers."

"I thought you were thwarting excisemen," Janet said.

"Same thing," said Rab. "But it's also not talked about in the way some people don't like talking about their favorite books or movies. Too much talk diminishes them. Dilutes the pleasure."

"So, it's basically a secret club for people who like to drink," Janet said.

"Drink whisky, aye," Rab said. "Tom was a member. That's why we know the Ardbeg found with him is wrong."

"Ardbeg Corryvreckan," Hobbs said. "It's particularly dear."

Rab waved the complaint of expense away. "He was a man of strong opinion, and he hated the smoky, slap-ye-in-the-face taste of Ardbeg. I looked tonight. He had several whiskies, but no Ardbeg. Nothing peaty or smoky at all."

"Yet he drank it with the laurel," Janet said. "Why?"

"The whisky in the flask with the tea was different," Hobbs said. "He probably filled that himself. The extra bottle, the Ardbeg, made it look as though he'd brought plenty more to do the job properly."

"Window dressing?" Janet asked. "Or a stage prop? That means someone else was out there with him or went out later."

"Possibilities," Hobbs said.

"Why has Reddick been sniffing around your society?" Christine asked.

"Sam Smith had a photocopy of a letter in his rucksack," Hobbs said. "It was an anecdote about a Great-Great-Uncle Edward and his belief that a bottle of Laphroaig saved his life, on a voyage of polar exploration, when he was caught in a blizzard and buried in snow for three days with only his reindeer hide suit and the bottle to keep him warm. He didn't drink the bottle while buried. He saved it to celebrate if he survived."

"Always good to have a goal," Rab said.

"A penciled note on the letter said that Great-Great-Uncle Edward lived in Inversgail and belonged to the Deoch-an-doris Society. We're reasonably certain this was Edward Buchan. There have been no members of that family in Inversgail since he emigrated to Canada in 1903. As far as Reddick knows, Sam Smith didn't ask anyone about the society while he was in town."

"Tell us about Ian," Christine said.

Hobbs and Rab exchanged looks.

"Think of him the way you think of an exciseman," she said. "If we know what you're up against, then we can help thwart him."

"We think he stumbled across something while researching one of his books," Hobbs said. "It must not have been anything specific, but it convinced him a secret society exists, and he seems to think that his books, or his dream to own a wee distillery, mean he should be allowed to join, if only he can track us down."

"Silly question, I'm sure," Janet said, "but why not let him?"

"Because no one needs him," Hobbs said. "That sounds unnecessarily blunt, and membership isn't based on anyone's value to the society, but there are other ways of not needing someone. We don't need the aggro."

"Or the ego," Rab said.

"May we have a list of members?" Janet asked.

"Why?"

"It'll save further ferreting."

✍

Hobbs brought the membership list to Yon Bonnie Books the next morning, before any customers arrived. It was in an unmarked envelope. Janet promised not to share it outside the SCONES and to keep it safe. Even so, she felt a smidge of resistance when she took the envelope from his hand.

"Rab was the historian before me," Hobbs said as she took the envelope, "but his tasting notes tended to be too flowery. I took over to improve the tone."

"That was good of you." She ignored the renewed sniff in his voice and the smile Tallie hid behind a feigned cough. "Norman, do you know who died first? Was it Daphne or Tom?"

"I haven't read the official reports."

"A guess?"

"*My* report, after finding Ms. Wood Sunday night, included the information that she'd made a pot of stew after leaving the signing at your shop. The pot was still warm and on the stove. The kitchen hadn't been tidied, but parings and spills appeared to be fresh."

"That doesn't sound like the kitchen of someone planning suicide, does it? It's all so awful and shocking. Gillian wants to believe that Daphne poisoned Tom's tea and scones and then herself. But that doesn't account for the wrong whisky."

"Aye, to me, the stew indicates someone who was home all evening, not traveling up the glen with Tom or after him. Well, I'll leave you to your business and I'll attend to mine—more bad news, I'm afraid."

"Oh dear, what now?"

"Another crime of opportunity, Mrs. Marsh. They do happen frequently, ken. This time, Sharon Davis is the unlucky recipient. Someone broke into her house last night."

28

The burglary of the librarian's house seemed to prove Norman Hobbs's expertise on crimes of opportunity in Inversgail. Janet was ready to believe he might be right about the incident at Maida's house, and almost ready to be convinced that Rab and Gillian had imagined patchouli lingering like a sneak thief in Tom's.

"If for no other reason, we have a business to run, and smelling patchouli where it didn't belong complicates our investigation. It's a nuance we don't need."

"Patchouli is a pretty pungent and specific nuance," Tallie said. "*Nuance* might be another word for *clue*. I don't think we can ignore them."

"That's irritatingly logical. *Nuance* might be another word for *red herring*, too, but I suppose we won't know if any given nuance is leading us or misleading us until we've solved this thing."

"*Nuance* is to *clue* as *smirr* is to *thunderplump*."

"All right, I like that," Janet said. "We'll make it our new guiding principle. What's our next step?"

"If you don't mind, I'd like to park myself in the office. I want to read through Daphne's websites again. There might be a nuance or two that went past me earlier."

"Take this with you." Janet handed her Hobbs's envelope. "Heaven forbid it should fall into the wrong hands. I'll let the others know about Sharon's burglary, and I'll call if it gets busy."

"Champion pig calls only," Tallie said.

With no hint of smirr, thunderplump, or anything in between, Inversgail basked in a spate of sunshine for an hour or two that morning. While anyone with sense took advantage of it, the bookshop and tearoom grew quiet. Christine then took advantage of the lull and brought cups of tea for Janet and Tallie. She handed one to Janet and looked around. "Tallie?"

"In the office," Janet said. "On the trail of clues and nuances."

"Then she won't miss the tea." Christine settled herself on the stool behind the counter with the second cup. "This possibility that the scene of Tom's murder was stage-managed interests me. But if Norman is willing to believe that was staged, why not the break-ins, as well? They could have been made to look like typical crimes of opportunity. James and Martin probably know enough, from covering stories for the paper, to make a break-in look like the work of bored kids."

"Anyone who reads enough mysteries or watches crime shows would be able to," Janet said.

"Sharon-the-burgled-librarian could. Any more postcards from her?" Christine asked. "Do we *know* she left Inversgail? Her cards are electronic. What if she invented an alibi for herself?"

"That would mean she planned the murders weeks in advance, and part of her plot was a fake vacation. But why?"

"Fake or not, everyone needs a vacation."

"I'm serious, Christine."

"So am I. She's a master manipulator. She maneuvered level-headed-you into judging that literary contest when we first got here. And then here she came, complaining about Daphne's list of dos and don'ts and silly needs, and asked if *you'd* kill her. And then said she would if you didn't. Talk about stage-setting."

"We all say things like that from time to time. She was blowing off steam, not confessing."

"That's part of her cleverness," Christine said. "Creating a memorable scene to throw us off. Why should we discount her as a suspect just because we don't know why she'd want Daphne dead?"

"But we can't just lob accusations. We need evidence. We need motive. Even if she did kill Daphne, what about Tom and Sam?"

"Tom is easy; it made him look guilty. That motive works for any suspect. Poor Sam, though. He doesn't fit into any theory easily."

"So, then, what about the break-ins?" Janet asked. "Can you really picture Sharon creeping around and getting into other people's houses?" She stifled a giggle. "Actually, I'd like to see her try."

"If she's the one Ian saw at Daphne's, it's no wonder he thinks the information is valuable. Between him and Maida, what a pair."

"Why aren't we suspecting either of them?" Janet asked.

"We can work on them later. Continue with your objections to Sharon. This is useful."

"Why *would* she break in? What was she after? Did she fake the break-in at her house?"

"Yes, because she knows about opportunistic crime. She did it to remove lingering doubts about the other two. We don't know what she was after, but that would be true of any of our suspects. Think about it, though. Her house is more secluded than Daphne's or Tom's. Who else would know it had been burgled? She probably reported it herself through the anonymous tip line. What day is it?"

"Monday."

"There you go, she picked the obvious day for it. Everyone in Inversgail knows she goes to Fort William to do her radio program on Mondays."

"Monday afternoons. Norman heard about the break-in this morning or last night. And your theory assumes she heard about the lingering doubts. How did she hear that if she's pretending to be away, and where was she when Norman investigated?"

"You're so hung up on details," Christine said.

"They're called nuances, and the devil is in them."

With the afternoon came a soft, steady rain—a dreep, Janet decided, and marked it off her list of rain words. Tourists came in, happy to be out of the dreep, with books to browse and the possibility of hot tea and a scone or shortbread. Martin came in, too, and brought the article and interview notes he'd promised to share with Summer. She gave him tea, a scone, *and* shortbread in thanks.

"A file folder of papers?" Janet asked when Christine reported the exchange. "He can't be thirty; why didn't he zap over an electronic file? Or bring a copy of the recording? Surely he didn't take notes by hand?"

"You were going to take notes the other evening at Nev's."

"But now I'm with it and shocked by such backward ways."

"He's sipping tea and gazing at our Summer. I don't know if that's the only reason for the hand delivery of a paper file, but he's a bit like a puppy."

"Have you noticed how often we need to straighten the picture books?" Tallie asked at the end of the day. She corralled a drift of them on the floor in front of the fireplace and took them back where they belonged.

"At the library, we used to say that a discombobulation of books in the children's area is a good sign," Janet said. "It means children are reading. Here, we can hope it means parents will buy."

"Win-win. Long live discombobulation."

"Speaking of discombobulation," Janet said. The door jingled and Ian stepped in. "Hello, Ian." She wanted to leave the greeting at that, but her better nature insisted she behave. "What can we do for you?"

"Just browsing, for now."

He stuck his hands in his tweed pockets and started down the first aisle, attempting to casually whistle along with the jazz on the sound system. His whistle quickly died and his browse looked to Janet more like a reconnaissance mission. He walked each of the aisles and looked into the tearoom. Tallie left her shelf-straightening and followed him back to the counter, where Janet's better nature was rethinking itself.

"Perfect timing," Ian said. "I hope you appreciate that I waited until you were about to close to avoid upsetting customers."

"Waited for what?" Janet asked.

"To share my theory about Daphne's murder. Interested?"

"Sure." Tallie leaned her elbow on the counter next to him; he put two steps between her elbow and himself.

"Everyone's upset. Everyone feels like a suspect."

"Really?" Janet said.

"You hadn't noticed? You should get out more. *I've* been out and about, picking up the vibes of the community, and those vibes all say one thing: No one liked her. That fact gave me my clue. It's like Christie's *Murder on the Orient Express.* The police are stymied because they're looking for *a* murderer, when, in fact, multiple people are in it together. And then it struck me how appropriate it would be if Summer uses Mandarin oranges in her orange almond scones. That would make this murder with the Oriental scones."

"Ian," Janet said, "for so many reasons, don't ever say that again."

Tallie moved a step closer to Ian; Ian moved two more away.

"My offer still stands," he said. "Quid pro quo. I'll tell you who I saw in Daphne's house in exchange for information about the whisky society."

"What makes you think we know anything about a whisky society?" Janet asked.

"I have my sources. I know you have yours. As a good faith gesture, I'll share this tidbit with you. Did you know a cache of whisky was buried in Inversgail during the Great War? The secret of its exact location long lost. There, now it's your turn to share a tidbit."

"Sorry," Tallie said. "Now we're closed."

Christine and Summer arrived from the tearoom in time to see Ian huffing his way out the front door. "Not causing problems, is he?" Christine asked.

"Nothing a good lock doesn't solve." Tallie turned the deadbolt.

"We've had an idea," Summer said. "Why don't we stay here this evening?"

"Nev's will miss us," Christine said, "but we can eat toasted cheese, muddle through our theories, and toss accusations at people we think we know."

"And see what sticks?" Janet said. "Sure. Can we start with Ian?"

They settled into the chairs by the fireplace with Isle of Mull cheddar toasted on thick slices of whole grain bread. Tallie told them she'd added notes about Daphne's websites to the cloud. Summer gave them each a copy of Martin's file, which she'd made on the machine in the office. Janet had the Deoch-an-doris Society membership list, but decided to wait before passing it around. Instead, she shared Ian's theory.

"Of course there could be more than one person involved," Christine said. "Didn't we already think of that?"

"I'd wondered if Daphne and Tom were in it together," Janet said. "But if Ian's right, we're living in a whole town of homicidal maniacs."

"He isn't *right*," Tallie said. "He's a *writer*. Give him an inch and he'll see a crime in every cup of tea." She picked up Martin's notes. "What's good in here, Summer?"

"I'll give you the high points. Hang on." Summer set her toasted cheese aside and leafed through the pages. "She had no particular affection for Inversgail. Her memories of people are foggy. Her family moved on or died. She talked about trees and said as long as she had them, she was never lonely. Martin asked, 'Are trees a good substitute for filling one's life with another person?'"

"Did she bop him with her bokken?" Christine asked.

"She came back with, 'Does one need to fill one's life with the mess of another person?'"

"That's a complicated question," Tallie said.

"Which he didn't answer. They talked about her books. She said bookstores are anachronisms. He asked if she'd had any backlash from booksellers for saying that, and she said, 'Backlash doesn't worry me. I'm not a worrier. I'm a warrior. I'll stand up for anyone who's been taken advantage of, treated badly, beaten down, or killed. Physically, emotionally, or spiritually.'"

"Go, Daphne," Tallie said.

"Yet she thoroughly trod on Tom in public." Christine shook her head. "Then again, let she who is without inconsistencies be the first to pick holes."

"How far would she go to stand up for someone, do you think?" Janet asked. "And does a warrior use poison?"

"A poison-tipped sword, maybe," Tallie said. "But I thought we eliminated Daphne as a suspect because of Norman's stew clue."

"But he also thinks the break-ins aren't related, so let's keep—"

"An open mind?" Christine asked. "Such wise words, Janet."

"Learned from a wiseacre friend."

"Always glad to do my bit. Do we have a list of clues floating in the cloud?"

"Let's start one when Summer's finished," Janet said.

"Hold on." While they'd been talking, Summer had eaten the rest of her toasted cheese. Now she wiped her fingers and picked up Martin's file again. "I'm paraphrasing, here, but the warrior thing is why she wanted justice for Sam Smith. Then Martin asked something we wondered, too—why she said she knew Sam's family when there's no evidence he was related to anyone in Inversgail and Smith is the most common surname in Scotland. She said, 'Smith is Everyman.' He asked if she had suspects and if she was worried about the killer. She repeated her 'I'm not a worrier. I'm a warrior' thing and then said, 'I've killed bears. But I'm not an idiot. People are more dangerous than wild animals.' He said, 'So you're a worried warrior?' She accused him of laughing at her and ended the interview." Summer tapped the pages back into a neat stack. "Those are the highlights, according to me, but read the file, because something else might jump out at you."

"Did he record the interviews?" Janet asked. "It might be interesting to hear inflections."

"He must have," Summer said, "but he didn't offer it, so he might not be as willing to share it. Do you want me to ask?"

"It can't hurt."

"Could James have an ulterior motive for the cuts he made in the article?" Tallie asked.

"I doubt it," Summer said. "James wasn't looking for edgy. As far as I can see, he cut out the edge, reframed the piece, and ended up with a perfectly good article that fits the *Guardian*'s style. Still, I know how it feels to have your work chopped up." She took out her tablet. "But you move on. So, moving on to clues? I'll start with my least favorites: scones and tea."

"Stew," Christine said. "Electronic postcards."

"You're just guessing about the postcards," Janet said.

"We're guessing about a lot of things," Christine said. "Let's treat it like a game of associations and see what happens. Just sing them out."

"But sing slowly, so I can get them down," Summer said.

"Break-ins."

"Patchouli."

"Unhappy memories."

"Conversation stoppers."

Janet gave Christine a look. "What kind of clue is that? Oh wait— whisky society."

"The wrong whisky."

"Peeping Tom."

"Tom's temper."

"Sam Smith."

"Daphne detecting."

"Daphne defending."

"Daphne disappearing," Tallie said. "Daphne Wood, Daphne and trees, Daphne and Apollo. Whoa." She waved her hands. "Whoa, whoa, whoa."

"Whoa, is right," Summer said.

"Her website—"

"Whoa! Let me catch up." Summer tapped madly on the tablet, then pointed at Tallie. "And go."

Tallie did, ticking points off on her fingers. "That story you told us, Mom, about Daphne wanting to be called Laurel but not telling anyone. And Christine, your mum's memory of Daphne—that she had an idea Daphne would want to get away. She said something like 'they often do and come back later.' The rough patch Gillian said Daphne had their last year. And her *website*. She posted her own retelling of the Greek myth of Daphne. It takes place in a northern garden warmed by gulf winds, but in this version, Daphne is caught by Apollo. No one comes to save her, so eventually she saves herself. *She* turns *herself* into a laurel tree." Tallie sat back, the others staring at her.

Then Summer and Christine spoke at the same time, Summer saying, "Rape?" and Christine asking, "Who was this Apollo?"

Janet studied her daughter. "Fill in the blanks," she said. "Give us a clear trail to follow."

"I will, but I'll tell you where they lead. It's Gillian's dad. It's Alistair. He killed them."

29

A listair's pet project, before Glen Sgail, was restoring the
Farquhar garden, up there where the library and high school
were eventually built." Tallie said. "That's your northern
garden warmed by gulf winds. He worked there with Girl Guides and
Boy Scouts."

"Gillian and Daphne were Guides," Janet said. "Gillian said they spent
a lot of time in each other's houses, but Daphne spent more at Gillian's.
Alistair called them the two musketeers."

"At the ceilidh, Daphne called Alistair an old sinner," Tallie said, "and
presented the plaque on behalf of all garden gnomes. Then he told her
to walk carefully. That could have been a threat."

"Made so publically?" Janet asked.

"Made in Gaelic," Summer said. "That isn't exactly the same thing."

"It was taking a chance," Tallie agreed, "but anyone who understood the Gaelic probably didn't hear it as a threat or just laughed
it off."

"Rab didn't see it as a threat," Christine said. "He repeated it to her,
later, and he hardly takes time to threaten dust on the bottom shelves."

"Just her presence in Inversgail had to be a threat to Alistair, though,"
Tallie said. "Think of the damage she could do if she said anything. But
think of the damage he did to *her*."

"If it's true," Summer said.

"You're right. If. But it seems pretty certain she ended up pregnant, and the story of Daphne and Apollo isn't a happy romance."

"At the signing, Daphne commented on Alistair being attracted to a couple of the students," Janet said.

"Do you think Gillian knows?" Summer asked.

"She almost certainly *didn't* know," Christine said, "or Daphne wouldn't have been the author-in-residence. But, given the way Gillian reacted outside Tom's house, when Janet asked her about Daphne's 'difficult patch' in their last year, she's heard since."

"And I think I know when she heard." Janet told them about the afternoon Daphne invited Gillian to go hillwalking and share old memories. "Except Gillian talked about things Daphne didn't remember, so Daphne brought up something Gillian might not remember. Daphne didn't tell me what that was, but she said Gillian not only didn't remember it, but claimed it couldn't be true. Daphne said it ruined the afternoon. At the time, I thought she was exaggerating."

"Alistair's fit enough to hike in and out of the glen," Tallie said.

"But why the break-ins? Why kill Tom?" Janet asked.

"To silence him, because Alistair found out Daphne told him. Or it's what we've said before—he killed Tom to make him look guilty."

"Or it's both," Christine said, "and killing him solved two problems."

"As for the break-ins," Tallie said, "what if Norman is right and they have nothing to do with the murders?"

"What about the patchouli?" Janet asked.

"Sneak thieves might go in for a dab behind the ears," Christine said.

"Do you know where else you find it?" Summer asked. "Insect repellents. Handy when you hike in a wooded glen."

"Sam," Janet said. "Could Sam be Daphne's child?" She shook her head and answered herself. "Sam was too young."

"If Alistair knows Tom likes whisky, but doesn't know much about whisky, he might choose the wrong bottle," Christine said. "Where's that membership list? Have you read it?"

Janet held up the envelope. "I did. I don't remember seeing his name, but he might have gotten lost in the ones I didn't recognize."

"Who *did* you recognize?" Christine asked. "I know what *I* recognize when I see it—that look on your face. You're hiding something you think is funny."

"That might depend."

"It usually does." Christine took the envelope, opened it, and scanned the list. "*Maida?* That almost makes my head spin."

"Keep reading." Janet turned to Tallie and Summer. "It isn't just the members' names. It tells how each of them became a member, who they inherited membership from or if they were invited." She glanced at Christine. "Ah."

"Mum?" Christine let the list fall to her lap. "She inherited it from her dad some years after Tony and I settled in the States. Not that I look forward to the day my old dears are gone, but won't that make an interesting inheritance?"

"Will you tell them you know?" Janet asked.

"No, why spoil the secret? And suppose Mum decides to leave the membership to someone else? I do wonder if she can tell us anything about Daphne and Alistair. Maybe the Farquhar garden will give us a footpath into her foggy memory."

"Is there time to go this evening?" Janet asked. "Only, we don't want to tire her."

"Early evenings are good for her," Christine said, "and company might stimulate her memory. She'll think it's a party. I'll give Dad a bell and warn him."

∽

Helen McLean smiled around the room at David and Christine and their three guests, and then she asked David if she'd remembered to bake. David assured her the house had smelled wonderful, and he'd bring everything *ben* when the kettle boiled. Christine had brought fairy cakes and shortbread from Cakes and Tales, made from Helen's own recipes, and she and her father felt the deception forgivable. Christine had told Janet she hoped the rest of their deception was forgivable as well.

"Mum, we walked around the Farquhar garden today."

"Lovely!"

"And I told these three that you helped with the restoration. Did I get that right?"

"No, I don't think you need a reservation. You don't need a reservation, do you, David? Oh, he must have gone to get the tea. Call Alistair, he'll know. You'd think *I* would know; I spent hours enough up there."

"With the Girl Guides?" Janet asked.

"Aye, Guides and Scouts. Lads and lassies."

"'Bonnie bairns among the blossoms.' That's what you called them," David said, as he brought in the tea tray. "You taught them the names of the plants."

"I did! Some of them never took to it, of course, but it rubbed off on one or two."

"Daphne Wood?" Christine asked.

"The names, aye. She loved the common names and the Latin. But she was one of those pernickety girls. Didn't like digging in the dirt."

"But then she surprised us, didn't she?" Christine said.

"Aye," Janet said. "Such a surprise."

"She went to Canada," Tallie said. "Isn't that right?"

"Much farther than some girls go," said Summer.

"*Such* a surprise," Helen said. "I'm glad you remember, too. I tell David the fairies come and play tricks with my memory." She took the plate David handed her. "Och, well, I *did* bake fairy cakes. I'm so glad."

"I was just as surprised to find out who the father was," Janet said.

"Now that is something she never would tell me, though I had my suspicions."

Christine exchanged looks with the other three. Janet interpreted the look as, *Tread carefully.*

"Of course, we never went in for palm trees," Helen said. She took a sip of tea and smiled at Christine.

Janet saw a twinge of sadness in Christine's eyes. Christine recovered, and smiled back at her mother, but the smile showed defeat, and Janet decided to step in. "Why didn't you have palm trees, Helen?"

"Colonel Farquhar never had them. They can grow along this coast because of the Gulf Stream and he had other Mediterranean plants, but he never took to palms. *Agapanthus africanus, Pogostemon cablin, Erithroniums,* and lucky or unlucky, he loved the flowers and fragrance of flax-leaved daphne."

Janet saw Summer sneak her phone out of a pocket, tap something into it, and then wince.

"Is that what Daphne took?" Summer asked. "The flax-leaved daphne? I always wondered."

"Aye, one of the spurge-laurels. Nasty, messy, and effective. Lost the child and nearly herself."

"Then why did she go to Canada?" Tallie asked.

"She couldn't bear it otherwise, I suppose. She needed a new life."

"Daphne and Daphne," Summer said.

"Sad, isn't it? He called them his flax-leaved and flaxen-haired beauties."

"Who did?" Christine asked. "Colonel Farquhar?"

"Tcha. And you complain my memory is bad. It's who we've been talking about. Alistair, the old goat. I had no proof—"

"You said you only had suspicions," Christine said.

"Even a strong suspicion, without proof, is only a suspicion. But he up and quit teaching at the high school at the end of the term, and she suddenly had the money to go away."

"'Old goat' seems too kind," Janet said.

"No excuse." Helen clamped her lips and rocked for a moment. "But it was only the one lass or the last lass for him. As far as I know."

"And how far is that, Mum? How do you know?"

"I made sure he never worked with Guides or Scouts or bairns of any age again."

∽

"So that incredibly awkward award presentation at the ceilidh was even more awkward than we thought," Janet said, as the four said good night on Christine's front stoop. "Do we sit on this overnight and see what we think about it in the morning?"

The other three shook their heads.

"Good." Janet looked up at the stars. *Scarce to be counted*, she thought, recalling lyrics from *Les Misérables, filling the darkness with order and light*. "Good and bad, both. Poor Gillian. I'll call Norman when I get home."

"How did your mum manage that?" Tallie asked. "Making sure Alistair never worked with kids again?"

"She's isn't just a mum, she's *Mum*."

Janet and Tallie dropped Summer back at the B and B, then went home. Tallie was silent. Janet drove, glad to concentrate on gears, proper lane, and legal speed instead of the sad story they were about to tell. She saw the light in Ian's writing room, and Ian briefly silhouetted there, as they pulled into the driveway.

"I wish we didn't have to share this with Ian," Janet said. "Not that we're going to tell him, but we're exposing it, and he and all the other numpties will hear it. It doesn't seem right."

"We'll close the curtains as soon as we get in," Tallie said.

"That won't make it better. It won't help Gillian."

"No."

They went in the front door and through to the living room. Janet looked briefly toward Daphne's house before Tallie drew the curtain. Then she took out her phone.

"You don't want to sit?" Tallie asked.

"It isn't a comfortable call. I don't want to be comfortable."

"Do you want me to call?"

"No."

Tallie stood with her mother and listened as she told Norman Hobbs what they knew and what they suspected about Alistair Gillespie. Janet spoke slowly, clearly, softly, stopping only here and there to repeat something or to answer a question from Norman. At the end, Janet asked him what he planned to do.

"You won't go speak to him alone, will you? It could be dangerous. I can meet you there if you like—oh—yes, of course. Yes, that makes more sense." Janet disconnected, blew out a long breath and shook her head. "That's done. He'll call Reddick and they'll follow up."

"And you offered to ride shotgun?"

"Don't laugh at me."

"Never. Ever. I'm proud of you."

∽

Janet didn't sleep well, imagining others sleeping less or not at all. Norman Hobbs called as she cradled her coffee the next morning. The coffee wasn't doing its job, and she wondered if the caffeine had crawled back into bed where she wanted to be. After she hung up with Hobbs, her sleepless night seemed like a waste.

30

"A listair has an alibi," Janet told the others when they met in the doorway between the bookshop and tearoom.

"That sounds like the beginning of an alphabet book by Edward Gorey," Christine said. "Except Gorey was funny and Alistair's alibi is annoying."

"And not just alibi, but *alibis*," Janet said. "He was at an AA meeting in Fort William, with plenty of witnesses, the night Sam was killed. The day of the signing, immediately after he left here, he drove to Glasgow for a two-day seminar at the university, with time-stamped receipts and more witnesses to prove it. Norman says he was gracious about being suspected, and he thanked them for believing Gillian that Tom didn't kill Daphne or himself. I guess, considering the ceilidh and that he did show up for the signing, he didn't feel threatened by her."

"I didn't know he goes to AA," Christine said.

"He told Norman that's why he goes to Fort William."

"Does this leave us looking like nosy eavesdropping snoops?" Summer asked.

"No," Janet said. "It doesn't and it won't. Even the thought makes me want to stamp my foot. In fact—" She raised her foot and looked at the others. They each raised a foot and they brought them down together. "So there."

"So there, but what now?" Tallie asked.

"Now for something harder, but it might have been in the backs of our minds all along. We wondered why Tom went back to Nev's the night Sam died, and we wondered if Gillian went back with him. If she did, some of the pieces we've been wondering about might fall into place."

"But Danny didn't see her," Christine said.

"I know. There are other *but*s, too. *But* every clue that pointed to Alistair also points to Gillian. Let's take today and try to identify the *but*s. Think about the *if*s, too, though. See what we come up with. I'll start a new document."

"Call it 'Let's Hope Not,'" Tallie said.

"Narrative or list?" Summer asked.

"Any way you want. Use your initial when you add something."

"I'll let Mum and Dad know they're on their own again for tea," Christine said.

⁂

As Tallie unlocked the bookstore's front door, she glanced at her mother. "Do we know what we're doing?"

"We aren't hurting anyone," Janet said. "At the moment."

"I thought you were going to say, 'as far as we know.'"

"That, too, but ask me again later."

"Do you want me to take care of orders this morning?"

"Sure."

Janet had brought her laptop from home. She put it on the counter, then cleared a space on a shelf below where she could slip it out of view when her attention needed to be on business. She opened the computer, turned it on, and created "Let's Hope Not." Tallie watched her from the office door before going in to run the reports she needed.

Rab and Ranger arrived before any customers. Ranger nodded at Janet and headed for his chair. When Rab had him settled, Janet asked after Rachel Carson.

"She's a bossy wee bisom," Rab said.

"Oh, dear. I'm sorry."

"No need. I ken someone who might take her. Do her some good."

"Do Rachel Carson some good, or the person?"

Rab considered. "Could be both." He nodded at the laptop and then the cash register. "I can watch this, if you've work."

"Sure, for a while." Janet nodded toward Ranger. "He and I will be over there, if you need us." She took the laptop and sat in the chair next to Ranger's. She began the new document with the *buts*, hoping she'd find enough objections to Gillian's guilt to close the laptop and feel foolish, without ever getting to *ifs*. Ranger sat up when she started typing, as though taking an interest.

"I'm looking for answers for what happened to your housepest's friend," she told him quietly. "Wish me luck."

The *ifs* began popping in almost immediately and brought a slew of *whys*, *dids*, *what ifs*, and *could haves* with them. She deleted her work, gave it some more thought, and then saw that Christine had lobbed in three questions. Janet answered them with two of her own.

C: Why did Tom go back to Nev's?

J: Maybe he went back because Gillian did and she needed him there? Danny didn't see her, but she could've been in the passage or the alley.

C: Why did he get involved in the fight?

C: Why did he stand at the entrance to the passageway?

J: Answer to both—was Tom running interference for her while she poisoned Sam?

Janet felt sick. She grimaced at Ranger. He lifted his lip. She didn't know if he was commiserating or trying to make her laugh. She gave him a slow, double-eye cat wink in return, and he turned his back on her. When she looked back at the screen, Christine had added another question. She answered. Then Tallie made a statement in Gillian's defense. Janet was glad for her daughter's loyalty, but felt compelled to add her *buts*.

> C: *Why* would Gillian kill these people?
>
> J: Daphne—to protect Alistair's name? Or for revenge, because her image of Alistair was destroyed?
>
> J: Tom—because he had a fling with Daphne? Or so he'd take the blame for Daphne's death? Is she that heartless? Alistair is into restoration; what if Gillian tried to restore her life to the way it was before Daphne came back? Except, how does that work with killing Tom?
>
> T: Gillian is an advocate for strong girls and women. She's been teaching for 20 years and brings more enthusiasm and energy to a classroom than most brand-new teachers I've met. I burned out in 15 years teaching adult law students. She spends her days with teenagers.
>
> J: She's a wonderful teacher, but she's human. What if Daphne rubbed her nose in the fling with Tom and told her she'd told Tom about Alistair? Scenario—Gillian went to see Tom after the signing. She'd already left poisoned scones and tea with Daphne. Tom confirmed everything. She gave him poisoned scones and tea, too.
>
> T: And followed him with the Ardbeg?
>
> C: Or went with him and left it. Tourist bus. Cheery-bye.

The door jingled and Janet was glad for the onslaught of tourists. Even if they only shuffled through the postcards, she was happy to stow the laptop and its suspicions under the counter for a while. Tallie came out of the office and Rab went to see if they needed help in the tearoom.

"All right?" Janet asked Tallie.

"Playing devil's advocate and getting surprisingly shaky. But, yeah, all right."

"We can stop," Janet said.

"I don't think SCONES quit."

For the rest of the morning, they didn't. As they found time, they added to the document, and when Janet looked it over, just before noon, she saw they'd created a sequence of short conversations.

T: Her grief over Daphne seems real.

S: Maybe her grief isn't for the Daphne who came back. Maybe it's for the Daphne who used to be.

S: Gillian walked home with Daphne after the signing. Opportunity.

C: Maybe the break-ins were Gillian being clever. She knows kids and how they think. She created a different story to throw off the police.

J: Daphne had a notebook. Do the police have it?

T: She's good at organizing, good at details.

C: A killer needs those skills. Maybe she arranged the visiting author program to get Daphne over here.

J: Starting with Daphne's list of demands and the miscommunication over our meeting at the school, and then not knowing she was bringing the dog—did Daphne and the stress of her visit put Gillian in a dither? Or was she laying groundwork? Smoke and mirrors? I heard that phrase somewhere recently. *Tom* used it, talking about the new school building.

T: Arranging the author visit so she could kill Daphne? Way too elaborate.

T: The change in Gillian, after Daphne must have told her about Alistair, was believable.

S: Sam doesn't fit any of the story lines. Unless he was practice, an experiment to perfect the poison recipe?

J: But why *him*?

S: What if he was in town and saw that Daphne was coming? He had one of her books in his backpack. Maybe he contacted the school for details. Gillian talked to him? Arranged to meet him?

C: Who misses him?

C: Why did Gillian call Janet when Tom went missing? Doesn't she have closer friends? Did she call for Janet's help? Or more smoke and mirrors?

C: Who *did* Ian see at Daphne's? Where did he hear about the Deoch-an-doris Society? Is the 'lost case of whisky' real? Who is this source he claims to have? His own imagination?

C: Is the society a clue or synchronicity? Is synchronicity another name for red herring?

S: This was done by a good liar. The best lies are almost true and not too complicated. Too complicated = too hard to keep straight.

S: This was done by someone good at thinking in terms of stories.

C: Word association—stories, clever, conniver, manipulation, orchestration

J: Daphne said the story you tell depends on which one you believe or which one you like better.

T: Gillian teaches literature.

J: Did Gillian and Alistair plan this together?

Shortly after noon, Rab and Ranger folded Ranger's second-best towel. As they left, Rab held the door for Alistair. He smiled and nodded,

and didn't act in any way as though he knew they'd called the police on
him. But he'd rarely set foot in the shop, and Janet worried there might
be hidden meaning when he bought a copy of Daphne's *The Deciduous
Detective*. Alistair didn't stay long, and when he left through the tearoom,
Tallie wiped an imaginary bead of sweat from her brow.

Janet wasn't surprised to get a text from Christine a few seconds later
that said, "Heart attack." A few minutes after that, Christine sent another
text: "Coast is clear and Martin's here."

Martin came through from the tearoom during a lull, habitual scone
in hand, and wandered over to the window display. "She was brilliant."

"She was complicated, but she'll be missed," Janet said.

"Complicated, yes. That's exactly how I plan to couch a more in-depth
piece on her life. I really want to get into the psychology of being an
environmentalist of her caliber."

Janet had forgotten how excited Martin got when he talked about
his writing. Tallie hadn't; she'd been on her way back to the counter
and did an abrupt about-face. "Will the article be for James?" Janet
asked.

"No, it's not his style," Martin said. "The *Guardian* is brilliant, of
course, but safe and cozy. James would want Daphne's recipe for cherry
pie where I'd want to ask if the use of cherry laurel was mere happen-
stance or meticulously planned."

Martin only paused briefly when Janet started coughing into her
elbow. She didn't hear the rest of what he said because she was too
busy pretending she had a tickle in her throat and wondering how well
that disguised her shock. To her relief, the door jingled for a couple
coming in. Martin popped the rest of his scone in his mouth, waved,
and was gone. When Tallie came back to the counter, Janet was sitting
on the stool.

"There's one more cloud note from Summer," Tallie said. "Have you
seen it?"

Janet shook her head and Tallie passed her phone to her.

S: No dice on Martin's recording. He said the interview got personal—wink, wink, nudge, nudge—and he doesn't have time to edit.

"I need to call Norman," Janet said. She took out her own phone, handed Tallie's back to her, went into the office, and closed the door. While she waited for Hobbs to answer, she wondered which way Martin's interview with Daphne had ended. Cut off by a huffy Daphne, as his notes indicated? Or with the wink and a nudge he'd just told Summer?

"Norman, hello, Janet Marsh. A quick question. Has the cause of death been released? You're sure? Will you please find out if anyone at the paper has been told about the cherry laurel? Thank you."

She disconnected and waited not more than five minutes before Hobbs called back.

"I spoke to Reddick. The answer is no. So, tell me Mrs. Marsh, who knows about cherry laurel who shouldn't?"

"Martin Gunn."

31

"I know we had it wrong last night about Alistair," Janet said, "but now we have real evidence against Martin Gunn."

"That he knows about the cherry laurel isn't *precisely* evidence," Hobbs said. "Could he have heard that detail from one of you?"

"Absolutely not." Janet wanted to shake her phone, as if that would shake sense into Hobbs. "We have very strong *nearly* evidence, then. And if you want to know why he killed Sam Smith, I can tell you that, too." Rather than wait for him to consider her offer and possibly say no, she launched into their theory for how and why Gillian chose her practice victim. It worked just as well for Martin. "You know this is possible. Martin is a personable and passionate young man. He has easy access to the alley. *Plus*, he's told us two different stories about how his interview with Daphne ended." Now that she'd said that last bit out loud, it sounded less than earth-shattering.

"A motive would be good," Norman said.

"So would an arrest." Janet closed her eyes and said "bugger" under her breath. "I'm sorry, Norman."

"I understand your frustration. I am taking this seriously, Mrs. Marsh, and I'm glad you are, too. I'll ring you when I hear from the specialists. But, please, don't any of you attempt to find or confront him."

Janet assured him they wouldn't and disconnected. Before leaving the office, she sent a text to the others. They reacted with various words of shock. She'd worried about Summer, because of her ties to the *Guardian*. She needn't have.

"It fits," Summer texted. "He talks about 'growing' story lines. Means bugger-all. Until you think about stage-setting."

Customers kept them busy while they waited to hear from Hobbs. They didn't hear, and after Tallie locked the door behind the last customer, she said she felt as though a cloud were hanging over them. Janet looked out the window. A gray cat sat on the harbor wall, predicting the weather with a lick and a polish to its ears.

"There's a fog bank beyond the harbor," Janet said, "lurking. Maybe that's what you feel. We should all bolt our doors tonight so we're not tempted to go find that wretch."

"Believe me, I'm not tempted," Tallie said.

"Neither am I."

"It's good that I knew where to find you, then," a voice behind them said.

"How on earth—" Janet said, turning, at the same time that Tallie grabbed her arm and said, "Martin—"

"*Stop.*" He didn't raise his voice. He didn't need to. "The shotgun is real. Listen carefully. Helen and David will die unless you follow directions. Christine and Summer will also die unless you follow directions. Understand? Now, walk over here where we can't be seen from the windows."

They followed his instructions, letting him tie their hands behind their backs and gag them. Then he tied Janet's upper right arm to Tallie's left.

"The gags are clean," he said. "Oh, except they might have been soaked in cherry laurel. Ha! *Brilliant* reactions. Sorry, bad joke. There's no poison. Come on."

He had them walk in front of him to the storage room at the back of the bookshop. Christine and Summer were there, also gagged and bound together.

"Keep listening," Martin said. "I'll repeat what I told Christine and Summer. It's simple. I know where Helen and David are. You don't.

If anything happens that I don't like, you will never find their pieces. Cooperate, and I'll take you to them. Yes?"

They nodded. Janet saw Elizabeth II try to assert herself, but she flickered out, unable to break through the misery on Christine's face.

He had pulled a panel van onto the pavement behind the bookshop so the rear door opened close to the shop's back door. He helped Christine and Summer climb in, then Janet and Tallie, arranging them on the bare metal floor so Janet and Tallie's backs were to the other pairs' backs. They jostled against each other when Martin lurched the van off the pavement into the narrow street.

Janet's mouth was already dry from the gag. Clean or not, it tasted foul. She closed her eyes and wondered how they were going to die. She opened them again when Martin started talking.

"That lonely death in the alley; Daphne's grieving dog and the warm pot of stew on her stove; the tragic suicide in the glen—did you know they were all vignettes that I set in motion? Watching the additional story lines that have developed as events unfolded has been fascinating, from both a psychological and creative point of view."

Fascinating if you're a psychotic monster, Janet thought.

"Daphne was brilliant, but she let negative experiences guide her decisions and she ended up alone and bitter—literally, considering how cold it gets in that part of Canada. But I, rather than complain about being stuck in my job in this town, create. I create diversions for myself. For others, too. Wee crises, slices of joy, longer narratives. It's a far healthier way to handle the reality we've been dealt."

You know bugger-all about health. You should try empathy meditation. Or sanity.

"Breaking into the houses deepened the story for me and the police. Norman Hobbs seemed to enjoy wrestling with the implications."

You are deep in denial and wrestling with the devil.

"I didn't want to create an unsolvable mystery. The police were meant to be satisfied with Tom's suicide, and the Major Crime muckety-mucks were. But then there's you lot—just had to stick your noses in."

Too bloody right.

"You've complicated my narrative."

We've scuttled it.

"That's why you're back there and I'm driving."

Bugger.

They drove in silence, then. Janet tried counting seconds and minutes but lost track. When the van slowed and came to a stop, she didn't think it had been more than twenty minutes, but if someone told her it had been no more than ten agonizingly long ones, she wouldn't have been surprised.

Martin rested his arm across the back of the seat. "I created a story line for Ian, too. He asked me about a secret whisky society, and I passed along the rumor of a case of valuable single malt, buried during World War One, in a sea cave along this part of the coast. My rumor, of course, and my contribution to Ian's entertainment. He bought a couple of boats—one to get him where he's going and another to get into close places. He moors them on this side of the headland so he can come and go without everyone round the harbor knowing he's looking for buried treasure. A bit of a gowk, our Ian."

He's our gowk and our Ian. Keep your myths and mitts off him.

Getting out of the van was more difficult than getting in. The metal floor hadn't been kind to aging knees and hips. Martin helped them out, and then led them down a set of stairs to a dock protected by a stone jetty. Two boats were tied there, an open motor launch and an ancient-looking wooden rowboat.

"You have a story line, too," Martin said, pointing to a wicker basket in the launch. "You're going on a picnic. Ian won't appreciate that you've borrowed his boat without permission, but his reaction presents possibilities for a whole new story line." He took the shotgun from the front seat of the van. "This next part is going to be tricky, so it's a good time for a reminder. If you refuse to cooperate, if you do anything I don't like, Helen and David will die."

He patted them down, took their cell phones, and dropped them in the water. He helped them climb into the rowboat and untied the ropes holding them together by their upper arms.

"I'll tow you in this bucket so I don't have to keep an eye on you. And I'm going to be kind and loosen your hands a wee bit. By the time we get where we're going, you might free yourselves. That'll be fine; you'll see."

He stepped back onto the dock, cast off the rowboat's lines, and dropped the fenders into the stern. He did the same for the launch, climbed in, started the engine, and puttered away from the dock at slow speed, heading toward open water.

And the fog, Janet thought. *The bloody fog.*

They tried to free their wrists by wiggling their hands, and then by sitting back-to-back and picking at each other's wrists. Janet was fairly sure it wouldn't matter if they were successful, but the activity helped pass the time. *And it gives us hope,* she thought. They hadn't made much progress by the time Martin shut off his engine.

"Still fettered?" he called. He pulled in the rope connecting the two boats, drawing the rowboat toward him. "Keep trying. There isn't much else to do in this fog, besides eat." He transferred the wicker basket to the rowboat. "And now for a wee plot twist. You get the picnic and the tub with no oars, I get the motor boat." He cast off the connecting rope and shoved the rowboat away.

"Your sense of loyalty to each other and to Helen and David is admirable. Unfortunately, it's worked against you, and made you easy to manipulate. Still, I salute you." He did just that, then restarted the engine. Over the its gurgle and growl, he called, "To set your minds at ease, Helen and David are safe at home. They were never in any danger. You, however—och, well, that's me, then." He saluted again and motored away.

❧

Sometime later, as they drifted in the fog, Christine said to Janet, "You're the one who said, 'at least we're dry.' And now the boat is leaking."

"We're still mostly dry," Janet said, "it's a slow leak and at least it isn't raining."

"Please don't say anything else helpful."

"I never knew you were so pessimistic," Janet said. "Well, if we'd had oars, I would have swung one like a bokken and knocked the evil grin off his face."

"If we'd had oars," Christine said, "I would have rowed us back to shore."

"Which way is shore?" Janet asked. No one answered her. "And to think I used to like watching the fog and the mist."

∞

At what felt like hours past suppertime, Janet nudged the picnic basket it was now too dark to see. "Do we dare eat anything Martin touched?"

"Sadly, no," Tallie said. "Do we dare hope Norman convinced the specialists to arrest Martin?"

"If he didn't, do we have any hope at all?" Summer asked. "He's the only one who knows we're out here, and by now, even he doesn't know where we've drifted to."

"Are you sorry you came with us, Summer?" Janet asked quietly.

"More sorry than you know."

"If we make it out of this, you can go back home, you know. No hard feelings."

"Back home? Why would I do that? I was talking about getting into this sorry excuse for a boat with you. Why would you think I want to go back home?"

"You seem stressed sometimes," Janet said. "Preoccupied. Unhappy."

"Do you want to know why?" Summer asked.

"I do."

"I seem that way because that's me. Sometimes I'm stressed and pre-occupied and I don't always smile. Unsmiling doesn't mean unhappy, though."

"She's a Summer of infinitely variable weather," Tallie said.

"I'm finding my way," Summer said, "and except for this sorry excuse for a boat, I'm not sorry I came. But, Janet? Thank you for worrying."

∞

"At least your mum and dad are safe, Christine," Janet said an unknown time later.

"Aye."

"You know, she mentioned another plant last night. Your mum did," Summer said. "*Pogostemon cablin.*"

"*Pogo—*"

"*Pogostemon.* It's patchouli."

"And it's that dog I never had—Pogo. Do you suppose she caught a whiff of it that night in Nev's? I'll wager this sinking tub that's where her mythical pup sprang from, and if she and Pogo were here now, they'd find a way to save us."

"Is that a light?" Janet asked so quietly she might have been afraid she'd scare it off. "Port side."

"What kind of light," Tallie asked. "Real or mythical?"

"Steady. Bright. Shore lights? There's more than one, but they're too far."

"Are we drifting closer?" Christine asked. "Because we're sinking lower and I hate to say it, but Martin might win."

"*Pig,*" Summer spat.

"Summer!"

"I'm not apologizing, Janet. Martin Gunn is a lousy, stinking, con-niving, delusional—"

"Pig! Girls, it's time for a lesson in state champion pig calling. It's easy, just follow my lead. Soooooooooey! Soooooooooey! Soooooooooooey!"

"I wasn't sure you'd hear us coming over that banshee cry," Danny said as he and Rab brought the four women back to Inversgail in a borrowed fishing boat. "That's a useful skill you have there, Janet."

Reddick met them at the harbor and told them Hobbs had arrested Martin Gunn. "Acting on the information you gave him yesterday. I'll need to get statements from you, but later this morning will be soon enough. Do any of you require medical attention?"

They looked at each other. They were shivering, thirsty, hungry, tired, and hoarse, and their feet squelched when they walked. They shook their heads.

"Rides home would be nice," Janet said.

Tallie handed Reddick the wicker basket. "Martin packed this picnic for us. It might be edible."

"Or it might be lethal. Thank you."

They thought about giving themselves the day off, but compromised by opening the bookshop and tearoom late that day. Starting that afternoon and over the next few days, as the story spread, they had a succession of visitors.

Hobbs came first, telling them they'd been right about why Martin killed Sam Smith. Hobbs said Martin had been happy to explain to the specialists how creative he'd been. He had planned to kill Daphne because she was the perfect victim. She was a celebrity, but not likeable and not unique. No one would really miss her. But he'd needed a guinea pig.

"That was Sam," Hobbs said. "I've had word from his parents. They can't afford to fly here to take him home. His body will be shipped." He handed Janet a notebook. "Daphne's. Reddick said it won't be needed as evidence."

"She had it with her at the ceilidh." Janet opened the notebook and looked at the first few pages, then flipped through them all. Every one of them was blank.

"Speaking of Reddick," Christine said, "there's something I've been wondering. What is his first name? No one ever uses it."

"Norman," Hobbs said.

"*That* will never do," Christine said. "We only have need for one. Reddick he'll remain."

James Haviland came in that first day, too, and told them he felt as though he should apologize. He'd suspected Martin had caught the ambition bug, but thought he needed more seasoning before making it in a bigger pond. "I had no idea he planned to create his own version of the pond. Or something like that."

Just before closing, the door jingled and Gillian came in, leaving Janet with a momentary sense of dread. But she told herself not to be silly; Gillian couldn't know they'd convinced themselves she was a murderer. Or that Alistair was. Or that she and Alistair were in it together.

"Is your offer still on to help with a memorial for Daphne?" Gillian asked.

"Absolutely," Janet said. "I'm so glad you asked."

∽

Ian came in to marvel over his brush with death. "To think that I saw him at Daphne's. I *thought* he was doing a spot of investigative journalism. If he'd seen *me*, there's no telling how I would have ended up." He also gave them the good news that recent events had put fire in his writing. "The book is practically writing itself. I have a new title for it, too. Forget *The Shillelagh in the Shed*. Are you ready? I'm calling it *Smoking Gunn*. Two *N*s."

"No, Ian," Janet said. "Please, don't." When the door closed behind him, she told Tallie she was making a vow, there and then, to work harder on her empathy meditation.

"It's hard to empathize with a gowk like Ian," Tallie said, "and even harder with a murderer. A lot's been thrown at you lately."

"But I've managed to stay on my feet."

"You're tough as nails, Mom."

Christine had a new theory about Ian and the Deoch-an-doris Society. "Meetings are held in members' houses. They move around, and he's probably been trying to find one. That's why Maida thinks he's a Peeping Tom. She's seen him looking in windows."

Sharon-the-librarian came to say hello and ask if they had enjoyed her postcards. Janet welcomed her home and said they had. "But we were so sorry to hear about the break-in."

"Do you know who reported it?" Tallie asked.

"Ah. Well. I did. I returned early."

After the door closed, Tallie said, "I like Christine's theory better, that Sharon never left."

"But there's no real reason to believe she'd lie, is there?" Janet asked.

"As far as we know."

∞

Later in the week, Summer announced that she'd like to take Wednesday afternoons off, starting in January. "I've been asked to teach a baking and business unit for the culinary class at the high school." The others congratulated her and said they'd make the new schedule work.

∞

Rab and Ranger came in one morning with more of a spring in their steps. Ranger looked around, but stayed by Rab and didn't go to his chair. Rab told Janet they'd only just stopped by to let her know they wouldn't be in for a few days. He had another deadline, he said, and he was behind because of all the extracurricular activities.

"We have a bit of good news, too. Rachel Carson's settled in her new home."

"Oh yes, you said you might've found someone. So that worked out?"

"Aye."

"Anyone I know?"

"Maida. Suited for each other."

Rab came back that afternoon, alone—or almost. A small, creamy yellow kitten slept in the crook of his arm.

"Where did it come from?" Janet asked, surprised by how high and precious her voice had suddenly become.

"Reddick and Quantum were on a ramble. Quantum found a bag tossed on the roadside. This wee lassie was inside. Not much bigger than a butter pat. Reddick can't keep her. Says he's allergic." He transferred the sleeping kitten to the crook of Janet's arm.

That evening, while Janet and Tallie were busy adoring the kitten now named Butter, a knock came at the door. Tallie went to answer it and Janet heard her laugh, and then she came back with Rab. With Rab was another cat.

"Because a wee moggie needs a steady friend," Rab said.

"But isn't this one of the ferals from the harbor?"

It looked very much like the gray cat she'd seen on the harbor wall, washing its ears so that everyone would know rain was coming.

"Not feral," Rab said. "Independent, for the short term. The old fellow belonged to another old fellow gone into care."

"So, this old fellow needs a care home, too?"

The gray cat flopped down on its side, stretching its back and waving its paws toward the solemn kitten.

"Has a lovely purr," Rab said.

The cat closed its eyes and demonstrated.

"Welcome home, old fellow," Janet said. "What's his name?"

"Smirr."

ACKNOWLEDGMENTS

Thanks to Cammy MacRae for the little bit of Gaelic in this book. Accuracy is hers, any mistakes are mine. Thanks to James Haviland and Sharon Davis for letting me invent completely different lives for them, and to Chris Thompson, Marthalee Beckington, and Pat Witt for lending Ranger, Quantum, and Pogo, respectively. Thanks to Uncle Edward, who went with Peary in search of the North Pole and really did survive being buried in snow for three days—although the Laphroig is my own addition to the story. Thanks to Linda Kupferschmid for sharing her firsthand experience with patchouli. This book wouldn't be here without my agent, Cynthia Manson, or the guiding hand of my editor, Katie McGuire. Thank you, both, for continuing to believe in me. Special thanks, also, to my stellar critique partners, Janice Harrington and Betsy Hearne. And as always, thank you to my Mike for ignoring dust and weeds, and for inventing the world's best grilled cheese sandwich.